Yorkshire Rose

The Whispers: Book Three

Tasha Sheipline

Tasha L Sheipline

Dear Reader

Dear Reader,

As a writer, music has always played a vital role in providing inspiration for the stories I tell. Songs not only stir the soul but capture the spirit of the characters as they grow. Below you will find a list of songs that helped to spark my creativity and bring this book to life.

"Landslide" *Fleetwood Mac*

"Gypsy" *Fleetwood Mac*

"If We Were Vampires" *Jason Isbell*

"My Immortal" *Eminence*

"Somewhere Only We Know" *Keane*

"Over You" *Miranda Lambert*

"Bigger Than the Whole Sky" *Taylor Swift*

Dedication

It's the third book. Can you believe we made it this far? So many people have been part of this journey, and surely there isn't enough space on this page to thank everyone, but I will give it a shot.

To my editor Eamon, of Clear-View Fiction Editing. Your wisdom, wit, and constant professionalism are unmatched. You hear my voice, from across the pond. You give me courage, when I need that extra little push.

To my husband, Tony. Thank you for always giving me your unwavering support, being my biggest fan, and putting up with all of my wild ideas. You do daddy daughter days, when I need to polish up a manuscript. You take the dogs to get their hair done, when I have book events. You the perfect husband in every way. You can do better than me, you know that don't you?

To my daughters, Gabby and Ava. Thank you for being proud of me. Those words mean more than you will ever know. You are talented, educated, and strong young women. You know your worth. You bring kindness and compassion into everything that you do. Your only fault, is that you don't think the Christmas tree should go up on November first, but I can overlook that flaw.

To my mom, who has single-handedly managed to make my books a cult following. Thank you for your incredible marketing skills.

To my Uncle Ron. Thanks for being the only person who doesn't run away when I start talking about the Norman Conquest.

To all of my students, both past and present. You have taught me that goals are not dreams to be put up on the shelf until you have the time to make them happen. I want to be you when I grow up.

To Darla. Thank you for two decades of good solid belly laughs, and even better friendship. May the Fourth be with you. To my work wife, Lynne. You are the bright side of life. Thank you for that daily reminder that life is short, to put on that cat sweater, and let the good times roll. You are the Cassandra to my Adelia. Finally, to the Corgis, Basil Rathbone III and Piper Countess of Barksbury. Please stop barking because someone sneezed three blocks away. That is all.

Contents

Chapter One

England 1966

Adelia crossed the threshold of the front door and dragged the strap of her heavy bag over her head before dropping it to the floor. She took in her appearance in the foyer mirror, crinkling up her nose in dismay. Her long day at the university had taken its toll, evidenced by the shadows below her eyes. She patted a few stray locks of her dark hair into place, then slid her arms out of her raincoat and hung it up to dry on the hall tree.

She had only managed a few steps deeper into the hallway when Daniel poked his head out from his study.

"Welcome home, love," he chirped.

There was something about these nightly greetings that never ceased to warm her heart. They had been married nearly five years now, and in that time, life had taken a rather unconventional turn. Before buying their old manor house, Daniel was an established professor back at Oxford—a solid four hours away. With her teaching in nearby Leeds, the long distance had wreaked havoc on their relationship for a time. However, after getting married, Daniel left his job, relishing his newfound passion for running the bed & breakfast that comprised half of the mammoth mid-sixteenth-century home. When he wasn't catering to their endless stream of guests, he dedicated his free time to research and writing, having retained his love of history. Over the five years, he had managed to publish several books, covering a wide expanse of historical topics.

As odd as it was for the time, Adelia maintained her job, rising through the ranks to become department chair at Leeds University. By now, they were both accustomed to the disbelieving looks of others at the revelation that Daniel was the stay-at-home spouse. It mattered little to either of them—they were both content with the roles they'd settled into.

"Do we have any guests tonight?" She felt bad not knowing, but had come to rely on Daniel's capable handling of the business affairs.

"No," he said, smiling. "We don't have anything booked this week. Don't get too used to the quiet because the busy season is fast approaching. June, July, and August will be teaming with the holiday crowd."

She released a quiet sigh of relief. With it being the last two weeks of the spring semester, she was looking forward to the break from teaching for the summer, even if that meant picking up extra duties at home.

Daniel squeezed the back of his neck. "I haven't prepared dinner yet, I'm afraid. I was caught up in some writing and time slipped away, but I will conjure something up in quick time." He stepped closer and touched her cheek. "You look tired. Why don't you sit down and rest yourself."

She was tired. Close to exhausted. But she had been waiting to discuss something of a pressing nature with her husband for days. Now they had the house to themselves, it seemed like the right time.

"I have been thinking..." She glanced up the stairs, then made eye contact with him. "Follow me. I have something I want to show you."

He arched a brow but she didn't linger long enough to elaborate. In a flash, she was bounding up the stairs, with Daniel making up the distance behind her.

As she strode down the second-floor hallway, she sidestepped a man clad in an emerald-green topcoat.

"Pardon me, William," she said, continuing on toward the room at the end. "You look dashing in that shade of green."

She knew Daniel didn't see the figure, and smiled when he followed suit, moving around the invisible obstruction with care.

Just as the manor was no ordinary home, she was no ordinary woman. Daniel was well aware of her extraordinary gift. Even in an empty room, she was never alone, as all around her stirred echoes of the past. The souls that once dwelt in a space were still there, repeating moments that had passed long ago. To anyone else, she lived in a house filled with ghosts, but to her, these were all just recordings of energy—a common occurrence anywhere she went. And after nearly a decade together, Daniel had grown as accustomed to it as she.

She swung the large wooden door open and slipped inside. Taking care in the dark, she made her way over to a bedside table and switched on the lamp. When she turned to face Daniel, he was leaning against the doorframe, his expression one of clear confusion. Even so, he cut a dashing figure, his sandy-brown hair glinting with a hint of auburn. His simple button-up shirt and wrinkled trousers didn't rival William's debonair look, but he was still a handsome man.

As she took several seconds to regard her husband, a wave of love flooded her heart. The way he loved her was something that could hardly be articulated in words. It took her back to her childhood days, when she would rush to the door to meet her father after his long day at work. He had been gone mere hours, yet it felt like days. She remembered the swell of excitement at his return, and the sense of safety and security at knowing he was there. Each time it happened, she was like a puppy, overjoyed at seeing "her person." It was that same unconditional love Daniel had for her, accompanied by loyalty, devotion, and an unreasonable amount of patience for her hairbrained schemes. No matter how high she climbed, or how far she went in this life, he was her world, and it was a better place to be with him in it.

"Hear me out," she said, raising her palm, as if to stop his objection before he even had the chance to make one. "What do you think about moving all of this furniture out and putting a fresh coat of paint on these walls?"

His features twisted as he scanned the contents of the room. Nothing in his expression said he was remotely thrilled at the prospect of moving so much heavy furniture. She could almost read his thoughts: Who's going to lift that mammoth bed? Where are we going to put the damn thing? Why does she want to do this anyway?

Part of the reason they loved Middleham Manor so much was its history. The original parts of the house dated back to the Tudor age, though additions and changes had been made in every era since. They called it the Frankenstein of houses, with each generation of change patched together to make it unique. Aside from fixing a loose slate or sealing a drafty window, they were opposed to making any major changes. This wasn't just a house to them anymore, it was a part of them—a thread of security that bound them together.

"What are you on about?" He pushed himself off the doorframe and took a step into the room, eyeing her in the process.

"What am I on about?" she said, as if asking herself the same thing. "I spoke to the dean about a leave of absence. It would give me more time to help."

Though she smiled, she knew he wouldn't be fooled. The bulk of this project would rest on his shoulders and he was well aware of that.

"You spoke to the dean about a leave of absence? Really? What is this about, Adelia?"

She didn't miss the concern in his eyes, mixed with a hint of suspicion. He knew her too well. Never in a thousand years would she take off work, unless it related to a matter of grave importance. Given her track record of sometimes reckless decisions, she thought it best to put him out of his misery.

"I was just thinking that maybe a new color might be nice. Something more fitting for a...nursery?"

The rise and fall of his chest stopped, and for a moment she worried that it had been too long since he'd taken a proper breath. Just as she feared he might faint, his lips creased into a huge smile, his face lighting up.

He stepped forward, met her toe to toe, and brought his hands to rest on either side of her abdomen.

"You m-mean...?" he stammered.

"Yes," she said, breathless, having no idea why she had been so nervous about telling him. His reaction put her at ease. "By the doctor's calculations, I am about six weeks along."

"Good Lord," he exclaimed. "I will paint the whole damn house salmon pink if you want me to."

"No," she said, her tone clipped. "There will be absolutely no salmon pink. What a terrible idea."

"I would hate everything about that color, but damn if I wouldn't do it for you."

"I know you would." She giggled. "But please don't. I'm thinking something neutral, like a light shade of soft green."

Daniel slid his arms around her waist and nuzzled his face in her hair, then eased his head back to meet her gaze. They stood for a moment, trading smiles, her fingers laced at the back of his neck.

"We have waited so long." His voice gave a subtle crack as his eyes took on a glossy sheen. "This...is everything. You are everything. I just can't believe—"

"I wanted to tell you earlier, but I had to be sure. Things will be different. I need to start thinking about scaling back at work."

"Things can be as different as you want them to be," he said. He drew in a deep breath. "You don't have to give up anything you don't want to. I am here, and we are in this together. We can make anything work between the two of us."

She should have expected that from her husband—this unwavering support. When she first suspected that she might be pregnant, thoughts of how she could juggle her career and motherhood dominated her thoughts day and night. Not only had she wanted to be sure before she told him, she needed a bit of time to wade through it all. She didn't want to give up her career, having worked so hard to get to this point. But the thought of being an absent mother didn't sit right either. Now that she'd struck a balance within herself on the matter, she was confident that her loving husband would be there every step of the way. Things could not have been more perfect than they were at this moment.

They traded a few more ideas back and forth on how the room should be transformed. Daniel was sure it would be a boy, and thought a pale shade of blue would complement the woodwork. He threw out some suggestions for décor: A suit of armor, some

lovely sketches of the battle of Tewkesbury he had recently acquired, and a medieval sword he'd found at an antiques' auction.

"No, no, and no," she said, her brows tight as she glared at him.

He raised a finger to protest but a loud grumble from her stomach cut him off.

"Dinner!" He slammed his palm to his forehead and dragged it
down his face. "You have to eat."

"Truly, I am starving," she admitted. "I'd do murder for a cup of
tea and some crisps."

"You need more than that. Why don't you go down and put
the kettle on, and I will drive into the village, make short work of
getting us something, and be back before you have even stirred in
your milk and sugar."

"Really, we can just put something together here," she said. "It's
getting late."

"The pub is still open. I can have Ruby toss together a few
sandwiches for takeaway. Let me do this one thing, will you?"

"Fine," she said, relenting. She followed him from the room and
down the stairs.

When he left, she scavenged up a few biscuits to tide her over
until his return. After her tea had fully steeped, she chuckled to
herself as she stirred in her milk and sugar. He hadn't made it back
yet.

She moved into the front sitting room and tucked herself into
the sofa's soft cushions, propping up her feet on the ottoman. In
the peaceful silence, her fatigue caught up with her, and her dreary

eyes fluttered shut. She didn't fight it. Just five minutes would suffice.

****

Thump. Thump. Thump.

She jolted up, blinking several times, realizing she had fallen asleep. Glancing at the window, with the sky now dark, told her it had been a long five minutes.

Another hard knock at the door had her bolting to her feet. As she made her way to the foyer, she looked around, expecting Daniel to dart out from the kitchen, or his study. No doubt he'd snuck in earlier, not wanting to wake her. No sign of him, though. The house was silent, save for the thump of her heart, and that knock at the door.

When she opened the door to the darkness, her body clenched at the sight of a policeman, tall and broad-shouldered. He towered over her, and she had to look up to meet his gaze.

"Mrs. Adelia Brown?" He pulled his hat from his head and clutched it tight to his stomach.

The foyer's dim light caught a bead of sweat on his brow. Something empty seeped through her, like a slow-moving wave, its icy tentacles snaking into her heart. Then the earth beneath her shuddered, and just like that her entire world stopped rotating.

Chapter Two

Four Weeks Later

When Adelia awoke from her deep slumber, she looked to the window to be met by gray skies painted with streaks of charcoal clouds. Night had descended on Middleham Manor. She pushed back the thick down comforter, her fingers aching from having it clenched so tight to her chest. The room felt devoid of air, its stifling dryness making her eyes feel as if they were filled with dust.

Blinking, she rolled onto her back, staring up at the ceiling as though the answers to all her problems might seep from the tiny hairline cracks. She closed her eyes against the sting of long-evaporated tears, having never felt so numb, removed from all emotion, unlike earlier when a cloud of infinite sadness filled every inch of her being.

The house was silent, quieter than it had been in days. Two weeks had passed since the funeral. Her family and friends had departed, leaving her with the inevitable solitude that followed. This was where things got hard, where her own life was supposed to begin again. The thought bore down on her like a truck filled with heavy stone. How on earth was she supposed to start over? For the first time in her life, she lacked the will to overcome. Without Daniel, nothing would ever be the same.

She tossed back the covers and swung her legs over the side of the bed, aware of the blood seeping into her Jell-O-like limbs as they dangled there. The gloom threatened to envelop her so she flipped on the bedside lamp, bathing the room in soft warm light, though she had to squint to adjust to it. Reticent, she let her bare feet touch the silky-smooth cool of the hardwood floor, her legs as weak as wind-torn leaves after the fiercest storm.

Bracing herself against the wood frame, she made her way around the bed toward the door. At the corner of the footboard, her little toe brushed against a small black mound on the floor. She stopped in her tracks, as if frightened by a ghost. There lay Daniel's socks, tossed at the foot of his night stand. In the five years they had been married, she must have picked up his damn socks every single day, muttering in annoyance as she tossed them into the laundry. As she stared down at the tiny mass, she resolved never to pick them up. They would stay in that spot until the threads disintegrated into fibrous fragments.

She walked down the halls of the centuries-old house they had shared, her pace slow, steadying herself against the cold white-plaster walls. They had bought the manor just before getting married—a serious leap from renting a room in it as she began her teaching career at the university. When the place came up for sale, Daniel spent every shilling in his savings to purchase it, for her, wanting her to flourish in her career. There wasn't an inch of this house that he hadn't poured his heart and soul into preserving. They shared a love of history, and living here fed their mutual passion all the more, with each loving the building for its past, and all the promise it held for their future.

When she flipped on the light in the kitchen, she peered around the room as if for the first time. The stone hearth on the far wall was still strung with the dried herbs they had harvested from the gardens. Bright copper pans with charred marks on their bottoms hung from the rack overhead, evidence of Daniel's tendency to burn just about everything. The white porcelain Belfast sink still held yesterday's dishes, a reminder that nobody was coming to clean up after her. As she pulled a glass from the cupboard, she caught sight of Daniel's favorite cup, the one he used every day for his morning tea. He was everywhere. Each room of their dream home held reminders of him—all she had to cling to now—simple moments that brought a gentle smile, even as they clawed at her heart.

She sipped cold water from the glass, the instant relief easing the dry burn in the back of her throat. Her empty stomach gurgled, and for the first time in days she felt hungry. Running her hands across her belly, she was reminded of something else: There in her womb, grew the most powerful reminder of Daniel—the reason he went out that night.

Her mind flew back to the moment she shared the news of her pregnancy with her husband. His delight still rested heavy in her heart. He had been overjoyed, to say the least. She hadn't put up much of an argument when he decided to head out to the village. He would not have let her win anyway. For all the relenting he usually did at the things she wanted, it was useless to argue with him when he set his mind to something.

On his way into Middleham, no more than a mile up the road, he came across a stranded motorist and stopped to help. His nature was unselfish, and his deed came as little surprise to her when she'd heard. That night, however, the saying "no good deed goes unpunished" came to fruition. There, upon the isolated road, in the ebbing shades of twilight, he was struck by an oncoming car and killed instantly. Just like that, the world as she knew it stopped spinning.

Now, more than two months into her pregnancy, she was a widow. She had lost the most loving, unselfish being she had ever known. It was so unfair, as was life, death, and time. Loss had a way of plaguing one's soul with regret. All those empty promises flooded back, and every wasted minute of every wasted day hung heavy in her mind. A million seconds of their life together could have been better spent. Had she known what was to come, she would never have gone shopping with her friends that one day. She would have come home earlier from work that week, or not gone to bed early and left him reading in the study alone. Every mundane task would have been shelved to spend more time with Daniel. Too late now, with no more time left to change things for the better.

Standing alone in the middle of this big lonely house was her life now. Nothing would change that reality, and she hated everything about this new normal.

They had made plans. Plans for Saturday, plans for next month, plans for forever. Now those were all just blank spaces on the calendar of eternity. It was like taking your favorite book, at the best part, slamming the cover shut and locking it away in a closet never to be touched again.

With the passing of her life partner, friends and family had flocked to be by her side. Her parents made the journey from Boston, and helped her to finalize the funeral plans. Being able to curl up in her father's arms for a good sob reminded her of her childhood. No matter the obstacles life threw at her along the way, she was always able to rely on their unceasing love. All the support she received was both wonderful and overwhelming.

Yet, as the days passed, one by one everyone departed, returning to their lives. Their departure evoked a welcome relief, but the loneliness of it all was kicking in now. What was she supposed to do to move forward? Did she have the strength to take the necessary steps into a new life? Somewhere beneath all this grief beat the heart of a woman who still longed to conquer the world. A woman who always set her mind to achieving bigger things in the future. She knew deep down that this woman would reemerge in time, but, for now, that seemed a long way away.

Chapter Three

Weeks passed in a slow steady creep, and an odd sense of calm settled over her, like a dreamless sleep, leaving her feeling like a listless soul trapped within a corpse, cheating her own death with each lingering breath. Minute by minute, she sliced through the unyielding hours but her efforts did nothing to thwart the brutal reality. It threatened her like a weary traveler with the promise of a new day's rise, robbing her long-awaited peace and thrusting her back into its cruel truth. Some days the pain was unbearable—a constant hollowness, which no amount of mourning could relieve.

As the end of another vacant day came to a close, she sat at the kitchen table picking at her meager dinner. At least with it being the summer semester, she had a few months off work, with classes due to resume in the fall. However, having this time to herself was both a blessing and a curse. Despite all the time spent grieving her loss, the endless solitude wore away at her. The realization had pricked at her all day. After roaming the empty halls for what felt like hours, she'd entered the kitchen and flinched when met by the vacant stare of her reflection in the window. She barely recognized the figure staring back at her, who far more resembled the gaunt Mr. Mortimer she had once known, than herself.

She drummed her fingers against the ancient wooden table, having reached a point where sadness no longer brought her comfort. It was time to begin the process of returning to some form of normal life. The prospect was frightening, as the steps would be anything but easy. While overcoming herself was something she had spent a good many years perfecting, this time her beloved Daniel would not be the force behind her, willing her forward when the road got too rocky. From now on, she was on her own.

After scooping the dishes from the table and placing them in the sink, she walked out into the hall, where she stopped dead, facing the heavy wooden door she had not dared to open since Daniel's death. It was his place, a large and drafty room he'd used as his study, spending countless hours in there laboring away, surrounded by all the things he held dear. She moved toward the door with uneven steps, pushing herself forward despite the urge to turn and run. Running from unpleasant things had been ingrained in her since her youth, a time when she had allowed her anxieties to get the best of her, with escape always her go-to resolution. Those days were far behind her now after she'd taught herself to be unafraid of the unknown, recognizing that no amount of worry would change anything that was bound to happen. It never changed the past and it damn sure wouldn't change the present. Worry was little more than a waste of precious energy—a luxury she could not afford to spare.

She traced her fingertips across the cast iron knob. With a screeching yet familiar turn, she eased it open and stared into the bleak dimness of the room. Closed up for weeks, an initial rush of dusty air brushed her face, smelling of leather-bound books and old wood—a scent both brutal and comforting.

The room was dark, so she crossed the floor and switched on one of the table lamps beside Daniel's favorite leather chair, where he'd spent many hours reading notes on his last two books. They each desired their own workspace, and she had set up hers in one of the old rooms on the next floor, used as a rental before they bought the manor. The few times she'd tried to work in Daniel's study, she soon found he was far too distracting for her to accomplish anything of worth. In many things, they enjoyed each other's company, but in work they always found separation more productive. In truth, they'd spent far too much time working, because it was something that brought them individual joy.

Her old tattered shawl, a gift from Daniel after visiting the Scottish Highlands, lay snug around her shoulders. She sat at the aged oak writing desk, with its messy stacks of papers and books littering the long dark walnut surface. This was Daniel's favorite spot, a place he could spend hours poring over his work. Shifting in the worn wooden chair, she pondered how he could spend so much time in this uncomfortable thing. Like herself, he was a man gifted with an impenetrable focus, and when he set his mind upon a goal, it consumed him in every way. It was a trait they understood about each other, but now, in retrospect, she swallowed back a swell of regret. As incorrigible workaholics, they had formed a mutual understanding, with neither ever bothered by the other's grueling schedule. It was just the way of things.

She couldn't help but wonder what they had missed in living for their work. In the end, what was it all for? As she looked back at those hours spent in academic toil, she struggled to find a point. No matter how much she and Daniel sought to accomplish in life, all roads led here. Had either of them known what was to come, they would surely have spent their time differently.

As she scooted closer to the desk, she closed her eyes, taking in the familiar creak of the casters rolling across the rug, a sound she had heard a thousand times, yet now it evoked such an emotion, she struggled to fight back her tears. Every insignificant detail about her husband seemed to matter so much more now he was gone. How long would it be before these moments faded from her memory, until every sight, sound, and smell no longer brought his face back to her mind? The sad reality was that, with each passing year, she would forget a little more, until one day there might be nothing more than a few passing thoughts to recall.

Sitting here at his desk was not helping her to let go, with her newfound ambitions dissipating by the second. Not that it mattered—she didn't want to let go anyway, at least not yet. Moving on would come in time but, right now, it was far too soon to even think of such a thing. For now, despite all the pain it brought to the surface, she wanted to burrow herself in his memory—surround herself in the things he once treasured. Any shred of him would suffice.

She looked at the stacks of papers, all higgledy-piggledy and pushed into small untidy towers against the wall at the back of the desk. Over the past few years, Daniel had published a series of books centered on various periods in history. He'd spent a great deal of time studying the Croyland Chronicle, producing a lengthy analysis of its historical significance in both medieval and present time. For his second book, he detailed the contributions of Thomas More to the justice system of Tudor England. While running Middleham Manor had become his center of focus, he never lost his love of history after leaving Oxford. During the off season at the bed & breakfast, he'd continued to travel for research purposes. Most were just short trips here and there, and she never minded, being busy with her own career. They had always been able to enjoy a marriage where they could pursue their own passions—one of the many things that made their life together so fulfilling.

As she scanned his notes, she smiled at the haphazard way he bounced from topic to topic, no doubt trying to decide what the focus of his next project would be. His mind was never at rest, with creativity and diligence always his strengths. There was nothing that man could not do when he fixed his mind upon something of interest. These were qualities she also shared, yet she doubted to that degree. Daniel was never as insecure as she, with things always coming to him with the least effort. Though she was now a respected professor of history at the university in Leeds, her journey had been anything but smooth, having faced rejection after rejection for jobs before landing the Leeds' position. Being a woman in the world of academia was still met with unspoken opposition in some circles, forcing her to scratch and claw her way to her goal, and though she had finally gotten her break, it felt unfair that she should have to try so hard. Thankfully, she'd landed at a university where her gender was not met with hesitation and resistance.

Daniel's path had been far less bumpy. Being the son of a well-known Oxford professor, his career path was almost an expectation rather than a choice. After some rebellious wavering in his youth, he'd settled on following in his father's footsteps and things progressed naturally from there. He hit the ground running, and everything he touched after that turned to gold.

She chuckled to herself, thinking back to the days before they married, when she had been the only real obstacle in his life. For four long years, he had chased her, and she'd done her best to keep him waiting.

They'd met when she was visiting her grandma at Hampton Court Palace. Daniel was there researching the death of Amy Robsart Dudley, and somehow, she managed to become as intertwined in him as she was in the mystery. Love blossomed, and she didn't return home to Boston at the end of that summer, and over the course of the next four years, they'd stayed together. Their relationship had not been without its struggles, though. Eight years younger than him, she was just beginning her college education and had so many career aspirations for her future. Though always patient and kind, there were times when Daniel found it difficult to understand why she was so headstrong, always wanting to do things on her own. She wanted to achieve her own success, without his influence, and that sometimes led to them clashing. It took time but, eventually, she came to terms with the fact that there was no one in the world more well suited for her than Daniel.

Five years ago, they got married here at Middleham Manor. Since then, she could only describe her marriage as something out of a fairytale. They had worked together to build the bed & breakfast business, with each able to pursue their own career interests. There was nothing about her real-life fairytale she would have changed, except for its tragic end. Being a widow was never a role she imagined having to play, yet here she was, sitting in his creaky old chair, clinging to any last shred of memory she could grasp.

She brought her attention back to the pile of papers, read through each one, following his neat scribble, before placing them back onto the desk in an orderly fashion. Time was of no consequence as she progressed from one pile to another, stacking scraps of paper with addresses and directions on top of his handwritten notes. Moving through a pile of books, she came upon a small sketch pad, its thick brown cardboard cover showing wear on its edges, with the top starting to come loose from the thick spiral binding, no doubt from years of use. She flipped it open and stared down at the words, scribed in beautiful, neat calligraphy.

"Yorkshire Rose," she whispered, tracing her fingers along the delicate swirls of script.

When she turned the page, she stopped on seeing the smooth, sculpted face of a pale-haired woman staring back at her. Her gray-blue eyes had been painted with a sheer dab of watercolor, and every angle of her face seemed perfect, with no flaw to be seen. She stared off into the distance, as though looking for something that might never come, her eyes conveying anticipation and disappointment in equal measure. There was a complexity to her face, as though her emotions did not exist to be deciphered. Adelia stared back at the woman, the portrait reminding her of a Holbein sketch, so lifelike the figure nearly jumped off the page.

Daniel was gone almost two months now, and since his death, the whispers had ceased. Barely a day had passed since discovering her Babbington gift that it had not presented itself. The whispers, passed down to her through the female line of her family, was a clairvoyance of sorts, giving her the ability to experience the energy of the past as if she were really there. She felt the emotions of those long departed, with entire conversations coming through as though people were beside her. Most times, she could watch events play out before her like a movie on a screen. Her second sight had given her a window into another time, placing her right there in the center of it all. Everything about her life had been dominated by the whispers for as long as she could remember—even before she understood what she was experiencing.

In the beginning, she'd branded herself the anxious sort, with strange emotions taking her over in a way she could never explain. When her grandma shared the secret of her gift, she learned to understand that what she was feeling and sensing had nothing to do with herself—it was the whispers all along. She revealed this ability to Daniel early in their relationship. Much to her surprise, he not only believed her but proved supportive. Considering he was a man who relied on definitive facts, his reaction was unexpected. Their relationship grew stronger because of that, built on trust and truth, or so she'd thought.

With Daniel's passing, the whispers had shut off like a light switch. When her world went dark, so did her window into the past. She was alone in this house now; even good old William had abandoned her. There might have been a time when she would have appreciated such quietude, with those characters of the past not always making life easy, often infusing complexity into just about every aspect of her existence. But, over the past few weeks, she'd found herself lost without the company of the long-dead companions she'd grown accustomed to. Though it pained her to admit it, she found herself wishing her ability would return, if only to see Daniel again. However, despite all her wishing, the whispers refused to surface. Time and again, they proved that they were not to be summoned at her will. She knew after long experience that they came through when they wished, their purpose always shadowed in mystery.

As she stared back at the image of the woman, she sensed a tinge of angst, so faint she wasn't sure if it was her own feelings or that of the picture-perfect image. She flipped to the next page and, once again, pale pastel images of the fair-haired woman looked back at her. Page after page brought more paint sketches of the same woman. Each one was different, yet somehow the same.

She leaned back in the chair, pulling lengths of her hair free from the shawl. It was obvious that her husband had taken a great deal of time to produce these curious drawings. Indeed, it was also clear as day that they were not drawings of his wife. Her stomach burned with jealousy as images of the woman Daniel had labeled Yorkshire Rose filled her mind.

A dark realization caused her to sit up: Was it possible that Daniel had held some fascination with the woman filling these pages? Or was it something more? Her heart pained at the possibility of such a deep betrayal. She dropped the pad, gasping as she brought both hands to her face. Had her husband, this man she never imagined to be anything but faithful, given himself to another woman?

Chapter Four

S he studied the sketches, her focus intense. The pale golden hair, her clear-blue eyes, the soft lines of her silky-smooth face. She sat up in the chair as a realization dawned. These images staring back reminded her of someone she knew. Someone both she and Daniel knew. This woman, the image of perfection, held a remarkable resemblance to Cassandra, her own cousin.

A flash of pain in her chest had her squinting, as if the tip of a spear was being thrust into her heart. Her memory floated back to that fateful summer when she had agreed to take Cassandra on as an assistant for a university-funded research project. The young woman would have driven her to the brink of insanity if it hadn't been for Daniel's easy and timely intervention. He came along in the nick of time and saved them from clawing at each other. As they traveled along from town to town, stopping here and there so she could investigate the physical and otherworldly elements of the area, there had been moments when she felt herself growing a little jealous of Cassandra. Her cousin had the unsolicited ability to turn the head of every man who crossed her path. While she'd scolded herself for thinking Daniel might have been smitten by the young woman's undeniable charms, perhaps she had not been so wrong.

As much as she wanted to dash the idea that Daniel and Cassandra may have formed some secret relationship behind her back, the second she glanced down at the picture in her hand, the prospect came at her renewed. Her thoughts bounced back and forth like a crazed tennis ball being whacked across a court. It was both possible and implausible at the same time. After that summer, they married and settled in Middleham. Cassandra returned to school in London before moving to the city of York after graduation to work. It wasn't as if both were in close enough proximity to carry on some torrid affair, at least without their efforts being noticed. York was an hour away, at minimum. On the other hand, Daniel had done quite a bit of solo travel over the past few years working on his books. He had never been gone long, but then affairs didn't take a great deal of time to conduct. No, it was impossible. However, even if it was out of the question that they were cavorting behind her back, there was still the possibility he had developed some fascination with her cousin on his own. Perhaps it was more of a one-sided betrayal. Was that better?

Blinded by her questions, her eyes filled with a flash of red and she flung the sketchbook across the room. It smacked against the wall with a shrill crack, landing with a dull thud on the floorboards. She stood there in utter disbelief, her hands at her chest as her breath quickened, but then she grimaced, feeling childish for her outburst. After groaning with shame, she crossed the room and picked up the sketchbook, doing her best not to look at the images within. With its cover closed, she returned to the desk and set it back where she'd found it.

All of a sudden, the room became stifling. She crossed the space again and pushed open one of the windows, relishing the cool breeze on her face. A summer storm, heavy with rolling clouds, hovered on the horizon, filling the air with an earthy scent of rain. As it inched closer, the low moan of thunder echoed in the distance, with flashes of light flickering against a foreboding gray landscape, as if it and her stoic reflection in the window were trying to out-gloom each other.

Just as she decided to leave the study, a violent flash illuminated the sky, and a loud pop from behind had her turning to see that the lamp had died, plunging the entire room into darkness.

A tingle spread up and down her arms, as though static from the raging storm was filtering through her. As she stood there in a shroud of pitch black, the room filled with Daniel's presence, the rain-heavy air now tinted with the cologne of his shaving soap. She stood stock still, allowing the energy swirling around her to settle in one direction.

The storm drew closer, with another flash of lightning filling the room with momentary stark illumination. Daring not to move, she raised her gaze to the windows. Her breath caught as, even in the darkness, she saw the shallow form. It was faint at first, barely detectable to the untrained eye, but with careful scrutiny, she scanned the ethereal blue outline. He stood as still as her, gazing out into the misty rain now trailing from the heavens. His form lit up and dimmed in such rapid succession it resembled a faulty lightbulb. She pondered why his image was so spectral. Through years of concentrated practice, she had gained the ability to see the departed just as they would have appeared in life, and often found it quite unnerving how lifelike her visions were. On a regular basis, she could detect the most minute of details, from the subtle flush in a cheek to the scent of salty sweat upon a person's brow, with their voice as clear as if it had been whispered right into her ear. She experienced every range of emotion, from the highest form of joy to the deepest heartbreak.

Being encased in a world where time layered upon itself was something she didn't consider abnormal anymore, and every day she lived, up to Daniel's passing, she was surrounded by the dead. They had become just another part of the fabric of her life.

Now, mere feet from her, Daniel's image felt so far away. A deep sense of longing crept through her, though she wasn't sure if it was only her own. Why was this vision of the man she loved so different? His energy was so strong in this room, yet it evaded her almost intentionally. She resisted the urge to stretch out her trembling hand to touch him, sure that any sudden movement would shatter the moment she'd been so desperate to experience these past few weeks. The scourge of tears welled in her eyes, and she blinked them back, not wanting the vision before her to blur. Perhaps she just wanted him too much. She knew too well that the whispers bore a cruel side. One could never be in complete control, but this was by far the most brutal game for them to play, thrashing at her deepest desire.

With a flicker, the luminescent outline evaporated into the humidity of the summer air. She almost called after him, but staggered back instead and sat into his armchair, not even bothering to seek out a candle to light up the dark.

Her brain was ablaze with uncontrollable thoughts—about Daniel, and the mysterious woman in the book only a few feet from her. As ludicrous as it sounded, she found her mood lifted, if only for a moment. It was the first time in weeks she had felt any other emotion besides sadness. While jealousy and hurt were not an improvement, she couldn't help but feel slight relief knowing she was still capable of feeling something other than melancholy.

For at least another hour, she sat in the dark room, allowing herself to succumb to this barrage of newfound emotions. Somewhere deep inside her, a flame had been sparked. Over time, the whispers taught her a great many things, and she now knew far more about death than life. Death was the ceasing of time for the body, but not the soul. The soul lived on like an unpolished ending to an intricately written novel. There was always a cliffhanger, leaving the reader wanting more.

Just once, she desired to live her life not embroiled in some sort of mystery. Even though the whispers had gone silent since Daniel's passing, the sheer drama of it all had lost its shine. Oh, what life must be like for those without such a cursed gift. To meander about one's daily business, not entrenched in everyone else's strife, must be heaven indeed. But such a peaceful existence was not her calling. Be it burden or gift, her duty would always be to channel the souls in her midst, shouldering their joy and sorrow in measure, as if such emotions were her own. Not even Daniel could offer her peace. Though he had always tried in life to do so, death no longer afforded him that opportunity.

Ghosts, much like the living, dwell in a space that is unfinished. It may concern business being left undone—words spoken in haste, or things left unsaid. There is always something that could have been done differently. Death does not change these things, nor the heart's desire for closure.

Chapter Five

The letter came in the post a few days ago, and it wasn't until this morning that she'd mustered the nerve to open it. She stared down at the beautiful scripted writing and the York postmark, knowing it was from Cassandra, who she hadn't seen since Daniel's funeral. With eyes closed, she thought back to the tight embrace they had shared that day, and the way she'd all but thrust her weight upon Cassandra to keep herself from crumbling into a heap on the church floor. Though total opposites in personality, they had formed such a strong bond that they were now more like sisters.

She crumpled the letter in her fist as visions of the notebook filled her head. A keen sense of her surroundings, and a sharp intelligence, were the two traits she had always been known for. Though humble about herself, much of her success in life had relied on those two qualities. Even so, it was a blow to her ego to think she may have been deceived by those she trusted most.

Whether the deception was on the part of Daniel, or both, mattered little, because the deep hurt would not soon subside. She never considered herself the jealous type, but the past few weeks had taught her much about herself. In truth, she was capable of a great many things, with self-destruction being one of them.

Like everyone else, she possessed traits that stood in her way at times—her inability to let things go being the worst of these, by far. As she reread the letter, over and over, her need to know the truth continued to rear its ugly head. It was an invitation to visit her cousin in York on the occasion of the release of her debut novel. A book-signing event was being held at one of the well-known local book shops there, and Cassandra was most insistent that she be there to share in this significant moment. While she expressed her understanding that Adelia might not feel ready just yet, she was certain that a change of scenery would do nothing but help lift her spirits. Had it not been for the lingering thoughts in her head, she would probably have agreed. One thing was for certain: locking herself away in her large empty house had not improved her well-being.

She smoothed her hand across the ever-growing curve of her abdomen. While she had struggled through some of the earlier days of her pregnancy, she felt well enough to take a drive to York, and maybe stay a day or two as Cassandra had suggested. While she didn't want to dampen her cousin's triumph with accusations, she knew herself far too well to assume that the topic would not arise at some point. She wanted answers, even if she was fearful of what might be revealed as a result.

Sitting at the kitchen table, she scribbled an acceptance to the invitation. She kept her tone light and cheery, despite the whirling churn of emotion brewing inside. No one wanted to spend a weekend with the angel of sorrow, least of all Cassandra, who spent her days surrounded by all things pleasing.

As she scrolled through the last loop on her signature, she felt resolution in her soul. The promise of putting to rest the endless days and nights of overthinking was in sight.

****

The evening before she planned to leave for York, she headed out to the hills beyond the back garden, wading through the tall grass, slow but with purpose. She pulled her familiar old shawl tight around herself, swaddling in it like a baby in a security blanket, its once-stiff fibers now soft from years of wash and wear.

Since the night she saw Daniel, the whispers had made a gradual return, at their own pace. While her sight remained hazy and thin, at least it was there, and day by day the energies grew stronger. She couldn't pass up this opportunity to try again.

When she reached the crest of the hill, she stopped and drew in a deep breath of cool night air. It felt good to be out beyond the manor's heavy stone walls. She nestled into the grass, the soft blades tickling her skin. Darkness had fallen so fast upon the wide-open land, its edges tempered by a hovering half-moon. To some, just being out here might have proved unnerving but she relished the bleakness of the solitude. The pitch-black helped to slow her erratic thoughts, and she closed her eyes and let her mind wander to a place only imagination could unfold. She would let her soul paint the picture.

It was here, in the shadows of her mind, that she dwelt in the valley of her discontent. She stared up at the highlands, their grassy hills peppered with rocky edges and swathes of purple heather, wishing herself strong enough to traverse their steep climb. All around her existed things that were lost, and time stood still and silent. No amount of worry could hasten it forward. The peeks stood stoic, as foes often do, a quiet reminder of all that was left unresolved. At some stage, she would have to climb, step by step, breath by breath, until she reached the top. What lay ahead, she could not be sure, but it would take effort to attain. Backbreaking, heartless effort.

Her eyes opened with a slow, easy flutter. She was back upon the sloping field, a place she and Daniel had visited many times before—a quiet refuge from the busyness of the day—where her heart's guard could take a break, and she could share her innermost thoughts without fear. If ever she and Daniel had a "place," these wide-open hilly fields were it.

She looked into the darkness, her heart calling out to him. Once, visions had come so easily to her, but now there seemed to be something blocking that energy. Never had her heart felt so heavy with a sense of longing. She called to him with quiet fervor. Just to know that he was still with her would be more than enough.

No, that was a lie. It was nothing more than a tale she told herself time and again. She wanted him home, to feel his heat radiate against hers as he slept at peace in their bed, and to see his smile in the morning as he poured her a cup of tea, apologizing for the slightly burned toast. Then there was his deep growling huff as he barked about some historical inaccuracy in a newly released movie or novel. No vision, no glimpse, no glimmer of him could ever replace those moments. Life without him was beyond unfair.

She shifted when she caught a faint shadow moving in the murky light of the half-moon. Its upright form felt human, its gait somewhat familiar. She was far too intrigued to be afraid. For someone who spent most of her days surrounded by images of long-departed souls, there was little to find frightening in everyday life. Fear of the dead was a dragon she had slayed long ago.

Was it Daniel? She couldn't be sure. Its outline was far too faded to be certain. Even from a distance, she sensed that it was not of the living. The whispers evoked a physical reaction—a distinct tingle that played upon her skin when her visions came. Her breath caught when a tiny flash of electric blue surged through the shadow. Though it extinguished as fast as it came, she recognized its ethereal glow—the same phenomenon she had witnessed back in Daniel's study. He was here, moving through the night, reliving some instance he had experienced before. Her presence was unknown to him, their existence within this moment on different planes.

She smiled to herself—it was either that or cry out, and she couldn't go there. Between them stood a wall, invisible to the eye, but it did not escape her acute senses. This barrier of nothingness was so strong, her own energy doubled back upon her like a blast of arctic air. She could not pull in his essence nor push hers out,

for the space between them was far too strong, as if the threads
of time had been weaved so tight she could only catch a glimpse
of him through its few weak spots. Never had she experienced
such an anomaly before and, at first, she found herself perplexed at
how she would even begin to break through. As she pondered her
dilemma, she realized that the answer might lie in Daniel's secrets.
His sketchbook. Right now, she needed to be closer to him than
ever before. She needed to dive into those inner thoughts he had
shielded from her all along. But how could she connect on that
level with her dead husband? The second sight she'd long relied
upon to reveal the past would prove no help this time. While she
had used her wit over her clairvoyance once or twice before, this
would be at another level. With the whispers being such a main
part of her life for so long, the notion of going it alone was now a
bit frightening. What if she couldn't do it?

If she could not use her abilities to reach Daniel, then she would
have to take a different approach. Where once death created the
window, life may instead have the answers. If she was ever to find a
way to break through to her husband, relying on those who lived
may provide the way forward.

Chapter Six

Adelia made her way to the bookshop, located in an area known as The Shambles, one of the most visited parts of York, and a haven for tourists passing through the famed walled city. The narrow streets were lined with timber-framed jettied houses that had stood since the Middle Ages.

She walked along the ancient stone street, marveling at the beautifully preserved architecture. Deriving its name from the many butcher shops that once called it home, The Shambles still held all the charm of a picturesque hub of medieval commerce. Having lived in England for several years now, she'd never had occasion to spend much time in York, which was a shame. Work and school dominated her life for so long, she rarely had the opportunity to travel for her own pleasure. York was a significant location when it came to England's vibrant history, forged by centuries of triumph and tragedy, each leaving their respective mark.

Due to her limited time for road trips, she had only visited the city twice. With so much to see here, she doubted this long weekend could even begin to quench her curiosity. She always said she would make a point of staying a few days, to take the time to really explore. Now, more than ever, she understood that "someday" was a quaint notion if one was promised an eternity. Since losing Daniel, she had become increasingly self-reflective about her life, no longer thinking she had an infinite number of days at her disposal. This mental shift increased her courage, to the extent that she now believed someday may as well be today. To wait posed far more risk than taking the chance.

She turned her attention back to the crowded street. Thankfully, it was far more hygienic than it would have been in the past. Now more of a tourist attraction than anything, tiny remnants of the old butcher shops still remained, visible to the trained eye. Now and again, one could spot metal hooks on overhangs once used for displaying slabs of meat, with shelves below them where cuts would be laid out, the shade of the buildings their only way of staying cool. Back in its heyday, when sanitation as we know it did not exist, these beautiful cobblestone streets held streams of animal blood, tossed out from the slaughterhouses in the back of the shops.

It was mid-July, and she cringed thinking of the stench on a hot day like today. Rarely did books and movies depict the harsh reality of medieval life. Elaborate costuming and chivalric tales of courtly love were far more appealing for audiences. The Shambles was a place where real lives had been lived, and this street saw its share of such harshness.

The buildings that towered above her on both sides cloaked the street in a perpetual shade. She'd never been one for tight spaces, and the looming exteriors, crowds of people, and dim atmosphere proved a bit too claustrophobic for her liking. As she darted through the oncoming foot traffic, she had a strong sense of the energies around her, and the familiar sensations that came with it. Icy prickles inched across her skin, like a spilled inkwell staining a crisp white sheet of paper. No sooner had her temperature adjusted to the cold, flashes of warmth followed. For a moment, her mind flickered with a need to escape but she pushed it into the background, as she had a thousand times before. She shuddered with discomfort, like a hundred tiny bugs were crawling over her skin.

"So what?" she muttered, having taught herself long ago that her distress mattered little in the bigger scheme of things.

Though the feeling was oppressive, she reveled in the notion that her gift had not been lost for good. Even if its return was slow, and the sense of it somewhat disagreeable, it was at least recognizable. The air felt thick, as though all the layers of time wanted to make their presence known at once. She moved around and through centuries of people, each clad in the clothing of their respective time. A young girl carrying a large basket braced against her tiny frame caught her attention. By the look of her dress, she was likely a kitchen girl, mid-seventeenth century. Her basket already heavy with her purchases, she tucked a cloth over its contents, doing her best to protect them from the intrusive insects clouding the air. Her image was crystal clear, her vibrant energy radiating around her in a colorful haze. A few feet away, unaware of her existence, a young couple stood chatting. The man's jet-black hair hung shaggy at his brow, his friend's long legs revealed beneath the high hem of her mini skirt.

The power of a person's energy never ceased to amaze her. Each soul had the ability to stay fixed in a place of importance after death, replaying days long gone. For her, the wonder of the whispers was not only in what they allowed her to see, but in the silent clues they revealed. There was an irony in how much could be said in absolute silence. Thoughts and feelings took the place of conversations, revealing a far greater story than words ever could. She had never seen evidence of life after death, her gift never taking her that far. The whispers, while not always unintrusive, gave her a much-desired sense of uniqueness. Every once in a while, the energy's intensity breached the fabric of time, revealing itself even to those who had no gift of sight. What some often referred to as a ghost sighting, was really nothing more than the momentary materialization of this energy.

As she walked among the afternoon crowd, both the living and the souls of the past, she had the sense that grief was such a solitary emotion. The emptiness of loss wasn't something that could be shared. While those in one's inner circle might feel empathy, even that was just a sliver of the rawness inside. Just like love, loss was an emotion that weighed in a unique way in each person's heart. No two people ever loved the same, and no two people cried the same number of tears where grief was concerned.

The smiling faces and soft chatter on the street reminded her that the dark cloud hovering above was unknown to anyone but herself. No matter her misfortune, the world still spun on its natural rotation, and people moved about their lives unaware of a passing stranger's inner turmoil. Time did not cease its unending quest to progress to the next minute. The only thing out of the ordinary was her silent suffering, nothing more.

Being surrounded by people, even if they weren't all alive in the now, made her realize how much she needed to leave the comfort of the shell she had created for herself. She needed to be around people, to surround herself with happiness—gleaning that energy for herself. Having hung onto sadness for far too long, she was now tired of it. Over and over, she'd told herself there was no guilt in healing; she wasn't disrespecting her husband's death by living. Initially, she had reservations about coming on this trip, but now she was here, walking the streets of York, she accepted just how much she'd missed the sense of empowerment that only came when she pushed herself beyond her desire to be comfortable.

She checked the address on her invitation, then focused on the quaint exterior of the bookstore up the street. Its candy-apple storefront stood out among the host of other shops. She sighed with relief on reading the bold white print on the narrow black sign above the door, knowing she had at last reached her destination. Though the walk from the car was short, dodging the living and the dead in the streets had left her somewhat fatigued. Even so, she couldn't help feeling a buzz of excitement at the prospect of being with her cousin on her big day. She tucked the invitation into her bag and made her way inside.

On entering, she closed her eyes as the smell of ink on paper filled her head. There had always been something safe and warming about the scent of books, new or old. The interior of the shop was neatly arranged, with carefully positioned displays designed to tempt patrons with all the latest publications. She thought of Daniel. Had he been here with her, they would both be shoving a stack of books into the trunk of the car by the day's end.

Trying to exercise a bit of self-control, she flagged down one of the sales clerks to ask where Cassandra's book signing was being held. She reminded herself that she had an enviable library of unread titles at home, and bit back temptation as she made her way to the rear of the store.

She smiled when she spotted her cousin. Cassandra had changed her look since their last meeting. In place of her long flowing locks of golden hair, she had opted for a sophisticated French twist, transforming her from a newly graduated college girl to a smart woman of business, clad in a creamy white dress that hit just above her knees, topped with a finely tailored shrug. To say the least, she looked polished and expensive, and it suited her. Indeed, she had always been a woman well-versed in the trends of the day, a reason why Adelia showed no surprise when she'd dropped her major in history to pursue an education in fashion.

Thinking back to the summer when her grandma had arranged, before she died, for Cassandra to come to stay and assist on a historical research project, it soon became clear that it was not a real calling for the young woman. She had feigned as much interest as she could, but it hadn't been convincing. Both were equally matched in intelligence, but their interests lay in different areas. When Cassandra came to terms with where her passions lay, it opened a world of new opportunities for her.

Her novel was centered around the fashion district in Paris, where two arch rivals, both consumed by their lust to be famous, resorted to murder to achieve their goals. It was such a story that only Cassandra, with her wealth of knowledge and love for an intriguing tale, could write.

Having grown up in London, she had somehow found herself more at home in York, where she'd landed a job at a publisher's and adapted to the slower pace in no time. She was young, single, and successful—things just about anyone could envy.

As Adelia stood watching her cousin's graceful movements, she felt a heaviness in her heart, understanding why no man could resist the woman's charms. She always had an easy confidence about her, and it wasn't difficult to believe why Daniel would have been smitten with her. It was understandable, though no less painful.

A small crowd had gathered, and after a brief introduction by the owner of the establishment, Cassandra gave a reading of the first chapter before sitting at a table to begin signing copies for the eager patrons. One by one they filtered through the line, each giving praise to the author. From her spot behind them all, Adelia found herself drawn to one woman in particular. She had a stone-faced expression, with no hint of amusement crossing the stern lines of her jaw. Her hair was a light shade of brown with dull spatters of steely gray. Its short-cropped style looked somewhat uneven, and Adelia guessed she may have tried her hand at cutting it herself. She wore a pale-pink sweater, with gaudy embellishments that had a way of attracting the eye. Something about the impatient way she fiddled in the line gave the impression she'd come with a purpose.

With each ticking minute, the energy of the room changed. It may have been slight but it was tangible. Adelia glanced up to see if her cousin had noticed, too, but she was far too consumed with her avid fans. Like her, Cassandra hailed from the line of Babbington descendants who had inherited the whispers. While her own gift was more fine-tuned to people and events of the past, Cassandra could read the energy of the present. Now and again, just as today, Adelia found herself also picking up on these fragments of change. It was so rare, she sometimes found it far too confusing to decipher. In all honesty, she avoided any attempt to use her sight in such a way. Quelling the urge to change something could prove overwhelmingly difficult, filling her with intense anxiety. Visions of the past were far safer, with everything and everyone at a comfortable distance.

When the woman with the gaudy shirt made it to the front of the line, Adelia edged closer to better hear the exchange. Just as Cassandra had done with the other patrons, she greeted the woman with a cheery smile, thanking her for her interest in the book.

"I wasn't actually a big fan of the book," the woman said, grimacing.

"And yet, you are here?" Cassandra said, raising a brow—brutal honesty being one of her character traits, even when it wasn't necessary. It was one of the many things Adelia envied about her cousin.

"I want to know why you would choose to put forth such historical inaccuracies. There was just far too much speculation for my taste."

"You are aware that this is a book of fiction, right?" Cassandra's challenge was clear.

"I just found your main character to be unrealistic, and I didn't particularly care for the liberties you took with the historical events."

Cassandra placed her pen beside the pile of novels. "Just to be clear, as this is a work of fiction, none of the characters are actually real. As for the historical events...well, every bit of history is trenched in creative license, isn't it? Unless you were actually there and lived in the moment, I think it's safe to say that all historical accounts have some shred of interpretation attached. Interpretations and creative license go hand in hand." Her face gleamed with a sense of accomplishment at putting the woman squarely into her place.

The women stiffened. "All I'm saying is I wasn't a fan of your work."

"Thank goodness I didn't write it for you, then." Her smile lit up her eyes. "If you want me to sign your copy, I will be pleased.

However, if you wish to storm out and say you will never see me again, I will be equally delighted."

With burning-red cheeks, the woman shot one last glare at her before turning on her heel. She marched over to the exit and shoved it open, with several of the patrons giggling, no doubt loud enough for her to hear before storming out into the street. In true Cassandra fashion, she brushed off the nuisance and continued on with her work. Not a soul in the bookshop would have thought she'd been ruffled at all, with the exception of Adelia who braced herself for the inevitable venting when they were alone later.

At the end of the book signing, she helped her cousin pack up her belongings. Cassandra had parked just a block or so away, which was more than enough time for a rant.

"Tell me why such hatred exists in this world. I haven't done anything to have it dumped upon my doorstep."

"Hatred is a perplexing thing," Adelia said after a heartfelt sigh. "People will hate you for a great many reasons, none of which aren't foolish. They will always despise you whenever your star gets too bright, and forget the world would be very dark without that brilliant light. It's an age-old predicament, and a great many people have been through such difficulty. I assure you, it won't end with her, though I imagine it felt good to give her a piece of your mind."

"I hate people sometimes," Cassandra said, her words almost spat out.

"Are you considering moving to one of the barrier islands and living life as a recluse?" She gave her best sardonic look. "That would be about the only way to completely remove people from your life."

Cassandra shot her a smoldering look of reproach, and she shrugged in response, realizing it was too early for sarcasm.

"What a vile little woman."

"Yes, indeed. Not to worry, though, you had an amazing crowd to celebrate your novel. Don't let yourself be troubled by one insignificant person. She is just bitter, that's all. Her anger has far less to do with you than even she realizes."

"Well, I suppose I would be pretty pissed off, too, if I had gotten that lot in life." Her nose wrinkled as she fumed. "She smelled like frozen peas and cats."

"Exactly how close did you get to that lady?" Adelia wouldn't have wished this unfortunate event on her cousin, but it was providing a fair amount of entertainment.

Cassandra was like most women in that her outward self-confidence wasn't always a reflection of what lay inside. She struggled to keep up with the image society had prescribed. Though she was blessed with beauty, it came with its burdens, not all of which could be considered pleasant.

She stood apart from most women, in that life never really allowed her the chance to lose. Growing up in a wealthy family never gave her the opportunity to fail at anything, with a safety net of some kind always present for her to count on. On one hand, this might be looked upon as a positive. She spoke her mind in all things, as she had no real reason to conceal her thoughts. Yet, a harsh reality lurked in the distance; she had never been afforded the chance to develop the grit that comes with failure. As with all people, she would someday, but a life of comfort had prolonged that inevitable growth.

"Let's not talk about her anymore tonight," she said with a childish eye roll. "I am so excited that you came to see me here in York, and I won't let that horrible woman spoil that for either of us. Besides, I am famished after all that work. Let's go find somewhere to eat so we can talk."

"That sounds perfect," Adelia replied. "I will drive. You just lead the way."

Cassandra responded with a slight scowl. "I am a much better driver now than you remember, Adelia. Just hop in the car and I will take us there."

Adelia hesitated, recalling a few near-death experiences as a passenger in her cousin's car. Not wanting to be rude, she smiled in agreement. Anyway, now Cassandra had lived in York for some time, she would be far better at navigating the busy city.

As she drove along, her improvement as a driver came as a welcome surprise. The last few years had brought about some maturity for the woman. Even as Adelia's own world had come to a sudden halt, things were still evolving for everyone else. It may have made her a little envious but it was something she needed to learn to accept.

After being seated at the restaurant and having their order taken, their conversation started out light. The last time they were together was for Daniel's funeral, which had not given them much of a chance to catch up.

"How are things going with the baby?" Cassandra asked, her concern genuine. "Have you been keeping up with your physician's appointments?

"Yes, Mom," Adelia said with a chuckle. "Things are going fairly well now. My stomach was a bit queasy at first, but that has subsided. It was hard to tell if it was the baby or just what I was going through at the time. I'm far enough along that things are starting to feel more settled. Halfway there."

"Good. I'm glad to hear that. I know you have been through a lot, but it really is important that you take care of yourself. You have so much ahead of you now—you have to stay focused on things to come."

Adelia shot her a reassuring smile, grateful for her concern. As they waited on their food to arrive, the conversation dwindled and she couldn't help but notice the way Cassandra gave her the occasional searching glance. The woman was intuitive about others—Adelia more than most. The bond they shared in being keepers of the whispers made it difficult to hide anything.

She was unsure how to ask her about Daniel. There seemed no easy way to keep from being rude. Not knowing the details of Daniel's obsession complicated things further. If he had harbored some infatuation with her cousin, there was a chance she didn't know. Perhaps it was something he'd kept to himself. What if she knew? What if he *had* shared his true feelings with her? Would Cassandra have kept it secret to avoid hurting her? Did she feel the same about Daniel?

"Cassandra..." Her voice trailed off before she pulled herself together. "Was there ever a time when Daniel acted anything more than cousinly to you?"

Cassandra stared back, her furrowed brows conveying her confusion.

"Did he ever say anything, or make a gesture of sorts that felt...off?"

Through the heavy silence, her cousin squirmed in her seat, even grimacing.

"What is it?" Adelia asked, unable to hold it in.

"I... I am trying to understand what you are asking me here." Cassandra's discomfort was evident in her pained expression.

"I found this." Adelia reached down to her bag on the floor and pulled out the sketchbook. She eased open the front cover and handed it across the table.

As Cassandra flipped through the pages, Adelia mustered the courage to speak again. "I'm just trying to understand why he would draw you over and over. Why the fascination?"

After scanning the images, Cassandra looked at Adelia, her gaze unwavering. At that moment, both women understood what was being asked.

"This is not me, Adelia," she said, the certainty of her tone solid. "She doesn't look like me."

"She doesn't?" Adelia turned the sketchbook around. "But how can...?" She flipped two pages over, doubts now flooding her mind. "Well, he wasn't exactly an artist by trade." It almost came out as a groan.

"I would say he was quite a good artist," Cassandra said. "These are beautiful pictures. It's just not me."

"But... I was convinced..."

Cassandra gave her an assessing look, as if the gears in her brain were moving at a slow and meticulous pace.

"I see what you are trying to do here, Adelia. You want to replace your sadness with anger. You want to convince yourself that Daniel was somehow unfaithful to you, so you can move on, being mad instead of grieving his loss. I don't know who this is, or why he drew her, but one thing I can be certain of is that Daniel never spent a day being anything but dedicated to you alone."

"So...he never said anything to you? Anything in the way of professing some affection for you?"

"My love for you as my cousin is the only thing that is keeping me from being completely offended right now." She leaned forward, her irritation at this irrational inquisition beginning to show. "Don't you think I would have said something to you if he had?"

Adelia groaned inside. "I guess I thought you might have held it in to spare my feelings." As the words came out, she heard how ludicrous she sounded.

Cassandra chuckled. "Haven't you learned by now? I am no good at sparing people's feelings." She patted Adelia's hand, no doubt an attempt at reassurance. "I would have absolutely told you if your husband ever made any attempt to come onto me. He did no such thing, ever! If you think I would hide such a thing from you, then the person I am, and the one you think me to be, must be two very different people."

"I'm sorry," Adelia said, the groan clear in her voice this time. She felt like a first-class idiot. "I just wanted some sort of answer. I know you would never do anything to hurt me. Ever since Daniel died, I don't seem to be able to use the whispers as I did before."

"You want to see Daniel, and you can't," Cassandra clarified, no doubt reading her cousin's feelings like a page in her novel. "He feels too far away."

"Exactly. I get these strange flashes of him from time to time but that is all. I can't seem to make him whole. I thought this sketchbook might hold the answer...somehow."

"Maybe it does. Who can say? All I know is that I am not part of your answer, at least not in the way you are insinuating."

"Fair enough," Adelia said, though she still felt dissatisfied. What her reaction might have been had Cassandra revealed some deep dark secret, she didn't know. Desperate for some form of closure, it was clear she would not get the answers her heart desired here. The mood had taken a downward turn, and she decided a change of subject was in order.

"Enough of this nonsense, tell me all about your novel. How on earth did you come up with the story?"

Cassandra's clenched jaw relaxed and her normal bright smile returned.

"Well, being a writer is much like hearing the whispers. Your brain is racked with the onslaught of voices that no amount of good therapy or medication can quell. It comes to you bit by bit, but eventually you just start putting those words down on paper, and then something truly magical happens."

"I can only imagine all those extra voices in your head make for a crowded existence." Adelia laughed at the irony of it all.

"The world is always a crowded place for you and I. Our minds are never really quiet. Sometimes I think that is half our problem. The average person only has their own issues to worry about, but you and I are forced to take on the burdens of everyone else who ever existed in our space."

Adelia nodded. "When you put it that way, I couldn't agree more. It's hard, sometimes, peering into someone else's life, when all you want is to get a handle on your own. Maybe I should be thankful for this disruption since Daniel...passed. As much as I want to see him, it probably won't help this pain subside. It may well have the opposite effect."

"Daniel will come through to you in time. We may not understand the why or the how, but the whispers know when it's the right time. You have put your trust in your gift before, and this isn't any different. For the time being, you need to focus your attention elsewhere. I think you are pushing yourself too hard to get to him. The more you want it, the less likely the whispers will cooperate. You are far too emotionally invested in Daniel for his energy to emerge. Yes, you need to take a step back and clear your mind."

"I wholeheartedly...agree with you." She toyed with her napkin, aware that her voice had cracked. "Everything you are saying makes perfect sense. I...just don't seem to be able to relinquish my need to see him. I don't know where to even begin."

Cassandra responded with a gentle smile, conveying her understanding.

"So, what is your next project?" Adelia forced the corners of her mouth into a modest smile, hoping to steer the conversation in a more uplifting direction.

"Actually, you are going to love it." Her cousin beamed as she straightened. "I happen to have become acquainted with a local man who owns an antique store specializing in rare jewelry. He has come into possession of some items he believes are from the medieval era, and they may have been owned by someone of high status, perhaps even royal."

Adelia leaned forward and rested her chin on her closed fist. "You have my attention now."

"I thought so. Given my background in fashion and history, he asked for my assistance in determining the provenance."

"Have you seen the pieces yet?"

"No, but I'm meeting with him later this week."

"Drat, I will be long gone by then, but you will call and fill me in on what you discover, won't you?"

"Of course. I will be sure to tell you everything. Besides, I'm not convinced I will not need your help along the way."

Adelia couldn't help smiling. The idea of some long-lost jewels being discovered held real appeal. Regardless of whether the pieces had been owned by anyone notable, any type of find this old piqued her interest. With next to no detail to go on, the options were wide open, and the idea of waiting several days for Cassandra's call felt way too long.

"York is a magnificent town," Cassandra said, snapping her back to the present. "Tomorrow, you and I will go exploring. It will be good to get your mind off everything. And it's not good for you or the baby to be wound so tight. No, we shall do our best not to talk about Daniel, or evil demons disguised in horrible pink sweaters. We will just be tourists for the day."

"As much as I hate busy streets and crowds, I have to admit that sounds perfect. It will be nice for it to be just you and I."

"Let's enjoy our dinner then, and I will get you back to the hotel. You will need a good night's rest for our adventure."

****

Though she swore to herself that she wouldn't, that night Adelia found herself propped up in her hotel bed going through the pictures of the Yorkshire Rose. Cassandra's eyes told her all she needed to know. If Daniel held some infatuation, her cousin hadn't picked up on it. She was far too intuitive to have missed such a glaring sign. If she could be ruled out as the woman, then that left every other blonde woman in England as a possibility.

With quiet determination, she scoured the pictures, taking note of every single detail. It seemed impossible to think that such a remarkable beauty as this could ever exist. The pale pink of the woman's cheeks gave off an ethereal glow against her perfect porcelain skin. Long ebony lashes cast a faint shadow beneath her eyes, giving her a look of some unspoken sadness. Adelia could almost feel the gentle gusts of wind as they blew her golden strands back from her face. Everything about this mysterious woman's looks was the exact opposite of herself. Her chestnut hair was always combed into meticulous waves that fell right below her shoulders, her dark-brown eyes a stark contrast to the baby-blue of the

Yorkshire Rose. Though the portraits only revealed the woman from the shoulders up, it was easy to see that her frame was not as full as her own. The sketches conveyed a wild and untamed spirit about the woman, though her far-off gaze spoke of some hidden vulnerability. Adelia couldn't help but think of herself—polished, controlled, ever the servant of a well-plotted routine.

She wondered if the qualities she saw in this woman were ones Daniel desired. Did he wish she possessed them herself? Maybe, deep down, he held some attraction to a woman who lived her life carefree, unburdened by the rules of society. If that were indeed the case, then surely he had found his wife's personality lacking. Such a brutal comparison pained her heart, thrusting her back to days of her youth and the constant awareness that she wasn't anything like the other girls. How a simple image, crafted by pencil strokes and vibrant watercolors, could bring out her insecurities in such a savage way was beyond her own reasoning.

As she stretched her arms up to touch the wall behind her, she felt a light flutter low in her abdomen. The sensation brought a welcome smile. These past few months had been so turbulent, it was easy to forget that she was pregnant. Being so wrapped up in everything around her, she had barely noticed time ticking by. She was more than four months along now, and nearly halfway there. There was so much to prepare for, yet up to this point she hadn't done a thing. She supposed by now most expectant mothers would have a nursery well underway. Her mother planned on coming to stay during her final month and a few weeks after the baby's birth. She could almost envision Elaine Grey's irritated scowl on seeing that she didn't have one thing ready for the baby on her arrival. That should be her first order of business when she returned to Middleham Manor. Though she was nearing her thirtieth birthday, she was still not too grown up to invoke her mother's disapproving glare.

She slid down in the bed to rest her head on the pillow, and smoothed her hands across her growing bump. Even if she couldn't see or feel Daniel, he would always be near. He had not left her to face the world alone after all. Every day for the rest of her life, she could gaze upon his face in the eyes of the gift he had left behind.

Chapter Seven

Just after breakfast, Cassandra arrived to lead Adelia on her grand tour of York, a vibrant city steeped in history. As they walked along the towering stones of Micklegate Bar, Adelia could not help but feel as though she was once again sharing a connection with Richard III. The House of York's history was deeply rooted in these lands. It was here at the city's gate that his father, the Duke of York, had his head displayed on a spike after being declared a traitor at the beginning of the Wars of the Roses. While Cassandra found this gruesome story enthralling, she still wrinkled her nose in disgust.

"Such savagery!"

"Not for the time," Adelia said. "We may think it cruel today but, in the mid-fourteen hundreds, spiked heads were something you would take the wife and kids out to see. The warring parties didn't have the media at their disposal, and this was one of the ways they used to spread propaganda."

Cassandra frowned. "I'd say placing a rotting head on a spike was a highly effective way of getting the message out. If you ever show your baby a public execution, even a reenactment, I shall never speak to you again. History is interesting and all, but you have to draw the line somewhere."

Adelia shook her head. "I shall take reenactments of public executions off my list of daytrips then."

Cassandra gave her a sideways glance, then pointed to another location on her map. Let's do the York Minster next. I know you have seen a great many of England's cathedrals but this one is truly breathtaking. I am sure you can find some dusty old graves there to pique your interest."

"If it includes death and despair, then I am in." She chuckled. "Oh, can we add the Treasurer's House to our excursion? I love the stories about the ghosts of the Roman Legion."

"Adelia, why am I not surprised that, in a city filled with wonderful shops and restaurants, you are more interested in hearing about Roman ghosts in a musty old basement?"

"You shouldn't be surprised at all. I guess I have a soft spot for things that are a little weird. Besides, I want to see them myself."

"It's right beside the Minster. We can add it to our list for the day. Just to be clear, though, I don't plan on spending my afternoon chatting up Roman ghosts. Unless they all look like Kirk Douglas in Spartacus."

Adelia chuckled again. "I suppose that wouldn't be all that bad, but I doubt we could get that lucky. Besides, you know very well we can't chat up ghosts. They wouldn't speak English anyway. All we can do is observe, nothing more."

Cassandra pouted. "That sure takes all the fun out of it. I hate the idea of even observing them. I have never found anything about the gift that is of any use to me."

"That's completely untrue, and you know it," Adelia said as they walked onto the grounds of the Minster. Its towering roofline cloaked them in its enormous shadow. She stopped to study the ornate carvings by skilled stonemasons, astounded by the building's breathtaking magnificence. While she had visited here once before, there was so much to appreciate in the old building that one visit could never be enough. "The whispers are just a part of our lives. Now that I find myself a little rusty, I see that we use it far more than we know. There is no way not to, for me."

"That is where you and I differ. I don't want it to be part of my life. I like relying on my own senses to guide me. I doubt that you and I are the only two people on the planet who have the second sight, but still, I want to function like the other ninety-nine-point-nine percent of the population does. I block them out as much as humanly possible. Unless it pertains to some insanely rich and handsome guy, which is when I really do want to know what he thinks about me." She winked, her smile bordering on devious.

Adelia let her cousin rattle on, knowing there wasn't a shred of truth to her words. The whispers could be pushed into the background, but never for long. Her sight had become so second nature, it was almost part of her subconscious. Over time she had developed a certain numbness to her visions, hardly registering that they were out of the ordinary, and adapting without thought. She doubted it was any different for Cassandra, though she wasn't likely to admit it.

As they entered the cathedral, she felt compelled to lower her voice to a whisper. The last thing she needed was for the other visitors to overhear the conversation of two women endowed with clairvoyant abilities.

"You are different from me, Cassandra. I have never really had the ability to read the energy around the living. My grandma didn't either. In fact, I think she would have been amazed to know you can, as she truly thought it wasn't possible. Sure, I get flashes of things when I am around people, but I chalk it up to intuition. It's more of a gut feeling, really, not like the images and voices I hear from the past. When the whispers come to me from someone who has passed on, it's like all five of my senses are at play. The images are so lifelike, as if I am there in the actual moment. That's why I can't understand Daniel not coming through to me."

"He will," Cassandra said. "You have to give it time. I might know someone who can help you."

"No one can know about the whispers, Cassandra." She caught the hint of agitation in her voice. "I'm sorry... That came out harsh. It's just that, I don't think there is anyone who can help me with this problem."

"I have an idea, but I need to do some checking first. Just be patient. Your gift is still with you. It's not like the whispers are broken. I mean, you can see that lady over there, right?" She flicked a glance toward the edge of the nave.

"The one in the English Gable Hood?" Adelia asked, casting a nonchalant nod at a woman clad in a plush velvet gown, kneeling in prayer. Judging by the cut of her attire, she believed her to be from the Tudor period—early 1500's.

Cassandra smiled. "That's the one. What about those two men over there?"

"By the look of their coats and trousers, I would say the Georgian era. Regency."

"Straight out of a Jane Austin novel."

"God, I love Jane Austin." She smiled as she watched the two men engaged in deep conversation.

"Me too," Cassandra said. "Anyway, to the point. Your gift is not gone. You can still do everything you did before, you just don't have the right to choose who and what you see."

Adelia spun around to face her. "I thought you said you try not to use your gift anymore."

"First off, I don't use it, I am simply showing you something for your benefit. Stop trying to sidetrack the conversation." She scrunched up her face like a snotty teenager would to their bossy parents.

Adelia couldn't hold back a giggle, which reverberated off the walls of the massive cathedral. Biting her lip, aware of the glances from living visitors, she grabbed Cassandra's hand and pulled her back out through the door.

"Lovely old cathedral," she chimed as they darted out, "but it's time to go...to the Treasurer's House for the Roman ghosts."

Cassandra threw her head back. "Uuuuhhhggg. Not the bloody Romans."

As luck would have it, the Roman ghosts were not so willing to reveal themselves. Though disappointed, Adelia just shrugged as Cassandra pulled her along to a host of other must-see sights.

After traversing as much of the city as their aching feet would allow, the two women, while exhausted, had enough energy for a quick dinner. Later, as Adelia slung herself onto the softness of her mattress, body depleted and ready for sleep, she couldn't remember the last time she had felt this good.

****

The next morning, Adelia set out on foot to explore a little more of York on her own. Cassandra had work to do, and they agreed to meet up that evening to share one last dinner together before Adelia returned home. She hoped her cousin would meet with the antique dealer soon. The suspense of knowing more about the jewelry was almost too much. In truth, she wished she had such a quest to occupy her mind. The sketchbook was intriguing but she would much rather have a mystery a little less personal to solve.

Just like the day before, the city was a hive of activity. For her first stop, she couldn't resist returning to the bookshop. As well as a couple of other titles, she purchased ten copies of Cassandra's novel, her plan being to donate them to the Middleham Library and the University at Leeds. It was the least she could do to get her cousin's hard work out into the world.

Later, on her return to the hotel, she placed her purchases in the trunk of the car, had a spot of lunch, then spent the rest of the afternoon meandering around the city enjoying the sights and sounds of centuries of its inhabitants. Just as Cassandra had so annoyingly pointed out, her ability to hear the whispers had just stalled for a bit, not ceased. She took solace in knowing that, someday, Daniel's presence would come back into her life. Nothing she did would expedite the inevitable, so she just had to be patient.

That evening they met at one of Cassandra's favorite restaurants. With her spirits lifted, and feeling a bit like her old self again, she'd dressed up for the occasion, donning her favorite navy-blue dress and a string of pearls. It had been a long time since she'd put such effort into her appearance, and she liked the way it felt to at least feel moderately human again.

As they finished up their last dinner together, Cassandra declared, "I have a surprise for you, Adelia Brown."

"What sort of surprise?" She raised a cautious brow, almost afraid to receive the answer.

"You will see. Just follow me."

They rose from their seats and made their way out onto the street. Cassandra was so filled with excitement, her long strides left Adelia trailing and breathless.

"Wait up," she called. "I'm still pregnant, you know. Not to mention about three inches shorter than you. I can't move quite that fast."

"God, I'm sorry. I forgot." Cassandra fell into a fit of giggles. "This is going to be so great."

Adelia caught up. "Then just tell me what we are doing, already. What on earth are you getting me into this time?"

"We are going to see a witch." Her tone was matter of fact. She spun on her heel and started walking again, a bit slower this time.

Adelia followed, shaking her head. "A witch?"

"An apothecary, if you like."

"What for?"

Her cousin had always been prone to hairbrained ideas, but even this was more eccentric than expected.

"You said you feel as if something is blocking your vision. Let's see if we can remedy that problem."

"I know I said that, but I don't see how a...witch can fix that for me."

"Apothecaries have been around for centuries. They understand the natural world far better than any physician."

Adelia pushed on to keep up. "Cassandra, I don't have a medical condition! I have a clairvoyance issue, and one I have not divulged to many. I don't think a witch, or an apothecary, as you say, can do anything to solve my inability to read and interpret my dead husband's spirit."

"Now, you don't know that." Her cousin angled her head as she looked at her. "This particular woman has helped me a great deal in the past. She is much more than a simple apothecary. She is well-versed in reading energy, and has a great deal of experience in the matter. It may come as a shock to you, but we are not the only people in the world who possess such a gift."

That did come as a bit of a shock. Not that someone else possessed the ability—that was most certainly plausible—she just hadn't thought she would meet someone who did, at least outside of her own family. The knowledge of how or with whom the Babbington gift had begun was lost to time, and such a guarded secret had never been documented in the family archives, likely because public perceptions could often be dangerous, proving fatal in some cases.

She did not know how far back in her ancestors the gift stretched. Throughout history, clairvoyance, especially in women, was often labeled as witchcraft, or some type of mental affliction. Neither would have equated to a desirable outcome. Even today, in the modern world of 1966, revealing the whispers would provoke mocking and disbelief, and it wasn't a topic to disclose to perfect strangers over evening tea. No matter how much society evolved, some things were best kept to oneself.

As they passed dark windows of shops closed up for the night, she caught sight of a dim light burning up ahead. There, tucked between two buildings, stood a narrow storefront with a small wooden sign hanging above its door: "Apothecary of York," its words bordered by two sprigs of lavender bundled with thyme. Cassandra gave her a devilish grin as she twisted the doorknob.

A loud chime of a bell signaled their arrival, its sound filling the quiet summer night like a ship's foghorn. It reminded her of Mortimer's bookshop back in Coldridge. She hoped this wasn't an omen of the icy reception she had received then.

Stepping inside, her head was flooded with the aroma of numerous herbs, all slamming her senses at once. The smell, while pervasive, didn't bother her. She had taken to growing herbs back at Middleham Manor, a pastime picked up from Laura Bickel, the former owner.

Long wooden shelves lined the walls, all filled with clear glass jars of dried plants. Tables were topped with bottles of various sizes, containing different-colored oils. It looked like a cross between a gardener's paradise and a mad-scientist's laboratory. The cocktail of scents evoked a joyful familiarity, and being surrounded by nature's bounty calmed her.

She knew she should be nervous about whatever wild plan Cassandra harbored, but she couldn't muster any level of apprehension. Peacefulness existed within these walls, with the shop's energy crystal clear to her. Perhaps the lavender scent was helping.

"Well, hello," a woman called, her soft voice emerging from the back. The short curvy woman approached, smiling at Cassandra as though they were old friends. "What a nice surprise, Cassandra," she said, reaching out to give her a hug.

"Meredith, this is my cousin, Adelia." She stepped back from the hug. "She has come to pay me a visit."

Meredith smiled back, her dark-gray eyes searching. "Adelia," she said, the word echoing with gentle resonance. "Cassandra has spoken of you before. I'm so pleased to make your acquaintance. In fact, I believe I have been expecting you."

Adelia didn't know how to respond to the woman's peculiar choice of words. Meredith was not what she had expected when Cassandra first announced they were going to see a witch. She'd pictured some raven-haired woman with wild eyes, dressed in flowing black garb. Meredith was far more polished, her silky brown hair, carrying hints of caramel streaks, rested on her shoulders. Her radiant skin made her age difficult to discern. The pale light of the room gave her face the well-defined play of shadows like a black and white photograph of a 1940's starlet. Something about her screamed "Film Noir." Even her short stature complemented her full frame with perfection. She radiated her own kind of beauty—natural and unapologetic—her eyes conveying confidence, as though her secrets were not tucked away as tight as her own.

Standing beside two women so pretty made her feel...well, less pretty, and she winced at the thought of being jealous of their good looks. She shouldn't have been surprised at her envy, considering how she felt about some sketches in a tattered notebook. If she were honest, she was being downright petty. Yet another thing to add to the list of undesirable character traits she had discovered about herself. Perhaps it was more admitting than discovering. Either way, it wasn't the woman she wanted to be.

In times like this, when her insecurities got the best of her, she relied on what she knew herself to be: an intelligent, highly accomplished professor with a list of accolades to her name. She was not a beauty in her own mind, but far from unattractive—naturally beautiful in her own right.

That had her straightening up. She was in an apothecary's shop, for what reason she still didn't fully know, but it had nothing to do with being in a beauty contest. There was no prize to win, and her insecurities about her looks were misplaced. Irrelevant.

She focused back on Meredith, whose soft gaze was fixed on her as though she could read her thoughts. A flush of warmth washed across her cheeks as she stared back. Even if the woman couldn't read her thoughts verbatim, she was picking up on her inner turmoil. She fumbled out of habit with the string of pearls around her neck, aware that both she and the apothecary seemed content on examining each other.

"As you know, Meredith," Cassandra said, "my cousin and I are quite similar in our paths. Yet, Adelia has found herself changed after the passing of her husband. Things just don't seem to be coming through to her quite the same now. Her mind is somewhat muddled, to say the least."

Adelia shot her cousin a disapproving look. "My mind is not muddled."

"You thought there may have been some secret relationship between Daniel and I." She arched her brows. "I think it's safe to say there is some muddle in your mind. Not to worry, though, Meredith can help you. Of that, I am absolutely sure."

They glared at each other, like two sisters at war, until Meredith reached out and took Adelia's hand into hers, breaking the tense moment between the cousins.

"Not to worry, dear. I saw your arrival in my cards just this morning. You are meant to be right where you are, and I am most pleased to do anything I can to help."

Adelia was then led like a helpless child to a small round table near the back of the shop. She couldn't understand why but there was something here that made her feel safe, even eager to relinquish control.

The three women took their seats, with Meredith looking at her. "Tell me what your last few months have been like. Spare no detail. If you hold back, I will know."

Without hesitation, Adelia found herself bleeding out her heart and soul to this complete stranger. She recounted, in excruciating detail, her last moments with Daniel and how hollow she'd felt since his passing. If that wasn't enough, she shared about the day in his den, seated at his old writing desk, and the discovery of the sketchbook that sent her whole world into more of a tailspin than it had already been. Sadness filled her while recounting how foggy his image came through, like the flicker of an old-time movie reel just before it came unwound. Though still embarrassed, she didn't bother to conceal her initial suspicions that the images of the woman in the sketchbook was Cassandra, and her sense of betrayal at not knowing who she should blame. As the words tumbled out, each revelation felt like an open wound being tended.

When every word was expelled, she sat there, amazed, and coughed once into her hand to dislodge a dry scratch in the back of her throat. She felt light as air, a feeling she could not recall experiencing in such a long time, even well before Daniel had died. There was such freedom in honesty.

"You have done well to come here tonight," Meredith said, her words coming slow and easy. "This is really just a matter of balance.

When the natural world becomes unbalanced, we are blocked from experiencing life in its purest form. All we need to do is rebalance things, and you will find your vision as clear as ever."

"Is it really that simple?" Adelia asked, relieved that the answer could come so easily.

"In theory, yes. In practice, not so much." The apothecary tilted her head and drew in a sharp breath, as if preparing herself for the honesty she was about to impart. "There are some things I can do for you here, but some of this you will need to work out on your own. Tell me, when you first discovered your gift of sight, did it come easy to you?"

Adelia raised a shoulder. "Yes and no. It took me a while to truly be open to accepting that the emotions I felt were from some external force, and not just my own personal anxiety. I had grown so comfortable in thinking things were my fault. When I finally came to terms with that, my gift developed quite rapidly. Even more so than for my grandmother, who passed it down."

"Adelia didn't figure out she had a gift until she was twenty years old," Cassandra added, her brow raised, as if Adelia could not see the gesture. "She spent most of her childhood thinking she was looney."

Adelia wrinkled her nose at her—a silent chide. "I can be a little resistant to listening at times," she admitted. "I have a tendency to want to do things my own way."

"Don't we all," Meredith said, her smile jovial. "The secret is that you have to learn to connect with the answers you seek. Your gift gives you the advantage of reading and interpreting the energy around you. That comes without will most times. However, when your senses are blocked, you will find that you only get part of the picture. Critical things are missing. Unfortunately, we don't know what we don't know, so we interpret a scenario as it is, and most times it's incorrect. We must remove whatever is blocking these senses so you can receive the full images you seek."

"I think I need that more than ever now." She lowered her gaze to her clasped hands. "I need answers from my husband."

"I must be honest in telling you that the answers you seek might actually be his questions and not your own. I get the sense that he had inner turmoil he needed to remedy. Perhaps in giving him that closure, you will find it for yourself."

Adelia shifted as a surge of resistance entered her body. If there was one thing she understood about her own abilities, it was that she could not do anything to change the past. Not only was it impossible, it was unthinkable. Such meddling in things could only lead to something catastrophic. Even if she could, she knew better. What was more, she couldn't interact with the dead. There were times when she'd felt an acute sense that they were aware of her presence, but it never developed to more than that. Deep down, she supposed there really were no rules when it came to the souls that breached the veil of time. Ghosts didn't have to be from the past.

All these thoughts aside, it was ludicrous to think that Meredith could give her the power to bring Daniel whatever closure he needed in life. Who was to say he needed closure anyway? For all she knew, the closure he sought was in the arms of another woman, and that was the last thing she wanted to give the husband she had loved so much. No, if that was what Daniel wanted, he was out of luck. If ghosts were about unfinished business, then Daniel's soul would have to stay that way.

A surge of anger welled inside her. On seeing Meredith's blank expression, she knew the woman could sense it, too, though she did nothing, nor uttered a word, letting her feel as she wanted. She made no effort to rush her, letting her mind spin in circles. Deep inside, she wanted to know the truth about the woman Daniel had spent so much time sketching in his stupid book. She wanted to know just how angry she should be at him. Had this been a love interest, long before they'd met? If it wasn't Cassandra, as her cousin had insisted, then who the hell was she? Every fiber in her being wanted to discover the truth, but she didn't know if she was ready for whatever the answer might be.

She let out a slow puff of breath as she set her gaze on Meredith once more.

"My dear, even if I could give you the answers you seek, I wouldn't. This is a decision you have to make on your own. You have to discover the truth, alone. It's all part of the process of finally healing."

Her voice was soft but stern, giving Adelia no other option but to accept what had been offered.

"I want to know, but I'm afraid." Warm tears prickled her eyes on hearing these words said aloud.

"Have you been afraid before?" Meredith asked. "Have you ever been so paralyzed with fear, you felt your skin crawl?"

"Y-yes," Adelia stammered. "I have felt like that more times than I care to admit."

"What did you do? How did you make it through? How have you survived so long that now you are here, a living breathing person sitting inches from me? Fear was not the death of you, I see."

"No, fear was not the death of me. I just pushed through it somehow."

Meredith raised a brow. "Every single time?"

"Yes, I suppose I did."

"Now here you are, a woman who has pushed through every bit of fear that ever plagued her before. You are here, facing something that makes your skin crawl to even think about it. I suspect this time won't be so different. You don't strike me as the type who will just go on and live her life with such a burning question in the back of her mind. If it's not today, fine. But someday you will wake up and decide that the answer is worth the risk. That your question has weighed on your mind far too long, and you will push straight through all of your hesitation to finally have the matter settled. It can be today or years from now, it matters only to you. My dear, you have the right to decide what you want from your own life."

As the words sank in, a tiny flame reignited in Adelia's chest—a burning desire to return to the woman she had been, who would no longer be hindered by the forces working against her. She could fight against a great many things, but not her own nature.

"To thine own self be true," she said.

Cassandra groaned. "Oh God, not Shakespeare."

Adelia gave her the expected eye roll. How on earth could her cousin loathe Shakespeare so much? So irritating.

She turned back to Meredith, swallowed her pride and took an unimaginable leap of faith.

"If there is one thing I have learned in my life, it is that anything is possible. I just want to be closer to Daniel, and whatever that means for either of us, I must be willing to accept."

Meredith grinned. "Well then, let's get down to business and set things back to rights."

She led Adelia to a long narrow table covered in soft linens, and asked her to lie on it. Drawing from her knowledge of ancient Japanese arts, she worked to perform a cleansing ritual. As she began, she explained in detail how she would work to rebalance Adelia's lifeforce by purging the bad energy to allow the good to flow without constraint.

An intense warmth traveled through Adelia's torso and along her limbs as Meredith hovered her hands over her body. She closed her eyes and, without warning, was gripped by a sudden urge to cry, with hot tears pooling beneath her eyelids. Though the room was quiet, the low hum of a faint vibration filled the air, but she kept her eyes closed, focusing on the rush of pressure surging through her in waves. Unable to hold back her emotions any longer, she shuddered and allowed the sobs building in her chest to escape, and in doing so, a new sensation of pure light seemed to fill her body. Though her eyes were closed, she visualized bright rays filling the room with a near heavenly glow. Never in her life had she felt so liberated. It was so overwhelming, and relaxing, she lay still for several minutes, even after Meredith had ceased her work.

When she opened her eyes, the whole room felt different. Where had that bad energy gone? She could not have cared less. There was no doubt in her mind that her body was no longer its vessel.

Meredith crossed the room to an old wooden cabinet with many small drawers. She opened several, pulled out tiny objects, then returned to Adelia. Without a word, the apothecary gripped her hand and slid the cool items onto her palm. Adelia looked down, blinking at the sight of several small crystals of varying shapes and colors. Each was polished to a fine shine, and she couldn't help but rub her fingertips along their smooth surfaces.

"Energy flows through us, my dear. The energy of light passes through you with ease. Darker energy struggles to follow the same path. It can quickly find itself trapped within us and its release is something that takes a great amount of practice and understanding. These will help you. Keep them with you at all times. Remember that, like you, crystals can become bogged down with energy. Now and then you will need to cleanse them with a good overnight soak in salted water. Learn to fill yourself with the true treasures of this earth. They are anything but material. Not everything that brings us joy is light energy. Not everything that brings us sadness is dark. It takes time to distinguish these things, but you will learn it if you listen."

Listening was always the key to the whispers. Since discovering her gift, she understood the importance of clearing her mind in order to hear the purity of their message. However, this had also been her biggest challenge. Perhaps a quiet mind came easy to a child, but proved more difficult for an adult. The grown-up world was full of worry, with every day bringing more and more challenges—maybe the reason the world was no longer so easy to silence. Now that Daniel was gone, everything about living and operating in adulthood fell on her shoulders only. Her summer sabbatical from work would come to an end in the fall, with the daily grind of life returning in full force. In doing so, the demands of maintaining her large old house might prove too much. Every bit of work she and Daniel had divided as a couple would be hers alone to contend with, but with a child to raise as well, the prospect of what lay ahead was daunting. But her inner peace had felt miles away before, and Meredith's hands had somehow lifted all these worries, pulling them from her heart and thrusting them into the atmosphere.

She gripped the crystals tight, the light of hope filling her. Closure felt closer, as though she was right on the cusp of its arrival.

Chapter Eight

In the morning, as Adelia said goodbye to her cousin, she was almost on her toes with the change in herself, as if Meredith's ritual had dispelled the weight of decades of anguish. If she had been skeptical before, she was a believer now. Though she still hadn't sensed Daniel, she was confident it would happen in time. As she reached the outskirts of town, heading for the road back to Middleham, she became aware of a physical pull in her hands as she gripped the steering wheel. She had experienced it before, and knew the whispers wanted her to follow their lead.

After pulling off to the side, she sat for a while in quiet contemplation, trying to decipher what she was being called to do. Several minutes passed but the answer didn't come. No, it wasn't going to happen here. Embracing her new sense of self, she let instinct take the wheel and easing the car back onto the road.

When she reached the crossroads of one of the main thoroughfares, she turned, without hesitation, onto the road heading south, taking her away from Middleham. For reasons she couldn't explain, she found herself headed straight to Oxford, bound for a small house on a lonely country road, where Daniel grew up, and where her father-in-law still resided. Something told her that was where her journey would begin. What answers Dan Brown could bring to his daughter-in-law, only the whispers knew.

A touch of guilt surfaced at the prospect of showing up unannounced. The poor man took the loss of his son as hard as she had in losing her husband. With Daniel's mother passing when he was just ten years old, he'd developed a close relationship with his dad. Like Daniel, his father was always a busy man, winding his way through the country working on his next big research project. Dan had been an old schoolmate of her father's back at Oxford. When she'd first arrived in England, for what was supposed to be a summer trip, John Grey introduced her to his old mate's son, never thinking the two would fall in love. After she and Daniel married and relocated to Middleham Manor, father and son did their best to stay in touch by phone and through the post. Though visiting with the elder Dr. Brown happened as often as they could manage, she never had the opportunity to spend much time alone with him. Being compelled to come to Oxford on a whim, she hadn't considered how strange her unexpected arrival would be until now. But the pull—this unexplainable sense that she needed to see Daniel's father—was far too insistent to ignore. And so, she did as the whispers beckoned.

With one stop for refueling, and a quick bite to eat, the drive stretched out just over four hours. It was early afternoon when her tires hit the long gravel driveway of Daniel's childhood home. Her father-in-law managed to keep the small two-story house with a gabled slate roof well maintained, though the bright white exterior showed some chipping paint here and there. The glossy-black front door looked as if, over many decades, it had been painted numerous times with thick lacquer, diminishing the wood's fine details. Although some of the grass surrounding the house needed trimming, the gardens were otherwise neat. And while there were few flowers to be seen, in Dan's defense, the old house had lacked a woman's touch for nearly thirty years. The property looked as good as one could expect from years of sole occupation.

As she pulled her car up to park near Dan's, she took notice of the two small outbuildings just behind the house. They had not received much attention in a while but were probably only used for storage. In reality, her father-in-law still worked a considerable number of hours teaching at the university. She categorized him the same as she did her own father, who was ten times more likely to be found with his nose in a book than tending a garden. Domestic chores were not a strong suit for either man.

She groaned to herself as she maneuvered out of the driver's seat, all too aware that what should be a simple task was becoming more difficult each day. Not even halfway through her pregnancy yet, she wondered what the coming months would bring. Perhaps it was best she'd made the journey to Oxford now, for who knew if she would want to do it later?

After tidying her hair and enjoying a much-needed stretch, she dropped her keys into her purse and walked up to the front door.

It was too late to worry about whether or not Dan would be surprised to see her, for she had already given two loud raps with the large iron knocker. As she waited, she surmised that the knocker must have been one of Dan's finds at an antique shop or second-hand market somewhere. It was old, and well crafted, but way too big for an aged cotter's home with a couple of late room additions, and looked out of place on such a small door. Another detail a woman was more prone to notice.

The sound of a latch being unsecured and a heavy tug on the door snapped her almost to attention. Before her stood Dan, a man of short stature, clad in starched dress pants and a stiff dress shirt. For a brief moment, he stood blinking at her through his tortoiseshell-framed glasses. She wasn't sure if the dusty film on his lenses impacted his sight, or if he was just as shocked to see her on his front stoop as she expected he would be. As she stared back at him, she almost kicked herself for not rehearsing what she was going to say on arrival.

"Adelia," he exclaimed. "What on earth are you doing here?" He adjusted his glasses, as though wanting to make sure it was indeed his daughter-in-law standing on the stoop.

She tried to force a smile but it didn't work. "I know I shouldn't have shown up unannounced—"

"No... No, it's fine, really. I am just so surprised to see you." He stared at her for a moment longer, no doubt trying to gauge whether there was something wrong. As if anything could have been more wrong than when they last saw each other.

"I went to see my cousin in York this weekend. I don't know, I just thought maybe I would come see you on my way home."

"I don't want to question your sense of geography, my dear, but Oxford is not exactly on your way home. Well..."—he looked up at the ceiling, as if he had a map tacked up there—"if I had to guess, it's about a four-hour drive in the opposite direction of Middleham."

Like a stray bolt of lightning, she was hit with an instant flashback of her husband, who had that same tendency to infuse over-analytical observations into conversations. That inherited trait was all the more apparent here. She'd never got the impression before, but wondered if Dan thought her a bit of a hair brain. The thought left her with an indignant taste in her mouth. After all, she was a highly educated woman herself, with the plaque on her office reading Dr. Adelia Brown, Professor of Historical Studies. Even if she sounded like an idiot now, in reality, she was far from it.

"What I meant is, I decided I would like to come down and pay you a visit, before I returned home." She nodded once to herself. "I know it's unexpected, and I absolutely should have called first." She took a steadying breath. "I'm planning on staying in the city, in an old inn I love. I just thought I would stop by and say hello while I'm in the vicinity."

"I'm delighted that you're here, my dear." He grabbed her hand and pulled her over the threshold. "I'd be a fool to let you stay in town when there is an empty room upstairs." He looked up at the ceiling again. "Ah, it probably needs a bit of tidying up. Don't worry, we can get it back into tip top shape in no time at all."

"Really, Dan, I appreciate the offer greatly, but I would really like to stay at the Golden Rams Inn. Daniel set me up in a room there the first time I came to Oxford. It's a sentimental thing. Foolish, I know—"

"Nothing foolish about being sentimental," he cut in, the corner of his mouth raised in a halfhearted grin. "The room is here if the inn is booked," he assured. "It's no trouble to me either way."

"Thank you," she said, grateful for his understanding. Her parents would have argued her response to the bitter end, but Dan seemed to know it would have been fruitless. Her independent streak had not been extinguished with Daniel's passing. In truth, it was returning all the more each day.

"Come. Come. Let's sit in the parlor and have ourselves a nice long chat. How about I get us a cup of tea going? Have you eaten?" he asked, his tone that of a concerned father.

"I had to make a stop midway to put petrol in the car. I grabbed a little lunch there. Tea sounds great, though."

He led her through a narrow doorway just off the hall. "I will be right back." With a broad smile, he scampered off to the kitchen.

She moved over to the olive-green sofa and dropped onto it like a ton of bricks, which she regretted. The long drive had left a slight ache in her back, but the sofa was harder than expected, with lack of use never allowing the cushions to be broken in properly. It was like sitting on a showroom sample. After another stretch, she nestled into the most comfortable spot she could find. As she fidgeted with the clasp of her handbag, faint sounds from the kitchen filtered through the silence, reminding her of times when her husband prepared a pot of tea. Even if she appreciated the gesture, there was always the knowledge that he would leave a mess behind. She imagined her father-in-law wasn't so different.

A few minutes later, Dan returned with two piping-hot cups. He handed one to her, then sat in the chair opposite, that broad smile still stretched from ear to ear.

Despite her intrusion, it was easy to see that her father-in-law delighted in having someone call for a visit. Beyond a few work colleagues and friends, he spent most of his time alone. All of his mannerisms spoke of a somewhat lonely soul stuck way out here in his little country house. He had adjusted to the life of a bachelor after his son left home, keeping himself occupied at work and doing whatever he could to stay busy.

"Tell me all about your trip to York. And how is your dad getting along?"

"He is very well, busy as always." Even though she had no immediate intention of packing up and going back to Boston at this stage in her life, she couldn't deny missing her parents, and her heart always pulled at her whenever she thought of them. "York was enjoyable, and it was refreshing to get away after being cooped up in the house for so long. There certainly was no shortage of things to see." She sipped her tea, letting the hot liquid ease her dry throat.

"Did you visit Micklebar Gate? The Minster?"

"Cassandra nearly walked my legs off over the weekend. I was keen on seeing the old Treasurer's House as well. York did not disappoint."

"Oh, the Treasurer's House," he said, his eyes full of fond reminiscence. "It has been such a long time since I was there."

"Well, if you are in the market for the ghosts of Roman Legions, you will be out of luck. They were not cooperating the day I visited."

"Ghosts," he said with a hearty laugh. "You know, I have been to just about every place that held any significance in English History, and I am pretty sure I never once saw a ghost. That is not to say that I wouldn't have wanted to if I actually thought such a thing existed. I have many questions I would love to have answered, that's for sure."

Adelia responded with a coy chuckle, not obliged to correct him on his assumption that ghosts didn't exist. To the best of her knowledge, he had never been told about her gift. It was something she and Daniel agreed to never share with anyone outside of their trusted circle. There were far too many skeptics looking to disprove such things, and besides, it could never really be proven to another. She could share the information she witnessed, but without good hard evidence, someone could just as easily refute her claims. It had been in everyone's interest to remain guarded on such a sensitive topic.

"Sometimes I find my own life haunting enough," she said after sipping more tea. "I honestly didn't need to add the ghosts of the Roman Legion to the fray."

"I think about you often," Dan said, his smile now empathetic. "You and I are not so different in our losses. Of course, Daniel was a little over ten years old when I lost my wife. You going through this with a baby will undoubtedly be more difficult than what I went through. Just the same, I can understand how tough this has been on you."

For a moment, she focused on the heat from the cup. "In the beginning, I didn't think there could be much of a life for me without Daniel. I wanted to just throw in the towel on every hope and dream I had for the future." She blinked away memories of those first hopeless days. "The baby has made me realize that is not a choice I have the privilege to make. I have to move on and make a life for our child."

"It was the same for me, when I lost my wife. There was my helpless son, grief stricken and unsure. I had to put all my worries on the shelf and forge ahead for him. I felt I owed that to his mother."

"It's sad how much we want to do for our spouses after they are gone." She took a moment to sip the last of her tea before placing the cup and saucer back on the table. "One can only hope they knew our love and devotion fully in life."

"I loved my wife with every fiber of my being," he said, his eyes full of sorrow. "I'm not sure how she would have known it, though. I'm afraid I never told her as much as I should have." He looked down at his cup. "We were just like you and Daniel once, young and in love. But I was no good at putting her first, at least not when it came to my own ambitions. When I finally got my big break at the university, I spent my days in my papers, locked up in my study. I was far more dedicated to my work than being a good husband."

Adelia didn't know what to say, or what words of reassurance to offer. She'd never had such an intimate conversation with him before; he was always locked up tight within himself. In many ways, they were as good as strangers.

"I am sure your wife knew you loved her," she said, unhappy that her words sounded a bit generic, though it was probably a response anyone would have used to such a melancholy statement.

He gave a halfhearted quirk of his lip, no more convinced by her response than she. "My son loved you dearly, you know."

"I do know." She struggled to fight back tears with a fragile smile. "He told me often."

"I'm glad he was a better husband than I. It is good to know he learned from my mistakes."

"Daniel never thought of you as anything but a great man. His mother's death was difficult for him as a child, I am sure, yet he always felt that you stepped up to fill the void of her loss. He admired and loved you greatly."

His cheeks lifted for a moment above a slight grimace. "He might have thought differently had he known the truth."

Adelia stared at him. Just what did he mean by that?

"Just how did your wife die?" she asked, feeling a little insensitive at such prying. Daniel had told her the story long ago, but now she suspected that version might be the one deemed appropriate to tell a ten-year-old child. Perhaps it wasn't the entire story.

"The day Daniel's mother died, I had taken him into town to an antiques' fair. The weather was warm and sunny that morning, so we rode our bikes. Rosalind opted to stay behind, which was not out of character. But what happened next was." He turned his cup on its saucer, then turned it back, looking down at it as if the words he needed were inside. "Not long after we left, she got into the car to leave." He placed the cup onto the coffee table and wrung his hands in his lap. "She had never driven before. Driving scared her, and she never had the desire to learn. She never made it to her destination." He glanced at the open door, then back at his hands before looking at her. "No, she misjudged a bend in the road a short way out and the car rolled off a steep embankment. When Daniel and I returned that afternoon, the authorities were waiting for us. That was the hardest thing I ever had to do, telling my son that his mother was gone."

Adelia lowered her gaze to her own cup, now empty. The story was just as Daniel had recounted several times before. He'd always said his father blamed himself for his mother's death, but that made her wonder why, because nothing in the accounts of that day were his doing. It was a simple accident and nothing more. But it struck her as odd that Daniel's mother chose to drive, when it wasn't something she'd done before.

"Why do you think Rosalind chose to leave that day and take the car?" she asked, cautious about her wording, not wanting to stir up any more emotions than were already disturbed.

He released a shaky breath, then straightened. "I never told my son the truth. He was much too young to understand any of it then. After her death, I found some letters tucked away in her handbag." He glanced at the door, then looked right at her. "My wife was on her way to meet another man. I have every faith that she was leaving that day for good. They'd made plans to meet in a nearby town and run off together. Even if I didn't want to believe the letters, the packed bags in the boot of the car were hard to dismiss. She would have left Daniel and I that day, had the accident not happened."

"Oh, my goodness." It came out as a muffled gasp. "I never would have imagined—"

"Perhaps you think I was wrong never to tell my son, even as he grew older?" He shrugged one shoulder. "I didn't want him to think ill of his mother. It wasn't her fault. She lived a loveless life with me. She was lonely. Very lonely. It hurts me more to know that I drove her to such desperate measures than to know that she was unfaithful. I could never bring myself to blame her as much as I blame myself."

She set her cup and saucer down on the coffee table. "Honestly, Dan, I don't think you were wrong for not telling Daniel the truth. That would have brought him much pain, for no real purpose. I hope I don't sound harsh by saying this but I don't think you should blame yourself for your wife's death either. Infidelity takes a lot of effort. Perhaps more effort than working on a struggling marriage. I think your wife had a clear choice, and the one she made for herself was her own."

"Please, Adelia, I do not think you are harsh. After she died, it was so easy to see all my shortcomings as a husband. I only wish they would have been so clear to me before."

A long moment of silence lingered between them. She pondered what words she could say to help mend this old wound that had been reopened. Even after so many years, Dan was still hanging onto this deep-rooted guilt. Would her own grief be as strong after so much time had passed?

"I'm sorry that you never got the chance to really grieve for your wife. I have no doubt that such a revelation complicates things so much more."

"Grief is the hardest emotion to master," he said, the softness in his voice making her think of Daniel all the more. "You will think you're making progress, then wake up one day lower than ever before. In time, you will come to realize that you are never completely alone. All around you are people willing to lend you support if you are willing to let your guard down long enough to accept it. Healing is not all about strength, Adelia. It's about vulnerability too. You have to acknowledge your weakness if you are ever to manage it properly. I know that all you want to do is be alone now, and believe me I understand that very well, but you need people in your life more than you know."

"I suppose you having Daniel to look after made it both difficult and easier in some respects."

"Yes," he agreed. "I did not have the option of dwelling in my sorrow. I had to be strong for us both, and it gave me focus when I needed it most. You will have the baby to do the same for you, though with every milestone your child reaches, you will grieve for what Daniel is missing."

That hit hard, and had her cupping her abdomen with one hand, as if to soothe the baby after hearing such words.

"I am sorry to tell you that you cannot fight against grief. It will be an ever-present part of your life from now on. All you can do is manage it the best you can, and don't ask more of yourself."

"I will try." She smiled, knowing it was an empty promise. "Dan, I really am sorry that things ended the way they did for you and Rosalind, and that it caused you much pain over the years."

"Rose was a free spirit, an artist too. She spent a good deal of time in the garden shed. It was her art studio. She was a constant daydreamer. Not the kind who could easily settle into the everyday monotony of domestic life. I wanted to change her, wrap her up in some neat little package, always knowing full well that she could never be happy that way. I may have been hurt, but I could never be mad at her. If anything, I can only be mad that I took her happiness away just to satisfy my own."

Adelia sat up. "Rose...?"

"Yes, it's what I always called her. She actually preferred it. She always thought Rosalind was too stuffy."

Adelia steadied herself as the realization washed over her. "I...never knew all that much about her," she said. "Daniel had been so young—I suppose he didn't have many memories of his mum. Was Rose from Oxford?"

"Oh no," Dan replied with a smile, "she was from a little coastal village called Robin Hood's Bay. It's up near Whitby, north of

Scarborough. It's a quaint spot, really, but far too small for the likes of Rose. She much preferred city life."

"In Y-Yorkshire," she stuttered. Had it not seemed an ill-mannered thing to do, she would have clapped in utter joy. Her thoughts raced back to the sketchbook and the scripted words on its cover. "Yorkshire Rose," she said aloud, everything making perfect sense now.

"Yes," he said, his smile broadening. "My Yorkshire Rose. That's what I always called her." He looked away, as if his mind had wandered back to a time long forgotten, yet clearly still fresh in his heart.

A warmth engulfed Adelia as she watched him, no doubt back in some place that only he and Rose knew. A place where all the hurt of years spent lost in questions and guilt didn't exist.

"You know, I don't think I have ever seen a picture of Rose. Did she and Daniel look alike?" She couldn't help but feel guilty asking the question, knowing in her heart that she was robbing him of some memory when things were full of promise.

"Not at all," he said with a laugh. "Daniel got most of his looks from me, poor boy. Only thing he got from his mother was his blue eyes."

Her heart ached as she pictured Daniel's crystal-blue eyes. Something in them always drew her right in, close to mesmerizing her. Even now that he was gone, the recollection had the same effect. She imagined that, in this moment, it was something she and her father-in-law shared—a sense of longing for what was lost and could never be again.

Dan got up and crossed the floor to a small dry bar along the wall. As he opened up the cabinet door, Adelia wasn't surprised to see that it contained no liquor of any kind. Instead, it was stuffed with books and papers. The men of the Brown family were rarely inclined to partake in spirits, so stuffing a liquor cabinet with books was far more their style. Dan pulled out an ornate photo album that looked late-Victorian in age. She almost laughed to see such a gorgeous antique wedged in among stacks of old papers, as though it had no real value. That reminded her of Paul, her old friend, an antique dealer she had met when she first moved to Middleham. He would cringe to see such careless treatment of a fine treasure like this.

When Dan returned to his seat, he opened the front cover of the album, now resting on his knees. He thumbed through a few of the thick board pages, until a photo stopped him in his tracks. Something in his eyes glowed, which was nice to see. After a silent few seconds, he passed the album over to Adelia. "That, right there, is Rose."

He went on to tell her the story of how they had met, a tale that seemed almost cut from some flowery romance novel. As he spoke, she stared down at the familiar face she had studied far too many times—the one she had envied and loathed. Long golden waves dressed the delicate shoulders of the thin-framed woman. Every curve of her porcelain face was molded to perfection. Even in the black and white photo, the light shade of her eyes glowed back with commanding presence. Rose was something beyond the measure of beauty, and she looked almost exactly like Cassandra, even though her cousin said she didn't. This woman had unwittingly haunted her dreams for weeks on end. All this time, she'd convinced herself that Daniel suffered an obsession with another woman, and in reality, he had, laboring hours upon hours drawing pictures of the mother he could barely remember, recreating her image out of faded memories and old black and white photos. He brought her to life with a lead pencil and watercolors. All the relief she felt at discovering that her husband had been faithful was replaced by an enduring sadness.

She had not been wrong, feeling that she didn't really know her husband as well as she thought. He had not betrayed her, and guilt gripped her heart for thinking it could be so. At a deep level, though, he'd harbored feelings of loss for his mother that he never shared with her. He must have experienced so many conflicting emotions over the years—ones he didn't share with his father, and ones he couldn't share with her, his wife. If he had suffered in his grief, he did so alone, and that knowledge struck her a fierce blow.

In all their years together, she'd envied his cool demeanor. He let things roll right off him, never dwelling on anything so much to be distressed. It irritated her sometimes how he navigated his way with ease through life's stormy seas, while she spent far too much time dwelling on the little things. Deep down, however, Daniel grieved for something he could never retrieve, wishing for all those moments he could have shared with his mother as he grew older, got married, and started a family of his own.

She shook herself out of it, making a conscious effort to stop herself thinking of their last day together, when she had shared her good news. Right now, she didn't want to think about how happy he had been. How much his eyes sparkled when he smiled. The memory was still too fresh, too raw, to want to recall.

"I'm glad I came here today, Dan," she said, handing the album back. "I thought it would be too hard to see you at first. I damn near turned around just a mile or two from the house. But I'm glad I came. You really have helped me see what I need to do now."

"I think you have helped me too," he said, hugging the album as he smiled.

Chapter Nine

The day had been excruciatingly long, and Adelia sighed with relief as the inn came into view. Her pregnancy was slowing her down and she needed rest far more than she cared to admit. Pulling her belongings from the car, she couldn't help but notice how heavy they felt in her weary arms. At this point, her only thoughts were of her body landing on a soft bed for the night.

She smiled at the familiar chime of the tiny brass bell above her head as she opened the front door. The fragrant scent of the front lobby—a mix of lavender and furniture polish—brought pleasant memories of her last stay to mind. As she glanced around, she found nothing had really changed after all these years, and so many recollections of her first trip to Oxford flooded back. Those were the days she never allowed herself to forget, even in the flurry of life's everyday demands.

A pretty red-haired woman in a dark-green dress popped up from behind the front desk, and set down the magazine that may have occupied her time on this slow evening. She greeted Adelia with an amiable look, as though pleased to have something to divert her attention from her boredom.

"Oh, hello," Adelia said, the woman's mannerisms reminding her of her mother. They looked to be about the same age, their physical build quite similar too. As she approached the desk, she fumbled to free her sagging shoulders from the two heavy bags, which she placed on the floor with the least impact possible. "I was hoping to get a room for the night. Maybe two nights, if you can accommodate me?"

The woman scanned the open guest register, tracing her index finger down the page. "I think we can do that," she said, her tone cheerful, "I have one at the top of the stairs. It's a small one, though. Will it just be you staying?"

"I think that's the one I had last time I was here," Adelia said, unable to hold back a gentle smile as she remembered her previous stay with fondness. "It's just me, so it will do perfectly."

"Great. Just sign here, and I will get my husband to look after your bags."

"I hate to ask, but I am curious about the proprietor who was here the last time I stayed. Are you the new owner, then?"

"Well, in a sense," she answered with a chuckle. "That's my dad, and he doesn't get around so well these days. My husband and I have taken over the inn, but you will probably still see Dad around from time to time. He isn't so good at taking it easy, like he's been told."

Adelia nodded with a smile. "Parents don't do so well listening to their children, I guess." She remembered the kind face of the older man when she came here the first time. It was the summer when she met Daniel, nearly ten years ago now. On break from Boston University, she traveled to England to stay with her grandmother. In a twist of fate, she and Daniel found themselves both involved in unraveling the mysterious circumstances surrounding Amy Robsart Dudley's passing. When he asked her to come to Oxford to visit the last place Amy lived, he'd arranged for her to stay here at the inn. One morning, she entered into a casual conversation with the innkeeper, who told her that his wife Mary had a deep interest in Amy's story before she passed away. As they chatted, he shared some of her poetry. He then made a comment that stopped her in her tracks:

"She loved to write. Said it quieted the whispers, whatever that means."

Later, he revealed that Mary hailed from the Babbington family. At the time, they could not determine if it was the same line as her own. She mentioned it to her grandma when she got home and, as it turned out, Mary was a distant cousin, and may also have been gifted with the same abilities as other women in the family. Adelia soon became aware of how powerful her own gift was at altering her life. Beyond the complexity that came along with seeing into the layers of time, she realized that the whispers had the ability to lure her into the path of people and places, as if for a specific reason. Naturally, it took her some time to acclimate to the idea of her entire life being driven by some unseen force. This knowledge was difficult to grasp, and at times caused her to overanalyze every single event, trying to derive some deeper meaning. Then again, there was a solace in knowing that her life's journey always had purpose; each and every day, she inched closer to some new discovery.

Up until that summer, her life had been in utter turmoil, with her personal anxieties leading her toward darkness and isolation, and her stay became life changing in so many ways. She discovered the gift of the whispers, which helped her to overcome the inevitable self-destruction facing her. Most importantly, she'd met Daniel, which transformed her life in every conceivable way. This place held a particular fondness for her, and the energy within its walls—the sights, sounds, and smells—evoked pure contentment.

After she finished at the front desk, she climbed the narrow staircase to her room. The place had not changed a bit. The inn's floors had a slight lean from years of settling, giving a muffled groan with each step she took, as if she were a little old lady unsteady on her feet.

The room was small, just as she remembered from all those years ago, its decor conveying a cozy sense of warmth. Deep crimson hues were stitched into the beautiful damask coverlet on the bed, and the rich mahogany furniture made the space feel intimate but not crowded. The small wooden table against the far wall doubled as a writing desk and dressing table, and an aged gold-framed mirror hung just above it.

After her bags were delivered, she sat on the bed, yawning as the day's journey caught up with her. On the drive in, she thought she might like to take a walk around the city to explore the favorite places she and Daniel visited back in the early years of their relationship. She had shared a flat with a fellow classmate a few blocks from here while she finished her studies, but she and Daniel spent every waking moment of their free time together, and there wasn't an inch of this city she didn't know by heart. However, for all the nostalgia she felt being back in Oxford, she couldn't deny that she was dog tired after such a long day, so there would be no exploring this evening. She slipped off her shoes and scooted her weary body back on the mattress. The heavy bed frame gave out a slow creak, but she hardly noticed, her eyelids already closed.

****

When she awoke, the room was still filled with light, though it was clear sunset would soon arrive. She was annoyed with herself for sleeping away her short time here, even though she'd been too tired to do much else. Now fully awake, she rolled to her side, flinching when the bed gave out a sharp groan. Not a room well suited for a newlywed couple. She lay there for a moment, considering how she might spend the last shreds of daylight.

She got up and crossed the floor to her bag, grimacing as she rummaged for the dreaded sketchbook. This hadn't been on her list of things to do, but something inside drew her to it, and she'd learned through experience not to ignore such feelings. She sat at the desk, propping the book open on its smooth surface, her chin resting against her clasped hands as she stared at the image of the golden-haired beauty, as if she hadn't done it innumerable times before.

With her new understanding that Rose wasn't her rival, she found herself filled with questions. Maybe because of that, the pictures revealed subtle messages she hadn't noticed before. These were no longer just sketches of a beautiful woman. For one thing, her eyes radiated a heartfelt emotion—one that nearly projected itself straight off the page into Adelia's soul.

She thought about Daniel, and how she believed she knew him better than anyone. As her husband, he knew her inner workings too. He was a man who loved history, but not just for facts and figures. What drew him in was the emotional state of people—those underlying feelings that made them act upon their situations. He was the type of person who wanted to know the things that could never be known. It had been a curse of sorts. When he discovered her ability to channel those emotions in people long gone, it fueled his fire. He never sought to push her too far, knowing her gift took its toll on her at times. Yet, whenever she offered up information—some window into a person's soul—he listened with full focus. She could never give him enough detail.

It perplexed her that he never asked her to reveal anything about his mother. She could have done it with ease. Perhaps he would have asked her in time, if things had not been cut short for them. How much did he really know? Did he listen to the idle gossip of the locals through the years? There had to be far-fetched stories about Rose's tragic death. He must have felt overwhelmed at times, trying to sift through fact and fiction. She knew him too well to think he'd stopped wanting to know more about his mother, and the sketchbook before her was proof enough of that.

She traced the delicate line of the woman's face with her finger-tip. "Who *were* you, Rose?" she whispered into the stillness.

As she pondered the question, a faint wisp of movement startled her, and she sighed with relief at the sight of the ivory-colored curtains wafting at the window. She looked back at the page but stopped, realizing the window wasn't open, with not even a draft in the room. In fact, it was a little stuffy. She should have found this disconcerting, but she didn't because, in that moment, she knew she had asked the right question, and sensed that, of all the things she wanted to know most in the world, this was the one that needed answering. From this moment, she would not rest until she solved the mystery of the Yorkshire Rose.

Pen and paper in hand, she set about plotting out her plan. Dr. Adelia Brown was a honed scholar, well-versed in the finely tuned craft of researching the lives of her given subject. With precision, she jotted down important dates and locations that may have played a role in Rose's life. While she didn't have much to go on, she wasn't worried, it being a problem she was accustomed to encountering any time she did such work. Over the years, she had developed a methodology of using the whispers to fill in the blanks between factual information—a secret she'd hidden from the academic world, and for good reason. There were few who would accept her abilities, what with her gift being too removed from scientific reason. Yet, this profound sight had been the catalyst that led her to more and more provable data, and she used it to her advantage whenever possible.

Considering what she knew of Rose, the only logical conclusion was that she would have to start where it all began—back to the place that shaped the woman as a person: Robin Hood's Bay. She was born there, spending all of her youth in a cramped cottage just a stone's throw from the sea, only leaving before her twentieth birthday, never to return, forsaking all those years of hopes and dreams as she embarked on a journey to a new future.

What life did she live at Robin Hood's Bay? When she looked out at the vast seascape, what dreams filled her head? Was she sad to leave anything behind? What drove her to escape? When she took hold of Dan Brown's hand and turned her back on the place that molded her, what world did she envision? These were the questions no official document could dare to answer, and the ones Adelia wanted to know most of all.

Chapter Ten

Cassandra's familiar voice greeted Adelia on the other end of the phone, with music and laughter in the background. She brought her palm to her forehead. Unlike herself, Cassandra had a far busier social life. She should have known her cousin would not be spending the evening curled up with a good book.

"I'm so sorry to interrupt, Cassandra. I can call back another time—"

"It's fine, Adelia. I can spare a few minutes."

"I just wanted to call you before I head out to Robin Hood's Bay tomorrow."

"What the hell are you doing going to Robin Hood's Bay?" Cassandra's demand echoed down the line. "Should you really be out traveling across the country in your condition?"

"I'm pregnant, not infirmed," Adelia snapped in return. "You sound like my mother. Besides, what are *you* doing carousing with your friends at this late hour? Don't you have to work in the morning?"

"Yes, I do. It's not that late anyway, and now *you're* starting to sound like my mother."

Figuring they were both right on that account, Adelia decided it was best to get to the point. "It's a long story, but let's just start with the news that I figured out who the Yorkshire Rose is. Was. Yes, who she was."

"Good, I will patiently wait for my apology," Cassandra said, a clear edge to her voice.

"I'm sorry!" She bit back the growl behind the words, feeling like an annoyed teenager addressing her parents.

"Do it more like this: I'm sorry, dear cousin Cassandra, for thinking that you might have been having a torrid affair with my husband, as I now see I was wrong."

"Yes. Yes. All of that." Adelia rolled her eyes, waving her free hand in the air as though Cassandra could see her. She drew in a breath and gritted her teeth. Her cousin had a real gift for drawing out the nub of a conversation longer than necessary. "Can we get to the point here?"

"Now that my feelings are adequately repaired, you may proceed."

"Okay." She closed her eyes for a moment as she shook her head. "It was Daniel's mom, Rosalind. His father's pet name for her was Yorkshire Rose. Daniel must have gotten some solace in drawing her image, from what little memory he had left."

"He wanted to capture it so he wouldn't forget," Cassandra said, real warmth now in her voice. "That sounds like something he would do. Goodness, doesn't that ever hit you hard? It's like the sweetest and the saddest thing I have ever heard. I don't even know what emotions I should be feeling right now."

Adelia leaned her elbow on the phone table. "Personally, I feel a little relieved. It is nice to know that my husband wasn't entertaining thoughts of another woman in the romantic sense. Still, it bothers me to think that I never really paid enough attention to know he was going through this grief alone."

"Hmm, I never knew Daniel to be an overly emotional sort." Cassandra sounded cautious. "He wasn't unfeeling, mind you, he just wasn't the type to lay all his inner thoughts out for the world to trample on as it pleased. We all have a way of guarding ourselves, Adelia. Old wounds have a way of making us vulnerable, even if it's only to yourself. Some feelings are just better left unshared. I am sure he would have confided in you when the time was right."

Adelia believed he would have shared his feelings eventually. He must have needed time to work through them on his own.

"The whole thing is tangled up. The more I learn about Rose, the more layers appear in her story. I guess Daniel just wanted to know where he fitted into the whole thing." She still couldn't understand all the moving parts. Had Daniel puzzled it out himself?

"That's the way it is with all great stories, the ones that burrow into our soul. They are never singular. All the jagged pieces of the characters' lives intertwine until they fit together into something so perfect, it leaves you wondering if it was all by some heavenly design. Elizabeth Bennet's story would be nothing without Mister Darcy, and Mina Harker would have been a dull subject if it weren't for Dracula."

"You do have a point," Adelia agreed with a laugh, marveling at the two odd comparisons. "I suppose it would be rather boring if it weren't for the other characters."

"You have to think of your Daniel the same way as any of the people you have studied. Everything about him is a product of something he has been through in his life, and the lives that intersected with his have left some indelible mark. Some more profound than others, but a mark just the same. If there is anything I knew about Daniel, he loved a good mystery. He always wanted to know how every last detail of a story led to the next. If his mother's death was the ending, then you have to retrace the steps in reverse."

"That's it, Cassandra," Adelia said, her voice carried on a burst of excitement. "Dan said he never shared the full details of Rose's death with his son. However, I think Daniel would have picked up bits and pieces of the story as he grew up. Idle town gossip, at the least. He just wanted to sort out the facts from the fiction."

"Is that why you want to go to Robin Hood's Bay? To find out more about Rose?"

"I have no idea what I'm looking for, but I feel drawn there."

"Then that is where you should start. I am really trying not to sound like your mother when I say this, but...do be careful." Her voice had lowered to a near hush. "You and I both know the whispers can be powerful. You have to remember not to push yourself too far. It's draining emotionally and physically. It's not just you who will feel that impact."

"I know," Adelia said, weighed by guilt for all the emotional turmoil she had undergone over the last few months. "I can't let my curiosity get the best of me. I have the baby to think about now."

"All my scolding aside, I have to say, I am pretty impressed that you went home and figured all of this out in such a short time."

Adelia clenched her eyes shut, knowing what she was about to say wouldn't be well-received.

"Yes—about that. I am actually in Oxford right now. I never went home."

"You grate on my nerves, Adelia Brown. You really do. I assume you went to see Daniel's dad, then?"

"Yes, that's where I figured out about Rose. It was a good visit, and Dan wanted me to stay there but I opted to book into the Golden Rams Inn, just for nostalgia, really. Do you remember me telling you about the older chap who owned the place when I first came here years ago?"

"Wasn't he the one whose wife was a Babbington?"

"Yes, that's him. He told me she used to talk about hearing the whispers, though I never got the impression he knew exactly what she was talking about. Well, anyway, I decided to stay on an extra day, just to rest up before I head to Robin Hood's Bay. As luck would have it, I stumbled upon him at teatime this afternoon. It's probably been nearly a decade since I saw him last, but he is still just as I remembered."

"You must be on the right path, then."

"Come again?" She had no idea what to make of her cousin's comment.

"It's just that the first time you met him you were right on the cusp of solving Amy Dudley's case. Maybe he is a good luck charm."

Adelia couldn't hold back a smile. She finished up the conversation with a promise to keep in touch over the next few days.

She placed the phone on its cradle and looked at the window, the curtain as still as could be.

****

Daniel's mother was the only thing on Adelia's mind on the long journey to Robin Hood's Bay. Something about this mysterious woman captivated her thoughts, and it was no surprise that it had been the same for Daniel. Though she never knew her, something about Rose's spirit rooted itself into her own. Something that spoke to all of her senses, like a long-suppressed air of discontent.

When she reached the edge of the tiny, but renowned village, she made a conscious effort not to take Cassandra's advice, and to release her grip on control. She would allow the whispers to take over from here, leading her in the direction of whatever was to come. The process had taken considerable time to come to terms with. Letting go of one's will was not so easy for a woman as headstrong and determined as herself. Through time and failure, she had learned that fighting against the whispers did little good. Sight was her gift, not patience.

Images of the dimly lit apothecary shop in York flooded her mind. Meredith provided ample proof that she hadn't managed yet to fully perfect the art of relinquishing control. No matter how much progress she thought she'd made, there was still some subconscious will she would find herself struggling against.

As she drove along a narrow street, she found herself glancing up at a small fish and chip shop. Her stomach responded, indicating that it was well past lunchtime. The building was unremarkable, its plain exterior only accentuated by a basic sign with large red lettering. Time to eat. However, today, Robin Hood's Bay was a bustling haven for visitors craving a seaside excursion, and finding a place to park proved challenging.

She drove up the hill, finding no available space, but luck smiled upon her on her way back down, and she eased into a spot just big enough for her car. As she stood in the heat of the summer sun, she couldn't help but feel a little breathless at the sight of all the old buildings bordering the hill. Such a picturesque place, like something cut from a travel magazine.

For a moment, she contemplated finding something more enticing than fish and chips; there were many other options along the main thoroughfare. As she considered her next move, a light swirl of air caressed her midsection, nearly pulling her forward. She watched as the energy materialized into a vibrant stream of colorful waves working its way across the street and into the small diner with the red-lettered sign.

"Fish and chips it is then," she muttered to herself. Through the years, she had seen the demanding force of the whispers in many forms. Controlling where she dined was something new and unexpected, but she listened just the same.

The inside of the diner was like a scrapbook of days gone by, its decor consisting of everything one might expect of a local favorite. Retired fishing nets, aged by years of service, covered the walls, and old black and white photos of weathered fishermen and boats tethered to rickety old docks filled the spaces between. The whitewashed wood-paneled walls soaked up the scent of the day's catch and well-used frying grease. For her, the place oozed nostalgia, and she recalled holidays along the American east coast as a kid.

She toyed with the lid of the salt shaker as she waited for her lunch to arrive. The emotional connection here was as unexplainable as it was tangible. There were moments that felt as if they remained unforgotten, not by herself but by Rose. Something about this diner was unchangeable. Rose was within these walls, with everything stamped by her spirit. Adelia released a long exhalation and let the whispers guide her back to a sunny day much like today.

Chapter Eleven

C assandra slammed the car door shut and glanced down at her watch, smiling at the sight of the hands reading 4:57 p.m. She was to meet Basil Duncan at his jewelry shop at five, and she loved the idea that she would arrive right on time. By nature, she had always been late to just about anything of importance, her charming demeanor always assuring that she was soon forgiven. Though she had established long ago that life as a historian wasn't her forte, this project somehow managed to spark her interest. She was a diehard lover of jewelry, especially a piece that may have been owned by someone of prominence. A couple months ago, she was fortunate enough to hold a bracelet once owned by Marie Antoinette. There was something captivating about holding an object once so personal to the ill-fated queen. Her mind ran wild with what awaited her at Basil's shop. It was obvious from their phone conversation that he suspected this piece of jewelry to be of importance, and was eager to establish who had owned it, no doubt looking forward to fetching a good price for its sale.

If she could establish its provenance, she was promised decent compensation for her trouble. Being a single woman, no longer under the financial support of her parents, the prospect of extra cash was too good to pass up. Convincing her parents that she was no longer a child, and quite capable of supporting herself, had been a hard sell. She wasn't about to go crawling back for money anytime soon. Being a fashion journalist and now a published author, while both were paying jobs, did not provide her with enough to live with any extravagance. She did her best to give off the image that she was doing well for herself, but the truth was she still needed to find ways to earn extra when she could. An opportunity such as this fitted that need just right.

When she entered the tiny jewelry shop, she took a quick look around, scanning the cases brimming with sparkling trinkets. Basil prided himself on being a dealer in antique pieces, but her keen eye saw that, while many of these were aged, they were mostly costume jewelry. Probably less than half the pieces on display were real gemstones.

After a brief wait, a short balding man, dressed in a gray tweed suit and matching cap, emerged from the back. He looked like the perfect example of someone's jolly old grandfather—just as she'd imagined he would be.

She introduced herself and, after a few minutes of polite conversation, Basil rubbed his hands together. "I finally think I may have found a treasure. I have been in this business a very long time, and I have never been so lucky."

"Well," she said, giving him her best smile, "let us hope this is your lucky day."

She stood there while he reached under the counter and fumbled with the combination of a lock box. After a fair bit of rummaging and grumbling, he straightened, holding a plain wooden box, with no visible markings of any kind, and placed it on the counter. Cassandra watched as he pulled out a dark bundle of cloth and set it onto the glass. He lifted back the corners of the black-velvet wrapping, and looked up at her with wide eyes as a dazzling gold necklace was revealed.

Before she could say something, he held a weathered forefinger up, then unfolded the necklace. A large ruby pendant hung in the center, with four rectangular sections on each side, each artfully molded with elaborate scrollwork bordering a heraldic badge. She leaned closer, hovering her hands over each section, afraid to touch something so precious.

The heraldic badges were all the same—two sections of fleur de lis lying opposite three golden lions. At the top were five tiny banners, two of split ermine and three more of fleur de lis. She knew she was looking at something of great historical significance, yet whose badge it was, evaded her. If only she possessed half the knowledge of Adelia. Without doubt, she could look at these markings and identify the lineage without hesitation.

She pulled a pencil and paper from her bag and set about sketching the image with care so she could describe it to Adelia later over the phone.

"What do you make of it?" Basil asked, his voice edged with excitement.

"Aside from it being one of the most beautiful pieces I have ever seen?" She smiled, her face no doubt etched with disbelief at the extravagance of such a work of art. "I don't know where you got this, but I think you have found a treasure after all, Mister Duncan."

He smiled, beaming like a schoolboy who just found a twenty-pound note on the ground. "Is there anything about it that tells you something of its origin?"

"I would say there is definitely a strong French connection. That's evidenced by the use of fleur de lis."

He picked up an eyepiece and leaned closer to study the necklace. "Judging by the clasp, I am inclined to think it is Middle Ages."

"I would agree," Cassandra said, continuing with her sketch. "The key to its provenance is in the heraldry. Each one is indicative of a specific family line. Often, you will find that sons and daughters would alter theirs ever so slightly, sometimes merging their own symbols with that of their spouse, or even to document some achievement. I have a cousin who is quite astute at identifying these badges. That will get us off to a good start in tracing its provenance."

"I have taken a few photos. You can have some to use as reference."

She looked down at the rudimentary sketch, giving a halfhearted laugh. "That would be more helpful than this masterpiece I am producing. I will get to work right away, and hopefully have some information to bring back to you within the week, maybe two."

Even though she knew that to be an unrealistic timeline, Basil's desire to have the information as soon as possible was clear.

"I will grab them from my desk. Won't take but a minute." He turned and disappeared through the narrow doorway that led to the back of the shop.

Peering down at the necklace, Cassandra once again hovered her hands over its magnificence. A pulling sensation in her fingertips drew them down until the precious metal brush against her skin. She flinched as a flash of heat thrust itself from her fingertips in a rapid climb up her arms. The room blurred, then filled with bursts of light, and no matter how hard she tried, she couldn't blink them away. She clenched her eyes shut, stunned as the vivid image of a lush green forest came into view. Her body was being pulled closer and closer toward a faded outline in the distance. With each step, it became clearer, and a peculiar sound emerged, resembling a mournful cry hidden within a slow monotonous hum that was not altogether unfamiliar.

Her hands trembled from the fiery heat, yet she could not bring herself to let go of the necklace. She was close now, no more than a few feet away from the foggy outline. Was it a person?

A faint bell jingled in the distance, and she scanned the surrounding trees and thick undergrowth. All was silent, except for the low hum now echoing in her head.

Seeing nothing to alarm her, she turned back to the figure, teetering on her heels at the realization that the dreamlike fog had cleared. Just before her, a large alabaster tub nestled on the mossy forest floor. Before she could contemplate the oddness of its placement, the ivory-colored form of a woman rose up from the water, her back to Cassandra. Her long golden hair was bone dry, billowing out even though there was no breeze, the woman humming her sorrowful cry to herself.

The sadness of that cry went through Cassandra—bone deep—and she shuddered, releasing a whimper. The woman's humming ceased, and Cassandra drew in a heavy breath as the figure turned. She stared in absolute awe at the face of the most stunning creature she had ever laid eyes upon. Her angelic features were only rivaled by her eyes, which gleamed of a pale gold that reminded her of the necklace.

She smiled at Cassandra, as though she had been waiting for her arrival. Cassandra stood in a paralyzed silence as something else rose out of the water before the woman. Through the billowing strands of hair that floated in the air, she made out a long, smooth deep-green shape. A tail—a serpent's tail.

Just then, the ruby-red lips of this dreamlike creature parted. "Melusine," she whispered into the woods, as though speaking to the trees.

"Melusine," Cassandra repeated. Then everything faded to black and the vision disappeared. She blinked several times and stared down at the necklace, which was now lying back on its plush base. From a young age, she understood her ability to see what others could not, but whatever just transpired was far beyond anything she had ever experienced. She could not begin to process what she had seen.

"Melusine?"

The deep voice behind her made her jump, and she spun to see the man standing there. Glancing toward the entrance, she wondered how she hadn't heard him come into the shop. The sight of the bell above the door jogged her memory, and she recalled the sound of it in the forest. As she looked at the man again, she was struck by how much he resembled a real-life villain.

He was clad from head to toe in black, his sharp-pressed dress shirt covered by a long finely tailored overcoat. An odd choice of attire for the heat of summer. His thick dark hair lay cropped against his temples, and he stared back at her, his black eyes burrowing so deep, she was sure there was no emotion he couldn't detect in her. They reminded her of the cavernous darkness at the bottom of an inkwell.

The stranger had asked her a question but her brain was still too foggy to process it. She just stared back at him. When at last he broke contact, she heard the shuffle of feet behind her as Basil returned from his office at the back.

"Here they are, my lady Cassandra," he called, holding a pile of photographs up.

She smiled, relieved to peel herself away from the stranger's scrutiny.

"Mister Fulcanelli," Basil exclaimed on catching sight of the dark figure looming behind her. "This is Cassandra. Let me finish up here and I will be with you shortly."

Cassandra stepped forward to collect the photos. Once Basil handed them to her, he folded the velvet wrapping over the necklace and stuffed it back into its box, then into the lock box under the counter.

She peered back at the man, gave him a subtle nod, and he smiled in return. Even as she turned back to face Basil, she couldn't help but repeat his name in her mind: Fulcanelli. Fulcanelli. It had such a ring to it, reminding her of one of the bad guys in a Sherlock Holmes' serial.

"I shall be in touch as soon as I have some information of use, Mister Duncan," she said, her voice still shaky from all that had transpired.

When she turned to depart, the mysterious Fulcanelli stepped out of her way to let her pass. Though she didn't look into his face again, his stare never left her. From the corner of her eye, she noticed a large black satchel clutched in his hand, its contents bulging against the soft fabric.

"My work is complete, Mister Duncan," he said, just as she touched the door handle, his voice deep and husky. "I think you will be quite surprised."

She didn't wait to hear Basil's response, unable to get out of the shop fast enough. The freshness of the air out on the street was exquisite against the heat of her skin. She was so hot, she could have mistaken it for a fever. As she walked, she drew the coolness of the evening deep into her lungs, trying her best to regain some equilibrium. Whatever just happened was beyond her comprehension. Only one person might understand her confusion, and she couldn't get home fast enough to call Adelia. As luck would have it, her cousin wouldn't be home to answer the phone.

Chapter Twelve

As Adelia sat at the table in the fish and chip shop, Rosalind Delaine's life materialized around her. Rose had been born and raised in Robin Hood's Bay. Even from a young age, it was clear that her vivacious free spirit could not be contained within the confines of the sleepy seaside village. While she didn't leave until she was nineteen, she had the heart of a gypsy, and was never content to stay in one place for too long. The Bay was a quaint location, its dreamy façade ripped from the image of a postcard. Its small, picturesque houses were crammed together, a testament to centuries of its inhabitants making the most of limited space. Nestled tight against the North Yorkshire coastline, this was a village forever trapped in a bygone era—the kind of place a person could live out their days wrapped in its peaceful serenity. However, as Rose grew into her adulthood, she began to feel as though an invisible dome encompassed this dreamlike place, with some unspoken force hell bent on keeping her from breaching the edges of the village, as if leaving was impossible. It made her restless.

As time went on, her days became a monotonous stream of repetition. Almost nothing here had changed for centuries, and she doubted it ever would. That notion haunted her, until the day a stranger walked into the café. Call it dumb luck, or fate, but her life was forever changed the afternoon she met Dan Brown.

The day started out just as every other one before. After graduating from high school, Rose took a job working in one of the better-known fish and chip shops along the village square. Sandwiched between the butcher and the chemist on the main thoroughfare, it was a place frequented by the locals as well as the occasional visitor passing through en route to their holiday destination. As it happened, Rose was not due to work that day. At the last minute, her employer phoned to ask that she cover for another waitress who had come down with a sudden illness. Though she had plans for the day, she was never one to turn away an extra few bob. Her family was not poor by any means but, at her age, there was still a limit to how far she expected her parents to go. She planned to work her way to self-sufficiency, providing for the little extras that caught her eye.

As she busied herself wiping down tables in the crowded café, the high-pitched jingle of the door's brass bell didn't cause her any distraction. No, it was the unfamiliar clack of his shoes on the worn wooden floor that caught her attention. When she looked up to see the stranger, her breath caught. She kept cleaning the table, surveying him with quiet interest. He was clad in a crisp white shirt, light-brown tweed jacket and trousers, with a shiny pair of dress shoes. The formality of his attire provided stark contrast to the softness of his eyes and youthful face. Despite the windy day, his cropped sandy hair was combed ever so carefully in place.

She met his gaze, and his hazel eyes sent a burning heat through her cheeks. He was young, no more than a year or two older than herself if she had to guess. But he was oh so sophisticated. Being raised in Robin Hood's Bay, she knew he wasn't a local. His polished appearance gave every indication that he was not from any of the northern counties, for he had *city boy* written all over him.

As he seated himself at an empty table she had just wiped down, she went to fetch a menu from the counter. The crinkled-up sheet rattled in her grasp, and she looked down to find herself trembling. She gripped the faded paper with both hands, trying to steady herself, scolding her hands for being so erratic. Crossing the floor to where he sat, she reminded herself that this was just another customer, the likes of which she had seen a thousand times before.

"Can I get you something to drink?" she asked, a tiny crack in her voice mortifying her.

"Tea and some milk would be excellent," he said in a creamy accent that nearly melted her.

London, or somewhere close. She nodded as she handed the menu to him. The village was always bursting with visitors, so new faces were quite the norm, yet something about this stranger was different. Whatever it was, it had her smitten.

Weaving her way through the busy shop to fetch his tea, a flurry of thoughts swirled in her mind: Just who is this man? What brought him here? In the minute or two it took to prepare his tea, she had prescribed him at least ten different scenarios, each more far-fetched than the one before, and her imagination nearly ran out by the time she returned to his table.

He slid over a leather-bound notebook to make room as she set the cup and saucer down. The small rectangular book was stuffed full of loose papers, making it so thick its gilded brass clasp no longer stretched enough to fully close it. Journalist, or maybe a travel writer of sorts.

"Have you had enough time to decide what you will have then?" she asked, not quite conquering the slight quiver in her voice. Pen at the ready to write his order, she flicked a glance around the room, wondering if anyone else noticed the temperature had gone up ten degrees.

"I think so, seeing as how there are only four things on the menu and they are all just variations of fish and chips. Yes, I think I will have the…fish and chips, but hold the mushy peas, if you will. I always hated those bloody things as a kid." He shot her a mischievous, toothy grin.

His brilliant-white smile did little to help her keep the temporary composure she'd managed to muster, and she gave a girlish giggle in response. No sooner had it escaped her lips, she decided she hated it. He was such a refined gentleman, and she must have looked idiotic in his eyes. Like a true and proper country idiot, to be precise. She wanted to snarl at herself, give her face a good smack, then knock her head against the wall a few times. No, those were bad ideas too. He would probably bolt out the door. Still, she would take him thinking she was a country idiot over the village crazy.

Nervous, she peered through her lashes at him, and almost choked, realizing that he was looking right at her. She was, by some accounts, a pretty young woman, and no stranger to the attention of the village's male inhabitants. Her fair skin, blue eyes, and long golden hair had some branding her as the Yorkshire Rose. While used to having a string of admirers, something about the way he looked at her felt different. Every bit of interest she had in this delightful new stranger seemed to be returned tenfold in his gaze.

"I hate them too," she said, allowing a shy smile. "After working here so long, the sight of them nearly churns my stomach."

"There now, we have that in common. There must be a list of at least a hundred other things too. I'm free tonight, if you have time to sort through what those might be?"

Caught off guard, she stood for a moment, her mouth open, until she snapped out of it. "Are you...asking me out?" She wasn't sure why she found his boldness attractive. Most of the time, she was put off by such attempts; however, today, she couldn't help but be flattered. The notion that she must have come across as a foolish small-town girl dissipated, leaving her with a brush of confidence. She stared at him, challenging him with direct eye contact.

"That's what I am trying to do," he admitted, somewhat sheepish, "but I think I am making a rather poor job of it, to be honest."

Whatever momentary burst of bravado he had mustered seemed to wane, leaving him shy and unsure. They had officially traded places on the courage front.

A slow creep of awkwardness developed between them. In Rose's mind, the proper thing to do would be to politely decline, but good sense had never been her strength. Again, she regarded the man who sat before her. He was unlike any of the local lads she'd fended off for years, and he came across as smart and ambitious. His physical looks didn't disappoint either. She had spent many years dreaming of the day a handsome outsider would walk into her life, freeing her from the drudge and predictability of her small-town world. Today, it seemed, was the day she had waited for, and though some might consider her a fool for saying yes, she knew she would always regret saying no.

"It's an unconventional way to ask a girl out on a date, I will give you that, but no less effective. I should be off by five o'clock, as long as the dinner rush doesn't start before then."

"I will personally stand outside that door and shoo every customer away," he said, in a tone that made her fear he might be serious. His persistence was flattering, and a delightful shiver fluttered up her spine.

"No need for that. Seven o'clock will be time enough."

"My name is Dan," he said after she turned to walk back to the counter.

"Rosalind," she called back over her shoulder. "Everyone here just calls me Rose, though."

For Adelia, the downside to the whispers had always been the inability to read the thoughts and emotions of the living. It was usually in instances like this that she learned to tap into her own personal experiences to make interpretations. Today was different, in a remarkable way, and had been this way since her fateful visit with Meredith. Even as she viewed the past play out in intricate detail before her, she could see Dan's energy with the same clarity as Rose's. It was clear from the moment he set eyes on her that he was a goner. Infatuation was not such a difficult emotion to detect.

If Rose felt intrigued by him, there was no doubting he felt the same about her. A force of energy surrounded them, only detectable to Adelia's finely tuned eye. She could almost see the spark's ignition. The dizzying sensation of new love floated between them like a warm breeze, diffusing the particles in the atmosphere and thinning the air. Its sheer power had her pulling in a deep breath to steady herself. There was no other emotion like this in the world. While it was Dan and Rose's love, she sensed it in her core. She smiled as she remembered the image of Daniel the first time they met. Though she vowed never to forget that day, time had faded the memory without her realizing. Now, seeing Dan and Rose brought back a flood of emotion. Daniel's presence captivated her the same way. She had been young, inexperienced, and wholly unsure of herself as a woman at the time. Something about his nervousness around her made her certain that at least half of what she felt in herself was not altogether abnormal. Daniel taught her many things in their life together but confidence in herself had been the greatest of these. Did he understand just how much he gave her? And did she give him anything back in equal measure?

Her heart ached as she longed to remember those good times. A place when learning to love Daniel took precedence above everything else. There were low times, too, as she recalled, but something in her wasn't quite ready to reconcile them within herself. They could not be described as perfect people, but they were the perfect match. Fate had been kind enough to bring them to this conclusion together.

Chapter Thirteen

Adelia watched the reaction on Dan's face as Rose strode up to meet him at the wooden bench across from the fish and chip shop. As long as he lived, he would never forget the way she looked that night. He stood to greet her as she casually took a seat, inhaling the sweet scent of her perfume. In truth, he'd doubted she would even show up. She had changed into the most perfect yellow dress with little lavender flowers, and shed the tight ponytail she'd worn at the restaurant, leaving her long blonde locks to fall upon her shoulders like a river of gold. Her blue eyes took on every color of the rich-hued sky. Rose was a vision in her own right, and an inexperienced college boy was no match for her charms. Even if she was a small-town girl, and nineteen, she had managed to enchant him with a mastery that left him feeling like a blubbering young lad.

"How long have you been in the village?" she asked.

"Not long at all," he admitted. "This is my first day, in fact."

"Tell me, what brings you here, Mister...?" She leaned forward, her head at a slight angle.

"Brown," he answered, with an embarrassed smile. "My name is Dan Brown, and I am from Oxford."

"Oxford," she chimed with delight. "I have never been there myself, but I imagine it's a grand place."

"I'm quite partial to it," he said. "I have lived there my whole life, though. I'm in my last year of college now. I suspect I will stay on, maybe do more schooling."

"You go to university there? As in, you go to Oxford University?"

Her mouth fell open, and he was unsure if she would be impressed or turned off by his response.

"Y-yes," he stammered in return.

"Well, I never met an Oxford man!" Her expression was a mix of awe and delight. "What on earth are you doing all the way up here then?"

"I'm working on a project. It's rather boring, really." He sighed, unsure if he should elaborate. Much of the work he did at university was uninteresting to most people. Outside of his inner circle of schoolmates, few if any took an interest in what he was doing.

"Go on then," she insisted. "Tell me all about your project, Mister Dan Brown"

"Well..." he said, somewhat sheepish, "I am doing a piece on Medieval through Elizabethan-age economics. I have covered some things on the Abbeys and Monasteries in the past, but now I find myself drawn to the smuggling trade. Robin Hood's Bay was well known as the Smugglers' Paradise, so I thought it might be a good idea to come up here to see if I could learn more from the local legends and such."

"I should say you are in the right place indeed," Rose said, giving him a thousand-watt smile. "I have been listening to these old stories for years. Just about every one of these old buildings has a smuggling past. This whole place is brimming with old tunnels and passageways." She sat up. "I believe I could fill your head with stories for days."

"I would like that very much," he said, his cheeks burning. "Very much," he repeated.

Well, where should we start?" She pressed her long delicate finger to her chin, sprung to her feet, and spun in each direction as she surveyed the layout of the village. "I know," she proclaimed, her eyes wide with excitement, "let's walk down to the beach. The tide is out now so we can walk out into the bay. It's just down the hill. I can tell you all the facts about the buildings we pass along the way. There are so many stories."

For a moment, Dan wondered if this was all a dream. The idea that he was here, with this impossibly beautiful creature, who took an interest in his work, was unfathomable to him. He wanted to give himself a firm pinch to make sure this was all real.

Rose stepped onto a steep stone footpath that bordered the narrow road leading through the center of Robin Hood's Bay. Dan took her lead and followed, keeping just shy of her heels as she walked along. Quaint old shops and stone cottages with ancient tile roofs butted right up to the footpath that snaked down the hill. He marveled at how the inhabitants of the Bay had maximized the space of the tiny village set against the sea. Here and there, the buildings would give way to reveal hidden alleyways and footpaths nestled between.

Every few steps, Rose stopped to tell a story about a particular inn or pub, then resumed her descent down the hill. Dan almost wished he'd brought his notebook, though he was sure he could never have scribbled down all the details she shared. All the more reason he should ask to see her again.

As they rounded a corner, the scent of the salty sea filled the air. Small fishing boats came into view, each pushed up against the foundations of the cottages, and he knew the beach was near. The only thing protecting the village from the ravages of the North Yorkshire sea was a high seawall of heavy gray stone. When the tide came in, the waves surged against the wall with fury but low tide revealed a sizable sandy stretch where locals and visitors could discover the treasures left behind. Not just a haven for tourists on holiday, this entire stretch of coastline was also well known as a paradise for fossil hunters. It was a place steeped in history, and Dan could not help but feel his own story somehow taking shape here. He could almost hear the slow turn of fortune's wheel.

As they walked along and talked, he still found it hard to believe that such a girl would give him the time of day. For lack of a better word, he was a nerd—a bookish nerd, to be exact. Even though he was only a few hours from Oxford, he had never ventured this far from home on his own. When he tried his hand at asking Rose on a date, he'd been a nervous wreck, never in a million years thinking she would say yes. It was the first time a girl had looked in his direction in that regard. Every second in her presence was something out of a dream. Whatever good deed he did to exact such good fortune on himself, remained a mystery. All he knew was, never in his life had he wished for time to move slower.

"I love when the tide is out, but I love when it is in just as much," Rose said as she slipped the low-heel shoes from her feet, allowing her toes to sink into the fine sand crystals. "It changes the entire way the bay looks."

Dan, all awkward, reached down to untie the laces of his loafers, then pulled them off along with his socks. As he looked up, Rose was already yards ahead. He trudged along, trying to keep up with her excited pace, aware that the bottoms of his trousers were soaked from the small pools left behind by the ebbing tide. Rose bent to pick up pebbles and shells, slipping them into her shoes as though they were priceless gems she couldn't live without. He could imagine her having amassed quite the collection of ocean trinkets after years of living here in the bay.

"Aren't those cliffs magnificent?" she called out into the wind.

As he looked up to the looming cliffs that embraced the bay, he smiled. Coming from a place as landlocked as Oxford, he'd always held a fondness for the coast. The Yorkshire coast held a majesty all its own, and he could easily see why Rose loved it the way she did. One could never tire of seeing such natural beauty. Standing on the hard wet sand, he gazed out into the infinite sea. Though he was far from a seafaring lad, he couldn't think of a single person who didn't love the ocean. It was so vast and mysterious, and it always would be that way. There would never be a time when man could explore its entirety. That's what made it so captivating, he supposed—it would always remain fully undiscovered.

"This breeze is just perfect," she said, raising her hands to let it tickle her fair skin.

She spun in circles, her dainty yellow dress clinging to her delicate frame as she danced along the beach, so light and free. The girl was a thousand colors, like butterflies in an Elizabethan garden, unmarred by the world and all its woes. As he started after her, he was convinced that she was everything he had searched for his entire life. Every bit of his painstaking diligence as a college student dissipated, and for the first time he felt his first touch of real freedom. All the conventionalities of life were a foreign concept to Rose, created to be a rambler, unbound by the strings of life. He only knew her for a few hours, but that was more than enough time to decide that he was in love. Never had he laid eyes upon a creature so magnificent. She flashed him a dazzling smile that melted his insides like a block of ice in the hot summer sun.

He imagined for a moment that this was what good old King Henry VIII must have felt the first time he laid eyes on Anne Boleyn. Well...maybe Catherine of Aragon, or Catherine Howard. Any one of the six wives, really. Except for Anne of Cleves. Poor lass was the lucky one. He stopped mid-thought to scoff at himself. No matter how hard he tried, he could never push work out of his mind. He looked at Rose, twirling in the salty sea air, bare feet in the sand, like a gilded doll in a music box.

Adelia sensed that Dan had always looked upon Rose that way. Though not his intention, she became a coveted possession, like an obscure treasure he needed to own. Thoughts of her plagued him night and day, clawing at his heart's desire. Rose was everything he wasn't—everything he could never be. In her, he saw some release from the world. She was the pure embodiment of freedom, and the realization that he could never let go of his need to control his own destiny was lost on him as he watched her dance across the sun-drying sand.

From Adelia's perspective, though, she could see it—two people drawn to each other in opposite attraction, but unwittingly bound to their natural wiring. This was an ill-fated romance, the kind Romeo and Juliet would have experienced had they been given a chance to make a go of it. All she could do was be the silent observer. Intruding on something so personal made her feel guilty for wanting to know what happened next.

As fast as the guilt came on, she dismissed it. Curiosity was always her weakness. The whispers had endowed her with the leverage to be a bit of a busybody, always wanting to know things in life that were not intended for her viewing. Something in her perception told her that these were the moments Daniel longed to know about his parents too. These moments in their relationship, containing knowledge that would never be bestowed upon a child.

Then it happened. Something in the energy of the air made her awareness peak, and she spun around. She was alone, but a voice inside told her that wasn't the case. As a cool shiver rippled down her spine, she caught the scent of an all-too-familiar shaving soap, and knew in an instant it was Daniel.

She didn't try to see him. There was no need—she knew he was there. She thought back to Meredith and that night in the apothecary shop in York. Whatever called her to follow the trail of Dan and Rose's ill-fated love had something to do with Daniel finding closure. It was confusing at first, trying to comprehend how she could be the vessel for him to learn the truth, yet, as she sat thinking, an idea began to surface. At first she dismissed it, suspecting that her desperation was giving her outlandish notions, but the more she considered the idea, the more she found herself gaining a better understanding. Meredith had told her she would have to learn to listen. Maybe she meant she needed to listen to her own ideas, not just what the whispers revealed. It wasn't the first time she had been told this, remembering how Cassandra scolded her for the same thing. This time was different, though. This time, her thoughts were coming on so strong, she could not ignore them.

As realization sank in, she understood what Daniel needed her to do. He had always been with her, every moment since the day he died. Now she thought of it, it was clear that he'd led her to the sketchbook. True, he probably didn't anticipate her thinking he was some nefarious cheater, but that was something she could take accountability for herself. From the start, he pushed her along, knowing she couldn't resist a good mystery, or that she would never get a moment's rest until she figured out who the Yorkshire Rose was and why he had taken such an interest in this woman. Even in death, Daniel wanted the answers to the questions that haunted him all his life, and knew his wife was the key to solving the mystery. Interacting with those in her visions wasn't new. It had happened before. Years back, she had been researching the life of Richard III in the village of Coldridge. Though the moment was fleeting, Richard had come through in a way that left no doubt he was aware of her presence.

Her connection had been strong with him, and she would find out in time that it was more personal than she first believed. But her attachment to Daniel was magnified tenfold. Even if it was up to her to discover the truth on her own, she took comfort in knowing he was still a part of the quest, just as he had been in every one before. Part of her wondered why he didn't just ask her to help him years ago. She would have been willing if she thought it was that important.

It didn't take much thought to come to a conclusion. The answer was clear. They were much alike, both scared to find the truth to their own question. Just as she hadn't wanted to shatter the image of their perfect marriage, Daniel didn't want to lose the adoring mother he'd kept so guarded in his heart. Like Adelia, he chose to conquer his fear in return for answers. Her constant awareness of his presence said it all. He was using her eyes to see the things he could not on his own. She was the vessel he needed to achieve closure. It was up to her to discover the truth about Dan and Rose, and she would have to do it all for Daniel so that, at long last, he could be at peace.

"Ghosts are about unfinished business," she whispered into the wind.

For a moment, the icy chill upon her skin was replaced by a sensation of warmth. Her eyes welled up as a swath of heat grazed her swollen abdomen, like the touch of the softest hand. He was right here, wrapping his arms around her, and telling her he hadn't forgotten.

Chapter Fourteen

C assandra was more than a little agitated at her cousin as she put down the phone receiver. She had called her several times over the past two days, with no luck. Adelia should be more responsible. Doesn't she know I am worried about her? More than that, doesn't she know I need her help?

Her irritation was interrupted by the realization that, once again, she was acting like her mother. She grimaced at the thought and looked around her flat. Damn it all to hell, she was going to have to go to the library. She hated being surrounded by dusty, boring books. If Adelia had been home, she could have described the markings on the necklace, and her cousin would surely have spat out the family connection in a matter of seconds. No, her all-too-pregnant relation was out traipsing around Robin Hood's Bay of all places, and now she had no other choice but to go to the library and drown in a stack of smelly old tomes. It would probably take her hours to find the badge, with her only thing to go on being the French connection. That was as good as useless considering most aristocratic families in the Middle Ages descended from French bloodlines.

Growling to herself, she grabbed her purse and stomped out the door. Finding the library proved a challenge in itself. As long as she'd lived in York, she never had occasion to walk through its door, and she just about remembered its location.

When she stepped inside, she pinched her nose in a futile attempt to block the wretched smell, and the droning silence was only broken by the buzz of overhead lights. Such a dreary place, like all libraries. With the sheer number of full shelves ahead of her, she decided it would be best to ask a librarian for help. Her initial hope that this project would be a quick payday had evaporated, and it was now proving to be more difficult than expected.

By nature, she was not a deep thinker. Not that she was incapable—quite the opposite—she could be intellectual when it came to things that mattered most to her. If it did not impact her life or stop the earth's rotation, it was not a topic worthy of her critical attention. She lived on her own terms, and life never really gave her reason to feel the need to adapt to any other way. For her, everything fell into two categories: things she liked, and things she did not like. Things she liked included what she found attractive, exciting, and adventurous. Things she did not like included what she found irritating, boring, or creepy. If it fell into the latter category, she would devote no time or energy to it. As a rule, she preferred to only concern herself with things that were of face value.

She had only settled down with a pile of volumes chosen by the librarian when a long shadow graced the page of the open book before her. None too pleased, she looked up to see the black-clad figure of the man from Basil Duncan's jewelry shop. His presence caught her off guard. He looked just as he had the day of their brief encounter—polished and pristine, and dressed with such impeccable fashion, he could belong to another age. His face, though stern and emotionless, was no less perfect. The man was attractive. Even she couldn't deny that.

"Have you seen her?" he whispered, his inquisitive eyes searching every aspect of her face for something that might betray the truth.

"Who?" She furrowed her brow at him, as if he had just spoken in a foreign language.

"She has come to you?" he asked, his expression remaining neutral.

"*Again*, who?" she repeated, conscious that her pitch was a bit too high for this silent tomb. She sat back in her chair, trying to evade his looming shadow.

"Melusine. She has revealed herself to you."

His comment stunned her, because she couldn't understand how he knew, until she remembered uttering the name aloud in Basil's shop.

"It was just a daydream. I don't know why I said the name. I don't know who Melusine is."

His blank façade took on a mask of confusion. He raised his brows, searching her face with an unnerving amount of patience,

no doubt trying to decide if she was lying. Despite whatever conclusion he came to, and she couldn't have cared less what he decided, the truth was she had never heard the name before that
day. Whatever image played out in her mind, the half-woman,
half-serpent was hardly real. By now, she'd reasoned her bizarre
vision to be a combination of lack of sleep, too much gin and
tonic the night before, and the humid English air. Beyond that,
she found it uncomfortable that this strange man had once again
managed to stumble upon her. Not so coincidental, and a bit too
creepy for her liking.

She knew she had a tendency to attract men's attention, and
even though it wasn't something she was all that fond of, it remained an unavoidable fact. While she had developed a certain
tolerance for the problem, she drew a line at outright stalking.

"Look, buddy, I get the whole dark, brooding, and gloomy thing
you have going on. I'm sure there are plenty of women who fall at
your feet, but this particular one,"—she pointed to herself—"isn't
one of them."

He responded with a chuckle that made her eyes burn with
anger.

"You have mistaken my intention, my lady. I simply wanted to
know about Melusine. If she has come to you. That is all."

"If Melusine has come to me? What importance is that to you?"

"I take an interest," he replied, his tone flat.

"So let me get this straight." She sat up. "You, a complete
stranger, want me to reveal the details of some obscure daydream
to you? Yet you offer no real information in return. I am supposed

to reveal my innermost thoughts to you, while you remain guarded. How very...male."

She looked down to the open book, acting as if she was reading to herself. He stood there, his silence grating on her nerves. When she could no longer take his hovering, she looked up at him through her lashes, seeing that he hadn't budged an inch, continuing to stare down at her with those coal-black eyes.

"Are you still here?" she demanded. "Look, I have a great amount of work to do, as you can see. I have centuries of heraldry to decipher, and your looming over me is not helping me concentrate."

In an easy sway, he nodded once and turned on his heel. Pleased with his ability to take the hint, she returned her focus to the book.

"Trace the descendants of Melusine," he said, his voice soft, as if at her ear. "She will lead you to the answer you seek."

Just as she raised her head, ready to deliver a sharp-tongued response, she discovered that her dark stalker was gone. She looked around but he was nowhere to be seen. The enigmatic Mr. Fulcanelli had departed just as suddenly as he'd appeared. She shrugged, disappointed that her vicious verbal jab would go unused. However, she tucked it away, ready for the next man who crossed the line.

This had been the strangest week. She sat still, more than a little confused. A few minutes later, as she closed the massive volume before her, something caught her eye on the table. A calling card, black except for a gold scroll lining its edges. She leaned forward and picked it up, turning it over to see one word, neatly scripted in gold:

Fulcanelli

Nervous that he might still be watching from afar, she gave the room another diligent scan. Again, he was nowhere to be seen. Agitated all the more, she scrunched the card up in her fist, intending to toss it into the nearest bin. Just as she was about to seek one out, a thought crossed her mind. Should her mysterious stranger seek her out again, she might well want to provide it to the authorities. She opened her purse and dumped the crumpled card in.

Wasting no time, she went up to the librarian's desk and asked for anything they might have that referenced Melusine. The request was met with a look of bewilderment. Even so, it wasn't long before the woman returned with several more volumes, she said contained the information required. Back at her table, Cassandra flipped through page after page, until she found what she was looking for.

Melusine, or Melusina, was the daughter of a water goddess. As punishment for seeking revenge upon her father, her mother placed a curse upon her, where she would become a serpent from the waist down every Saturday. In time, Melusine met Raymond of Lusignan, and married him on condition that he agreed not to seek his wife out on any Saturday. She would spend those days alone in her chamber. After giving him no less than ten sons and bringing him exceptional wealth and power, Raymond found that he could not keep his promise, under severe pressure from his family. He spied upon his wife one fateful Saturday and discovered her secret. When Melusine realized his betrayal, she is said to have fled, lamenting the downfall of her world with a mournful cry. It is said that she is not only the protector of her descendants, as an ever-watchful eye, but a portent of what is to come. Like the Banshee in Celtic lore, if one hears the cry of Melusine, it foretells a great tragedy.

The last sentence pulled her up, the memory of the vision in Basil Duncan's shop flooding back. She had heard that cry they described, and its melancholy tone still reverberated through her bones. But that day in his shop had not been the first time. She pulled in a slow steady breath to calm her racing heart, pushing the memory back out into the dark recesses of her brain.

She looked to where her fingertip rested on the page. Captivated by the story, she could not help but read on. A great many prominent family lines, from Luxembourg, France, and the low countries, claimed to be descendants of Melusine.

She slid her finger further down the page. "The House of Anjou, the Plantagenets, Limburg-Luxembourg…"

It was said that some of her descendants had inherited the gift of foresight, giving them the ability to predict events to come. In the modern age, the story of Melusine was regarded as nothing more than a fable—something told over a roaring fire by those who had little else to entertain them. In its medieval heyday, when tales of the fay and their powers were widely held as truth, this story would have been as logical as the notion that the sun will rise in the sky tomorrow. For Cassandra, a woman who spent a lifetime in the company of the dead, she did not consider herself a skeptic when it came to things that defied explanation. There was nothing in this story she could not believe.

So many questions swirled inside her head, she found it difficult to settle on one long enough to think it through. The vision came the moment she touched the necklace.

"Melusine," the woman had whispered.

Now she'd read the story, there could be no doubt that Melusine was the woman in her vision. But why did she call her own name out?

Chapter Fifteen

Adelia sat on a stone bench, watching the tide roll in at Robin Hood's Bay. A sense of exhilaration filled her as she narrowed her thoughts back to Dan and Rose. She swirled one of Meredith's crystals around in her hand and let out a muffled laugh at the memory of Cassandra calling the woman a witch. If that happened to be true, in any sense of the word, she was a damn good one. Nothing about her own life had been the same since that night. Where the whispers always kept her visions isolated to whatever place she happened to be at the time, they no longer held such constraints. Now it was as if they followed the person, no longer holding attachment to a particular location. She closed her eyes, letting the story of Dan and Rose filter through.

It wasn't long before Dan swept his Yorkshire Rose right off her feet. Not so difficult a task when it concerned a young woman who had spent most of her life with her head in the clouds. Rose was a dreamer at heart, her mind filled with visions of some exciting life in the city. Dan married her a few weeks after he graduated from college, plucking her out of Robin Hood's Bay. For a while, it seemed that a life in Oxford suited them both. He was busy climbing the ladder in his quest to become a professor, and Rose was all too happy to tag along. In the beginning, she accompanied him as he explored the country, doing research as a means to build his career.

Back then, Rose believed she'd found the adventure she had sought for so long. No longer bound by the confines of the village she grew up in, she embraced city life. She found a job as a waitress in a local restaurant, and Dan took on an entry-level teaching position. Finances were tight, but they always made do. Being young and in love, little else mattered.

In the early days, life for the young couple was exciting. The city of Oxford was always bustling, with plenty to do. Whether it was a late-night showing at the movies or a theatrical performance under a starry sky in the park, Rose and Dan went together. On weekends, they would pack a picnic lunch into the car and head out to wherever Dan's research drew him. In the romantic ruins of a medieval castle, they laid out a blanket and Dan scratched out his findings for the day while Rose lay on her back staring up at the clouds. They would return home, happy with the perfect end to another perfect day.

Dan doted on his wife. Even though they lived paycheck to paycheck, he showered her with tokens of his affection, leaving little notes on the kitchen counter, and if he couldn't afford to buy her flowers, he would snatch a bloom off a rosebush on the university campus. No matter how small the gift, he never ceased to let Rose know that she was important. It seemed the two young lovers, with next to nothing, found everything in each other.

It wasn't long before the conventions of society caught up with them and Rose found herself pregnant with what would be their only child, Daniel. With the blessing of a healthy baby boy came the inevitable slowdown of their romantic adventures, until it was only Dan moving about the country at will. Rose settled into the life of a homemaker as best she could, but the days began to get longer and longer. They moved out of their small apartment in the city to a comfortable family home a few miles into the countryside. The new location brought serenity, but also isolation, and the vibrant social life they once enjoyed waned.

Just like them, their friends were settling into the routine of family life. Outings and parties dwindled, replaced by stuffy dinner get-togethers with Dan's academic friends. Never having attended college, Rose realized she was out of her element. Feeling as though she had nothing of value to add to the conversations, she would sit in silence almost the entire evening. Wrapped up in the busy world of academia, Dan barely noticed his wife's discomfort. Soon, Rose began to refrain from participating in such occasions, using the need to stay home with Daniel as her excuse. Dan accepted his wife's explanation, happy that he could still attend. As he fulfilled his goals of rising in academic circles, his promotions at work followed suit. As a result, he ended up working long hours, and his elevated status meant his presence was often requested at various events, with most of his evenings spent attending museum galas, community lectures, and awards' ceremonies.

Rose's days, to her horror, developed the same monotonous routine she had fled from. As much as she tried to adjust, the hollowness only seemed to grow. With Dan's continued absences for his work, she found herself lonelier than she had ever been, and soon descended from her carefree self into a world of dark isolation.

Without warning, Adelia's focus shifted to Dan. She welcomed it because witnessing Rose's journey was such an exhausting task. The woman's emotions were a rollercoaster of highs and lows in rapid succession, and her constant discontent depleted Adelia's energy. She couldn't imagine what that would have felt like each and every day.

Channeling Dan was not a straightforward task, however. It was rare for the whispers to let her peer into the window of the soul of someone living. Until that night in Meredith's shop, her visions were always murky with someone still alive. She still couldn't read the present so well, having to rely on intuition in those instances, but as she learned to let go, allowing the energy to flow through her, reading Dan's past became easier, with the image clearer. Meredith's cleansing ritual had also opened up a new ability. Before, the whispers only allowed her to read the energy of a particular place, giving her a bird's-eye view of the events that transpired there. Now, the more she concentrated, the easier the images and sounds came through. Emotions and thoughts became the ancillary pieces to the puzzle that painted the whole picture. It was like watching a live stage production, only one that occurred long ago and the players weren't wise to her existence. She could follow them wherever the whispers wanted her to go, even if she wasn't in that particular location.

Dan had unwittingly conditioned his wife to be alone. Through the years, she learned to do most everything it took to run a household by herself. Though never his intention, Dan withdrew himself over time from his wife, and little by little she grew accustomed to his absence. His tokens of love diminished until they ceased altogether, and his presence in the house felt more foreign than when he was away. In his mind, his work was a means of providing for his family, and in his devotion to them, he lost sight of the important things. To Dan, they had reached a level of comfort in their relationship where effort was no longer required, as if he'd built a house, considered it complete, and forgot the need for its routine maintenance. He would come to realize his grievous mistake, but far too late.

Each time he returned from one of his trips, Rose found herself less and less excited. Somewhere along the way, she woke up emotionally numb; their once fiery passion for each other had gone, like a once-beautiful, colored painting that had faded to a muted canvas. Were it not for the love of her son, Rose was sure her heart would stop beating. She felt neither love, nor loneliness. Nothing.

Dan Brown loved his wife, but the depth of his affection was only realized after her death, a sad reality even Adelia could relate to. In theory, she believed marriage to be something that should continue to blossom over time. It had to be a lifelong commitment, where a couple became closer as each grew in themselves. Marriage was supposed to be a safe place, where insecurities could shed as each day filled with peaceful contentment with one another. If it worked, it was the place where contentment becomes disengagement. People move through their everyday lives, coasting through the good times and conquering the challenges. Somewhere along the way, marriage starts to feel easy, and that is forgotten. Like every other form of success, it requires work. Dan forgot this along the way. His mind was on providing a better life for his wife and son, and he let that take over. He never saw himself as an absent husband, until he wasn't a husband anymore. That day he discovered Rose's secret letters in her handbag, he realized the gravity of his mistake. The perfect life he'd crafted in his mind had been a comfortable illusion.

Through all his tedious labor to make a better life for his family, he always assumed they would know they were the reason he worked so hard. However, he forgot that his wife needed to know he loved her unfailingly. He stopped giving her gentle kisses in the morning, and failed to compliment her on the occasional new dress she wore. Above all, he never took the time to reassure her that she was, indeed, a good wife and an even better mother. He just assumed she knew that he adored her above all others.

When she died, and he was left with so much time to reminisce, he came to realize all the things he had failed to tell her. As a result, he could never bring himself to be mad at her for needing more. There were times he wished she would have told him so, but as he retraced their conversations, he saw that she'd tried more than once.

He had painted a picture in his mind of a perfect existence with Rose. More and more, he began to understand that all the signs of her unhappiness were there; somehow, he had missed them. As the days wore on, he recalled the little things: the empty smile she returned as he rattled on about his day, not so much as asking her about her own; when he reached for her hand now and then, and she moved hers away as if she was busy doing something; and those empty Saturdays when she asked him what his plans for the day were, and he rattled off a list of things, none of which included her.

No, he could not be surprised that she was unhappy enough to leave. He had conditioned her to fend for herself in the world, giving her an equal dose of loneliness and strength. Inevitably, she would harness that strength for herself. She had every right to want to leave—he was just sorry he had pushed her to that point. His regret for never taking notice of what she was going through bore heavy on him, as did him allowing it get to the point where she was willing to give up the life she shared with him and their son. In all the years since her death, he still did not forgive himself for his role in the mess. In a way, it was his penance for taking everything from her.

It saddened Adelia to think of the deterioration of their marriage. She wondered how much of their strife Daniel had witnessed as a kid. Being only ten years old at the time, there was a good chance he'd been somewhat unaware. Just like his father, he was probably too wrapped up in his own concerns to pay much attention, though, as an adult, he had an intuitive sense about him, being able to read a room without much effort. He also found it difficult to let things he felt were not settled go, suffering a persistent need to make sure such issues were set right. If she had to guess, part of that was from years of sifting back through old memories with his mother. As time passed, he must have replayed every recollection of his childhood again and again, trying to decipher the meanings. The more she learned about the relationship between Dan and Rose, the more she thought of the vulnerable boy stuck somewhere in the middle. Daniel was just a child in the minds of his parents—far too young to understand the world of adults. But they didn't realize that he was old enough to have intuition.

She recalled the black and white photos of Daniel in the scrapbook his father shared with her. His eyes held a sadness she had missed. Having grown up in a home devoid of true happiness, he probably assumed that was the way with every family. Yet, the Daniel she knew was far removed from the boy in those faded pictures. Somewhere along the way, he grew into the exact opposite of who he was as a child, wanting his own life to be different from that of his parents.

In that moment, she felt his courage. It must have taken a great deal of personal dedication to change his own path, and to be unafraid to show emotion and vulnerability, which she would forever be grateful for. Though these were things she always loved and admired about him, she understood now how much effort it must have taken for him to become that person. These were traits he had chosen, not ones that came naturally. For that, she admired her husband all the more.

Chapter Sixteen

Cassandra's stomach gave a low grumble—a gentle reminder that she'd neglected to have breakfast this morning before heading out to the library for the second time this week. She glanced down at her watch, seeing it was already past noon. It might be best to head back to the flat, grab a bite to eat, then have a much-needed nap. But when she did a mental survey of the contents of her kitchen, she shifted direction and headed toward The Shambles where, just off a side road, existed a quaint tea shop which boasted the best lemon scones and Devonshire cream in York. Coupled with a nice cup of hot tea, her afternoon was sure to be complete.

As usual, the shop was bustling with the early afternoon rush. She placed her order at the counter and turned to search for an empty table. Seeing that every seat inside was already taken, she stepped outside to the batch of small tables lining the sidewalk. A quick scan had her heart sinking at the realization that they were all occupied as well.

Just as she turned to head back inside, she caught sight of him, the back of her neck going cold. Fulcanelli was seated at one of the tables, staring up at her as he set his tea cup back on the saucer. She gave a muffled growl under her breath, not loud enough for him to hear. Or perhaps it was, as he smiled up at her, its radiance a flashing contrast to his olive skin. The natural light gave his dark eyes a glint of amber that, had she not known him as a creep, she might have found appealing. He motioned to the chair opposite him—the only empty seat in the whole place.

As she debated sitting, she couldn't help but spit out, "Why are you following me around, Mister Fulcanelli?"

"I was here already," he stated, his tone flat. "It was you who stumbled upon me."

She stared down her nose at him, biting back her admission that he wasn't wrong.

"I am right," he said, a hint of smugness in his voice. "It's alright if you want to tell me so."

With reluctance, she slid into the chair, giving him a deadly side-eye glare. "You are one of those one-uppers, huh?"

Fulcanelli looked perplexed, the vertical line between his eyebrows deepening. "I am not sure exactly what you mean."

"For someone who seems to know everything, I am quite surprised that you are unfamiliar with the term." She fumbled around in her handbag, needing an excuse to take her attention away from the absolute perfection of this beastly man's face.

"Knowledge is just something to be obtained. Never apologize for what you know, any more than you should apologize for what you don't know. If it is worth my time, I will learn it with ease. If not, then I won't waste precious time."

She stopped searching for nothing in her bag and looked at him, running through his words again. "Hmm, interesting. Finally, something we may agree upon." She shifted in her chair as her tea and scones arrived. They were smaller than she remembered, but that was probably because she was starving.

Fulcanelli eyed her as she prepared her tea and added a drop of cream to her fresh-cut scone. Too hungry to worry about politeness, she took a bite, catching the crumbs in her free hand.

"Tell me, my lady Cassandra, was your afternoon productive in your search at the library the other day?"

"Somewhat," she answered, covering her mouth as she chewed. She took her time, then washed it down with hot tea, which was perfect. "I think I have narrowed down the possible owners. Now I just have to trace each one until I find the right heraldry. It's time consuming, and I don't have the patience to keep at it for more than a few hours."

"Ah, but a great historian such as yourself will surely solve the mystery in short order."

"I am not a great historian," she replied, her cheeks flushing. "I majored in history when I started college, but switched shortly after. It just wasn't for me. I specialize in fashion now, but I have a passion for jewelry with a historic past." She turned her cup, half-wishing she could dive into her lunch but also intrigued with this mysterious, gorgeous man. Instead, she took another sip of her tea, placing her cup back on the saucer as she looked him in the eye.

"If you must know, I thought this job would be easy money." She rolled her eyes. "I'm not so sure now."

"I appreciate your honesty," Fulcanelli said with a chuckle. "Just the same, I have a sense that you are more capable of getting to the bottom of this than you think."

She stared back at him, blinking as she let the words sink in. Interesting. She couldn't quite recall anyone in recent memory having such faith in her ability. If so, they hadn't voiced it. She polished off the last bites of her scone, sipped more tea, then picked up the second one, almost wishing she'd ordered a few more. They were small but tasted far better than she remembered.

"Tell me, Mister Fulcanelli, what is your interest in the necklace?" Her ravenous hunger somewhat slaked, she took a more delicate nibble this time.

"I brought it to Mister Duncan," he stated, his voice lacking any discernible emotion.

She leaned back, raising her hand to cover her mouth again as she chewed and swallowed.

"You...brought it to Duncan?" She realized her mouth was hanging open so snapped it shut. "Then you must know something about its origins. Why on earth am I the one looking for a needle in a haystack?"

"Because you are capable of finding a needle in a haystack."

She almost growled back at him, far from happy that the man had just added an extra layer of confusion to her work. It was clear from their encounter in the library that he knew something of the necklace's origin, but him not offering that information to Duncan didn't make sense. Was he unsure if his information was correct?

"Are you going to help me out by telling me how you came into possession of this necklace?" she asked.

"No, dear lady," he responded, his sly grin dimpling his cheek. "How I came upon it has no relevance, but I think you are quite capable of getting to the bottom of its provenance."

She wanted to keep pushing him, but it would all be in vain. There was nothing about the man's demeanor that made her think he would change his mind. Whatever his intentions, he had no desire to help her any further. Once again, she was struck by the realization that she would be doing this all on her own. So much for easy money.

Lost in a swirl of questions, she nibbled at the remains of her scone.

"So, what does an ex-historian turned fashion expert do in a town like York?" This time, his voice was casual and friendly.

She sat still for a long moment, taking him in, or the little she knew of him. "You don't have to be a historian to enjoy the spoils of York." She couldn't hold in a smile as she looked around her. "I grew up in London but, since moving here, I think I might just like it more."

"Ah, a London girl. The city life suits you well. I should have guessed you were a Londoner at heart. You are both sophisticated and street smart. A perfect combination."

Her cheeks burned at another unexpected compliment. Something about him played upon her senses. Not so much what he'd said. No, there was more to it than that. Then it came to her. For once, she was in the presence of a man who didn't seem to assess her physical appearance to such an obvious degree that it made her skin crawl. Though his stare was probing, it felt like he was searching for elements far more important than mere looks, as if he saw something in her of value—some unspoken quality that only he could detect. Even though they had gotten off to a poor start—and that was mostly her fault—she found herself softening to him...somewhat.

"What is it that you like to do, Mister Fulcanelli? Perhaps I can suggest some of the city's sights to you while you are here."

One dark eyebrow twitched. "You assume I don't live here already."

She smirked in return. "Your slight French accent betrays you. A definite transplant, if I have ever seen one."

"You are very perceptive, Cassandra. I do not live here. Just passing through." He flicked non-existent dust off his lapel, offering no more information on the topic. "I have a passion for a great many things. I am what one might call a man of science—elements and metals mostly. I am a lover of the arts. A great patron throughout the years, and a bit of a dabbler. Most of all, I love music. I play many instruments, but the violin has long been my favorite."

"You are a violinist? When did you learn to play?" She leaned in, resting her chin on her hand. This man grew more fascinating by the minute.

A delighted smile lit up his face, as if he was pleased to have found a topic that drew her interest. She couldn't help being mesmerized by the dark shadow his inky-black lashes cast on his eyes.

"I learned as a child, having the good fortune to be taught by a great master in Italy. I picked it up rather quickly, and have been playing ever since. In fact, I am scheduled to perform at a private function this evening."

"For an audience? You must be highly accomplished then. Where have you played?"

"All around the world," he said, as though there was little to be impressed by. "If I had to pick my favorite spot, I would say the Palace of Versailles. The hall of mirrors has wonderful acoustics."

"You...played in the Palace of Versailles?"

"Yes. Madame de Pompadour especially loved my sonatas."

She cast him another sideways' glance, sure his reference was a test. Given that Madame de Pompadour was the mistress of King Louis XV in the mid-eighteenth century, it was a far-fetched boast, to say the least. She didn't dignify his cheeky attempt at humor with a response, choosing instead to move the conversation along.

"Is there anywhere in the world that you haven't been, Mister Fulcanelli? Thus far, your resume is *unbelievably* impressive."

He pondered her question, drumming his index finger on his chin. "Ohio."

"Ohio? The state? In America?"

"One and the same," he said with a nod of agreement. "I have never been to Ohio." He shrugged one shoulder. "I can't really say I had any reason to go."

She stared at him, not sure how to take his obscure response.

"You did ask where I haven't been. I told you Ohio. It is the truth."

"I have no doubt you are telling the truth, at least on that point," she said. "It was just a rather random answer."

His eyes widened for a split second, conveying his amusement, and betraying the fact that he was well aware how odd his response had been. In the short time she'd known him, it was easy to see that he was a matter-of-fact type of man. He offered no more information than he deemed necessary. She wasn't sure whether she found that irritating or admirable. In the end, she supposed it mattered little what she thought—Fulcanelli did not seem the type willing to change to suit anyone's pleasure.

"I have an engagement at the Treasurer's House tonight. Why don't you come and have a listen? I imagine you have a very full schedule, but I would be most pleased if you could attend."

Caught off guard by his unexpected invitation, she refrained from sharing that she had nothing going on tonight.

"I'm afraid I have dinner plans."

His brow twitched again. "This would definitely be worthy of skipping out on that."

"I thought you said it was a private engagement?" She gave him an expectant look. "It would be improper of me to impose myself on such an event."

"I just invited you. It is now slightly less private."

"The Treasurer's House?" She made soft eye contact, trying not to be drawn in by the exquisite lines of his face. Up to this point, he had taken every opportunity to toy with her. Under any other circumstance, she might have found herself rather annoyed, but something about him made her crave more. In truth, she was bored with the monotony of her usual encounters with men. For now, she had nothing better to do than play along. "I am not a fan of those dusty old Roman ghosts in the basement."

"They are very nice gentlemen, I assure you, Lady Cassandra. They are just doing their job, like you and I. If you like, I can convince them to stay downstairs."

"That would be most kind," she said, her words dripping with sarcasm. "If something happens to change my schedule, perhaps I can squeeze in a few minutes."

"Perfect. Let me write down the details." He retrieved a small black notebook from inside his coat.

****

When Adelia felt she had exhausted everything she could learn in Robin Hood's Bay, she pondered where her journey would take her next. So much had been revealed about the relationship between Dan and Rose. If she went on emotions alone, while she did not necessarily agree with the woman's choice, she understood why Rose might have sought comfort elsewhere. It was clear she was seeking the love she couldn't find in her marriage.

Dan had told her how Rose spent a great deal of time in the garden shed she used as a makeshift art studio. Rose took to painting in her last few years and, like any artistic endeavor, probably used it as a way to decompress. Her studio had become a refuge from the unhappiness of her life, where she felt comfortable enough to tuck away the secrets that would have destroyed the last threads of her fractured marriage.

Aside from whatever secrets the garden shed may contain, she was at a dead end—there was little else in Rose's story to go on. If she could get Dan to let her into it, she might pick up on something that could lead her to more.

When did Rose meet the man in the letters? If she didn't drive, how had she managed to see him? Who was this man who would steal her heart so strongly she was willing to leave her life in Oxford? And not just her husband but her son too. That was the part Adelia struggled with, what with her facing motherhood soon. The thought of leaving her baby was unthinkable, but then again, she and Rose were different people, with neither of their situations the same. That was evident in her inability to believe she would have ever found sufficient reason to walk away from Daniel or the baby.

Again, her thoughts shifting back to Dan, a man blissfully unaware of the undercurrent surging right under his nose. Sure, he wasn't the perfect husband—far from it—he was distant and selfish at times, and never really in tune with Rose's feelings of loneliness. Perhaps losing his wife to another man was deserved—a product of his continued inattentiveness. What steps might he have taken if he realized just how broken his marriage had become? Would he have changed? Would he have taken the steps necessary to get things back on track? It wasn't impossible. Or were things too far gone to repair?

One thing she had not yet considered was that Rose and Dan were a product of the time. No marriage or relationship was impervious to the social norms of the day. Their strife would have been subject to what society deemed acceptable. Though things were evolving, there was still a stigma to consider. Rose was born in a time where you bit your lip and kept your personal business to yourself. Unhappy wives were supposed to just learn to be happy, or at least get on with their lot. Troubling your husband with silly things like emotions, just wasn't acceptable. Husbands were supposed to be providers, and as long as they did that essential job, they shouldn't be asked for more.

If Rose and Dan had wanted to repair their marriage, it was something they would have to do on their own, to escape judgment. Neither would reach out for guidance, the image of a perfect family being far too important to maintain. Admitting flaws in ourselves is a difficult enough task, so having others weigh in would have made it harder. Besides, marriage doesn't come with an instruction manual, and from all accounts is nothing less than a lifetime of trial and error. But Dan and Rose were never able to get it right, and Adelia felt sure that neither would have known how to repair what was broken, even if they wanted to.

Somewhere along the way, Rose found what she thought was the answer to her problems. Tragically, her solution cost her dearly.

From Adelia's perspective, prying into Rose and Dan's painful past felt invasive, but she couldn't shake the notion that there was more she needed to understand before it could be fully put to rest. At this point, she wasn't confident she had uncovered the answers

Daniel wanted to find. So far, how this all played out around him hadn't been fully revealed. Reservations aside, deep down, she knew she needed to press forward.

The longer she considered the situation, the more she believed she had to push further into Rose's mind to better understand her motivations. Even if whatever she learned changed nothing, she needed this closure for herself now, not just Daniel.

Chapter Seventeen

C assandra did consider not going to Fulcanelli's concert. Her social calendar was rarely empty, and she was always eager to attend the city's trendiest events, embracing the opportunity to be seen, yet, something about this particular invitation made her anxious. A private soiree held at the Treasurer's House felt a bit too highbrow and formal for her taste. Even though she had been raised in an affluent home, with her parents' successful entrepreneurial ventures seeing her accustomed to more luxuries than the average child, there was a fundamental difference between her own family's wealth and the established "old money elite" in England. The people she expected to be in attendance tonight were in a league all their own—one she could not see herself assimilating into, even if it was only for the night.

She swung open her closet doors, convinced she had nothing appropriate to wear. As she scanned the interior, she stopped on seeing a covered garment tucked in the back. She'd forgotten about that, and smiled to herself as she pulled it out and laid it across her bed. In truth, she had only worn it once before, and remembered how it turned its fair share of heads on that occasion.

When she unzipped the cover, the contents sprung forth. She drew it out and held it up by its hanger. It was a cocktail dress of the finest quality satin in a beautiful shade of oyster white. The form-fitting costume fell just shy of knee length. As beautiful as it was, the attached cloak sleeves had to be her favorite feature, adding a touch of elegance that made the dress spectacular. She placed it back on the bed and returned to her closet to search among the stacked shoeboxes. Her target was buried deep, purchased specifically for this dress, and had also only been worn once, a long time ago. She pulled the box out and extracted the pair of high heels, each covered in a bronze brocade. The raised embroidery gave off a subtle shimmer that, placed against the matte background, made the footwear truly eye-catching on their own merit.

Should she take Fulcanelli up on his invitation, she might still feel out of her element, but this ensemble would boost her confidence. The right outfit always lifted her, and she was aware of the definite shift in how she was treated based upon her chosen attire. An event such as this required a certain amount of sophistication.

Having slipped into the cool sleekness of the dress, she stood back to admire herself in the mirror, holding her hair up, away from her face. Even if she ended up regretting attending the concert tonight, she would at least not be dismayed at wearing this fabulous costume. That was all the convincing she needed. Lady Cassandra would attend the ball.

****

She clutched her purse tight, like a child guarding their security blanket. Falling in line behind a couple, she entered the walled garden of Treasurer's House. The house itself was situated to the rear of the towering York Minster. Cassandra had visited just a few days ago with Adelia, but she was struck at how different everything looked in the long shadows of the fading sun. In the light of day, the manicured garden was bursting with vibrant hues, and the lush green grass, white marble statues, and the soft purple shades of wisteria blooms climbing up the side of the house brought on a calming serenity. Now, as the last vestiges of daylight dissipated, the towering roofline cast its gray shadow, and the statues loomed in their dark corners like eavesdroppers in a viewing gallery.

Built on the site of an old Roman road, the Treasurer's House had earned its name from the structure that existed at this location as early as the twelfth century. That residence had served as the seat of all the treasurers of York Minster, until the reformation put an end to the need for such an occupation. In 1562, Archbishop Thomas Young and his family began the work of rebuilding the structure. Like all of England's great homes, the Treasurer's House had undergone a fair amount of reconstruction over time, with each change adding another layer of magnificence to the previous era. The house fell into disrepair, and was even divided into several tenements, until it was purchased in 1897 by Frank Green.

Frank was a wealthy industrialist, and the restoration of the Treasurer's House became his passion project. Drawing inspiration from medieval-era estates, he resurrected the house to a level of glory that Cassandra had no problem appreciating.

The beautiful pearl-colored stone of its exterior was embellished with an abundance of large elegant windows along the façade. Its arched entry doorway boasted two carved columns on each side, and the interior held a stunning collection of artwork and furnishings. Frank Green, a stickler for detail, oversaw every aspect of the reconstruction and restoration work.

In 1930, the house was given over to the National Trust. The maintenance of such large and unique properties was expensive, and while tourism helped offset some of the costs, other means of fundraising were necessary. Tonight's "Concert by Candlelight" was one of the inventive ways the organization employed to ensure a steady stream of revenue for upgrades and conservation.

As she made her way to the front door, she felt a bit embarrassed for the minimal contribution she would be giving, assuming that some of the checks written tonight would be more than her monthly salary at the magazine. She doubted she would find herself in a position to be as generous with her wealth as some of the big players here this evening. Once again, she questioned why she'd chosen to come. By nature, she had never been the nervous type, but just being here peaked anxiety like she'd never experienced before, reminding her of the tales Adelia shared about her own condition before coming to England.

The line was slow moving as visitors gave their name at the door, and it took patience and discipline not to show her growing frustration.

At last, it was her turn. "Cassandra Laughton," she said, pushing back the nervous tension surging through her.

The attendant smiled at her, motioning for one of the ushers to come over. "This is Lady Cassandra. She has a seat marked per *Comte de Fulcanelli's* request."

This puzzled her. *Count Fulcanelli?* The man had an obvious aristocratic air to him, was clearly educated and well-traveled, yet she would not have pegged him to be titled nobility. She had the sudden urge to flee, gripped by an insecurity unknown to her before this. Glancing behind at the waiting line, she knew an abrupt departure was out of the question. She sucked in a deep breath, straightened her back, and followed her guide.

The interior of the house was even more beautiful in the evening than it had been during her daytime visit. Rich tapestries and massive paintings adorned the walls, and the opulent glass-blown chandeliers sparkled as the light played off the hanging crystals.

She tried not to look too stunned when they reached the great hall, with its high ceiling of oak beams and plasterwork, harkening back to Tudor days. The floor, of white marble tiles, was covered with an abundance of chairs, almost all full, and the flames of hundreds of long tapers gave the room an ethereal glow, filling the air with the rich scent of smoky vanilla. She was led to a chair near the front, where a small stage had been erected before the huge stone fireplace on the far wall. The massive mantle was filled with candles in crystal holders, sending a glimmering radiance in every direction.

After taking her seat, she fiddled with the beading on her clutch purse, and barely noticed the sudden silence of the audience. Sharp footsteps echoed off the walls of the jampacked hall, followed by a burst of applause. The guest of honor had arrived.

Fulcanelli, or rather, Count Fulcanelli, stepped up onto the stage and sat on the lone chair. Instead of his usual waistcoat over a black shirt, this one was of black damask, woven with fine gold thread. He'd left it open, its gold buttons glinting in the pale candlelight. His hair was smoothed back, accentuating the perfection of his features. To Cassandra, he still looked like a fairytale villain, if a villain had the right to be so dashing.

In true Fulcanelli fashion, he said not a word to the awaiting spectators. After raising the violin to rest snug under his chin, he pulled forth the bow and began, which is when something magical happened.

Coming to age in the 1950's, Cassandra developed a fondness for the new sound of rock and roll. She made a point of owning no records her parents would not have considered utter trash. Classical music was never to her liking, and she couldn't tell the difference between a concerto and a sonata, not even sure either term had anything to do with music. As she listened to Fulcanelli play, the feeling it evoked was indescribable. Each note stirred something deep within her, to the point where tears brimmed in her eyes. Hidden notes in each number brought her soul to the darkest night, only to plunge it back into a burning sunrise. She sat stock still, fearing any slight movement might cause her to miss the minutest detail. It wasn't until the gathering erupted in applause that she realized the concert had ended.

The attendant brought forth a long black case, stitched with shimmering golden threads and jeweled along the top. Fulcanelli placed his violin in its resting place, then, without even acknowledging his audience, headed right toward Cassandra.

She clutched her purse tighter as he approached, his tall lean figure seeming to glide across the floor, debonair, without effort. The ambiance of the room softened him somehow, chipping at his usual overt reserve to reveal a man who resembled a Hollywood star rather than the formal creature she recalled from this afternoon.

"Lady Cassandra," he said as he reached for her hand, which he brought to his lips.

His kiss was gentle and warm, flushing her cheeks with enough heat, she was sure it turned them crimson. She smiled up at him, blinking her pale lashes, feeling no more sophisticated than a young girl in the presence of her first crush.

She was accustomed to having an effect on men, but not with it being the other way round. Somehow, in the space of a few days, Fulcanelli had managed to weave his way right into her heart. No matter how much of him she soaked up, it wasn't enough. She could not say how it happened. Now she thought of it, she was certain it defied explanation. When it came to romantic involvement, she made sure she had the upper hand, impervious to the smooth-talking charms of men, and proud to be an impenetrable fortress against their powers of persuasion. She was a woman men desired and women despised, priding herself on owning her fate, without arrogance or lack of respect for the power it gave. Without fail, she never willingly dangled the heart of her admirers for personal gain, believing herself to be far better than that. She liked to keep love at a safe distance in the knowledge that someday she would come upon a man destined to change everything, deconstructing the wall she had built around her heart, to leave her vulnerable to all the things she'd guarded herself against. When that happened, she would take that leap by her own free will, accepting all the risks involved.

As she stared into his black eyes, muted golden at the edges, she realized that day may have come.

"I have to do some mingling," he said, his words followed by an exasperated sigh. "It would be very poor taste for me to leave abruptly, and I want to see the foundation do well in its fundraising tonight."

"Absolutely," she replied, leaving no doubt that she understood. "You are the guest of honor, after all."

"Would it be too much to ask for you to wait for me?" His voice was so soft, she felt sure no one else heard him. "I know that you probably need to get home, but I really would like to talk to you."

She went through her imaginary schedule for tomorrow. Being a writer, she had deadlines, but her next one was not exactly looming.

"I could stay around for a bit," she said, with a hint of dismissiveness, though a mix of apprehension and flattery waged war in her chest.

He gave her a conspiratorial wink, then departed to converse with his waiting admirers. She got up and walked away, doing her best to shield the unstoppable smile. Over the next while, she wandered around, pretending to find interest in the priceless paintings and furniture decorating the hall. When, on occasion, she caught a glance from Fulcanelli, a red-hot fire surged through her. Throughout the next hour, he moved about the room talking to the distinguished guests, never allowing her to be out of his sight for any great length of time. She liked the feel of his gaze on her, far too much than she should.

As the evening drew to a close, and people began departing into the night, she looked up to find that her handsome host had returned to her side. He stood silent, fastening the gold buttons along the front of his dress coat. For a moment, she just beheld him, and for a second, placed him in the same pantheon as Mr. Darcy from Pride and Prejudice, one of her favorite Jane Austen novels. Beneath his proud countenance and stiff demeanor lay the beating heart of a man who every reader rooted for in the end.

He led her out of the great hall and through the corridors that took them to the foyer. A man at the door tipped his hat to them, then pulled open the massive wooden door to the outside. The night air was cooler, in pleasant contrast to the heat of the after-noon.

"A cab, Lady Cassandra?" Taking her arm in the crook of his, his movement was so delicate that she almost didn't feel it.

She smiled at that, liking it more than she should. "There is no need. I don't live far from here. I can probably walk home just as quickly."

"It is far too late for you to be walking on the city streets by yourself," he said, stiffening, and sounding like an older gentleman lecturing a young woman, which *was* the case.

She could not contain her independent streak, no matter how smitten she had become. "I assure you, Mister Fulcanelli, I have walked these streets alone a great many times, and I have always made it home unscathed."

"Then I shall escort you home. I would not be an honorable man to let you walk alone."

She flashed him a questioning look, not liking the way his tone left no room for negotiation. As a single woman, who always resided in a large city, the prospect of allowing someone she barely knew to escort her home broke all the rules of common sense. While she respected his outdated attempt at chivalry, she still felt uneasy saying yes.

"I will take you a block or so away," he said, seeming to pick up on her indecision. "From there, you can complete the journey on your own."

Assessing his offer for a moment, she deemed it to be a reasonable compromise. In truth, she was in no hurry to depart his company. Besides, she knew this town far better than he, and if she felt uncomfortable at any time, she was confident she could shake him off with ease. If worse came to worse, she could lead him in the opposite direction of her apartment and he would be none the wiser. She smiled inside at her cunning.

"I suppose a few blocks wouldn't hurt," she said. Despite the air of stubbornness she exuded, she could not have been happier to be in his company. With the night being such a whirlwind, she was still dizzy with exhilaration. She doubted she would be able to sleep a wink later for replaying the whole evening in her mind.

She pointed off in the direction of her flat, and Fulcanelli fell in step with her. The night was serene, the cool air refreshing after an evening in a jampacked hall. As they walked, the street lights and shadows played tug-of-war, the comfortable silence broken by the gentle hum of the occasional car passing them. For her, it was a scene plucked right out of a peaceful dream.

"How did you like the concert?" he inquired.

"I must say, your talent is impressive. Each song was like a love story, with all the highs and lows. I especially liked the last one. It left me feeling like the story ended happily."

He responded with a wry smile. "The best love stories are the ones that don't have a happy ending"

She leaned away and studied him. "That is a rather dim view of love, don't you think?" She hadn't had much luck in the ways of romance, but there was still a part of her that remained ever the dreamer.

"Not at all," he said. "Romeo and Juliet didn't end well for either party, yet it is universally known as one of the best stories ever written. Wuthering Heights? Jane Eyre?"

"Hmm, I think you are reading some rather dark works. What about Pride and Prejudice? It gets off to a rocky start but Elizabeth Bennet and Mister Darcy end up together in the end."

"I would have liked a follow-up novel. Maybe a year or two into the marriage. Things may not have fared so well."

"Have you been slighted in matters of the heart?" she asked, aware that such a probing question might be taken as somewhat impertinent. But she couldn't help herself, wanting to break through his guarded façade. In the short time she'd known him, she had found herself perplexed by her inability to read this man. Had she tucked her gift away for too long, with her refusal to use it diminishing its strength? While it sounded logical, she knew it wasn't true. She used the whispers far more than she let on, but only when she felt a true need. Now that need was upon her, more than ever, absolutely nothing came of it. This must be how Adelia felt.

Her gift aside, her natural intuition made her well aware that, if he didn't want to entertain her curiosity, he wouldn't indulge it further. It was an approach to life they seemed to share.

"I haven't been slighted," he said. "I move around too much to ever find myself entangled in matters of the heart, for long. My work dominates my time."

"What exactly is your work? As I recall, you said science. Metals, correct?"

"Yes, it's a type of metallurgy. Taking a variety of substances to create something of greater value."

"So, you create different types of metals?" She wasn't sure why she continued, as science did not interest her too much, and she hoped he didn't go into great detail. It was just to keep the conversation going, as the former topic had struck a nerve.

He leaned closer. "We call it *The Great Work*." He nodded once, then straightened. "You see, there is an ancient school of thought that some base metals can be combined, in a precise concoction, to produce ones of significantly more value."

"Like turning lead into silver or gold?" A flush of excitement buzzed through her. "Like an alchemist?"

He stopped and turned to face her, his emotionless gaze telling her she had hit some button. Was he unhappy with her deduction? Those hints of amber in his dark eyes glistened back at her, and she swallowed hard as heat swept across her face.

"Yes...like alchemy," he said, resuming his progress along the sidewalk. "Are you familiar with the work?"

"Not exactly. At least, not in the technical sense. I am, however, a lover of fine jewelry, and I have spent some time studying the subject. I must admit to believing alchemy to be a myth—a bit of hocus pocus? The idea that it's possible to use elements to manufacture gold or gemstones...? Well, it has to be far-fetched. Still, I *am* intrigued that such a thing could be possible."

She'd downplayed her knowledge of fine jewels. While she had majored in fashion, jewelry was her specialty, giving her an in-depth working knowledge of construction and design, and allowing her at times to pinpoint a specific maker just by the look of a piece. More than anything, she possessed a keen eye for authenticity. From what she could tell, the buttons on Fulcanelli's coat were gold. Even the gold stitching of his violin case was the real deal. One of her college professors had referred Basil Duncan to her, and from the moment she laid eyes on that necklace, she could have given an immediate market value to the near-priceless piece, even before establishing its provenance.

"There is a great deal possible," he said, his voice soft, "if one is so inclined to devote one's life to its fruition. This world is filled with endless wonders. Things that defy the imagination."

"So, have you been successful in your...great work? Is it possible to create silver and gold from something like base metals?"

"I have been quite successful," he admitted, without hesitation. "Yet the secrets to my work must be highly guarded. You see, this work is meant to be for the good of all. It could easily be used for ill deeds if not in the hands of someone with pure intentions."

Cassandra thought of her own gift of sight with the whispers, understanding what he was saying far better than he might have guessed.

"I don't think I will be laboring over a forge in my apartment anytime soon, Mister Fulcanelli. You can keep your secrets." She gave a dismissive wave. "I simply wanted to know if it was true."

He responded with a gentle smile, conveying his appreciation for her not pressing him further than he wished to go. She was almost content to leave it at that, but as they walked along, she felt inclined to ask one more question.

"Is it true that a master alchemist can create fine gemstones? Even take several small ones and make one much larger?"

"It is possible," he answered, offering up no further elaboration.

"Then the myths about Nicolas Flamel must be true."

"Nicolas Flamel?" Once again, he stopped to look at her. The intensity in his eyes burned through her, and she knew right away she had struck a chord. Something flashed—an image she could not decipher at first sight, but the emotion of it was raw. It felt...honest.

"Legend tells that Nicolas Flamel was an alchemist," she continued. "It is said that he came into a great fortune, having found an ancient manuscript that unlocked the secrets of the great work. If what you say is indeed possible, then it stands to reason that the legends are not so outlandish."

"Forgive me for saying this, but I am astonished that you are familiar with the works of Flamel."

"Mister Fulcanelli," she snapped back in return, "are you insinuating that I am far too shallow to be interested in someone like Nicolas Flamel?"

"*Au contraire*, I am actually very impressed with your knowledge of the subject." The gold thread in his eyes glinted as he smiled. "This is not a conversation I have had the good fortune of having so often. Tell me, Lady Cassandra, what is your favorite gemstone?"

She wrinkled her nose, convinced he was trying to sway her attention. Even with his guarded nature, and his wholly unbelievable resume, she could not deny the sense of pure honesty about him. Had the whispers not taken an inconvenient holiday, she might have been able to read him like a book. Fulcanelli may be the master of evasive conversation, but she had something he did not possess:

a woman's intuition, and her gut could sense a lie as easily as the truth.

Just as they turned the next corner, she stopped and looked up at him, her breath catching as he turned to face her. The pale light of a street lamp cloaked him, and he stood there looking as polished and perfect as she had ever seen a man. While love at first sight was a notion she didn't believe in, infatuation at first sight was more than possible. Her physical reaction proved that: how he quickened her pulse; her temperature rising at least ten degrees, maybe twenty; and how the space around her heart was now filled with such airy warmth, she couldn't feel its thump anymore.

"This is where I take my leave," she said, disappointed that they had covered the short distance so soon. Truth be told, she could have burned another few hours with him. To hell with sleep.

"Then this is where I take mine," he replied. "You will be okay the rest of the way on your own?"

"I will be fine, thank you."

"Until we meet again." He performed a bow that reminded her she had been escorted home by none other than *Count Fulcanelli*.

As she walked away, she remembered she had not answered his question. Turning back, she nearly stumbled on seeing that he was standing in the exact spot she had left him, watching her.

"I like sapphires most of all," she called out, then turned and resumed her departure.

"They match your eyes," he said, his words coming to her so soft on the night air, she was unsure if he'd meant for her to hear them.

Her flat was just a block or so from where she'd left him under the streetlamp, but she still found herself checking behind every now and then. To his honor, he did not follow her.

When she made it home, she closed the door behind her and leaned against it like a giddy schoolgirl. She wasn't sorry she had gone tonight, even if it turned into the most bizarre experience of her life to date. There was no way in hell she would get a wink of sleep tonight.

Chapter Eighteen

Before Adelia knew it, she found herself right back in Oxford, standing at Dan's door once again. There wasn't time to think better of her decision, nor worry about what her father-in-law would think of her return. The summer would soon draw to a close, seeing her back in work, and the idle time she'd spent unraveling Rose's story was a luxury that wouldn't be afforded much longer, with her focus once again on juggling the demands of her job, and preparing for the baby's arrival in a few more months. She wanted nothing more than to finish this endeavor and resume her own life without the shadow of Rose plaguing her every waking thought. It was this self-serving desire that led her back to Dan's door, ignoring the fact that he might find her visit more than a little odd.

During the drive, she had drummed up a concoction of reasons for her return to Oxford, but as she looked into the older man's eyes, a sense of calm prevailed and she realized they wouldn't work.

She wanted to be honest, or at least be as forthcoming as she could allow herself to be, all the while knowing she was probably tapping into painful memories Dan wanted to forget. As much as she needed answers to her questions, she didn't have the right to hurt him in the process.

"Not long after Daniel passed away, I found myself sitting at his writing desk in his old study, which is where I stumbled upon this book of sketches." She pulled the frayed book from her bag and handed it over to Dan. "At first, I had myself convinced that these pictures were...another woman."

Dan's gaze shot up from the front cover to meet hers, his brows raised in surprise. Then his expression turned from disbelief to confusion. Adelia suspected that, like herself, he'd held tight to the belief that he knew his son far too well for such a thing to be plausible. She motioned for him to turn to the next page, and he did so, the action slow, almost fretful. As he looked over the words *Yorkshire Rose*, the corners of his mouth lifted in a subtle smile, the phrase no doubt striking bone deep into his long-term memory.

Adelia gestured that he continue to the next page, which he did. As the colorful images of the fair-haired beauty met his gaze, his eyes, filled with disbelief seconds before, softened, taking in the face he'd seen so many times before, yet so long ago.

"When I came here last, you showed me the photos of Rose. I knew right away this was her."

"It's unmistakable," he said, turning the page over.

"It took some time, but I finally came to understand that Daniel had held onto his mother far more than he ever let on to anyone. I think he drew these as a way to keep her in his memory."

"He and I never really talked about her much through the years," he admitted, his voice solemn. "I suppose that was more for my sake than his."

"I cannot explain why, but something about this book made me want to learn more about Rose. As if I could be closer to Daniel if I wanted what he wanted. I guess I started to approach it just as I would if I was studying someone's life—some historical figure I was doing research on for work."

Dan chuckled. "That is actually not so difficult to understand." He turned another page. "Such is the way with us historians. Everything is meant to be studied." He traced the outline of the portrait with one fingertip. "We cling to the process, diving in and letting our thoughts be consumed. It becomes an escape for everything wrong in our lives. Indeed, it might be described as our coping mechanism."

"In truth, it has helped me heal most of all."

He nodded, then eased the book closed, keeping a tight hold, as if unable to let it go just yet.

Adelia described her visit to Robin Hood's Bay, though she made no mention of the whispers and all they had revealed. "I find that being closer to the places Rose knew has helped me somehow. That is why I came back here. I wanted to spend time where she last lived—to connect with her spaces."

"Well...you are about as close to her as you can be in this house. We lived here a good number of years before she died. There isn't much left anymore, though. Over the years, I have given most of it away. Just a few things here and there now."

"What about the garden shed she used as a studio?"

He looked off to his right, thoughtful, then back at her. "I haven't touched a thing in there since she died. I just covered everything over. It is exactly as she left it. The only things of hers I have ever gotten rid of were those letters. I destroyed those long ago, not wanting Daniel to stumble upon them someday. No, I didn't want him burdened by that memory."

She considered what he said for a moment. As much as she had loved her husband, she could not imagine simply leaving all of his belongings to sit, collecting dust for decades. She was already resolved to pick up those socks from the floor in their bedroom when she got home. The whispers had taught her that the soul lingers in spaces—places where life was once lived—and sometimes with those whom we feel most connected, but objects rarely seemed to hold such strong bonds.

Unsure if she should press the issue further, she sat silent, feeling the conflict moving through him. A long time had passed since he'd been in Rose's studio. Though he was sure he'd moved on from his grief for Rose, there was something left—some untapped emotion long buried.

In the drawn-out silence, she feared he might refuse her request, and struggled to come up with a change of topic to lighten the mood.

"I suppose there would be no harm in taking you out there," he said, his voice quiet. "It's just sat there for far too long. Probably as dusty and dirty as you can imagine."

"You don't have to," she said, already regretting asking for something so personal. "I shouldn't have asked you. It is fine, really. I don't know what I was looking to find."

"From my experience, the greatest answers have come in the most illogical of places. Once, I found an old livery badge for Edward IV in an antique shop in Ireland. Who would have thought? You just never know what you will discover when you least expect it."

It was a point she couldn't disagree with. In her own career, she had stumbled upon a great many significant documents, tucked away in the most unlikely of locations. The truth had a way of seeking out the curious.

Dan patted his knees and released a slow breath. "It will take me a minute to find the keys. I honestly can't remember where they are. You just sit tight for a bit and I will find them."

As he left the living room, Adelia looked around the space. Rose's presence was still strong in this house. Her memory may have faded in time but had never been forgotten. As she focused on Dan's favorite chair, she felt those quiet nights when he sat here alone, his mind wandering back to those early days from time to time, or even to those warm summer days in Robin Hood's Bay, and the golden-haired girl who would hold onto his heart for the rest of his life.

She glanced up in time to catch the flash of a thin figure passing the doorway, long golden strands trailing behind. There was barely time to process the image when footsteps sounded in the hallway, heralding Dan's return. She blinked at the realization that Rose had just inhabited the space where her husband now stood. As he looked down at the keyring in his hand, fumbling to find the one to the shed, a deep sting in her chest almost had her grimacing. Dan had missed his wife for so many years, never knowing that she was always right here, moving through this space, just as she had in life.

He invited her to follow him out to the back garden. She kept close as he made his way to the small building, its walls covered in weathered canary-yellow paint. Almost right away, she guessed the color had not been Dan's choice. He was much too subdued for its loudness, and despite what little she knew about Rose, the hue had her personality written all over it.

The rectangular structure looked as though it had been built as a sizable garden shed back in its day, its two longest sides containing windows with a dusty film over them. No surprise considering Dan said he'd just covered the contents and left the place to itself. The old shed served as a relic of time, like a shipwreck resting at the bottom of the sea.

He approached the wooden door, still working through the keys, like he wasn't sure anymore which one it was. After trying several, one key slipped into the rusty lock. He jiggled the handle until a click rang out in the balmy evening air. At first, the door was hesitant to budge free from its long-resting position, but he encouraged it with his shoulder, and the old hinges gave way with protesting creaks. A strong scent of dust, old wood, and paint wafted out, and Adelia was sure nothing in this place had been disturbed in many years.

Dan stepped in first, one arm outstretched until he found the small chain for the light. The old bulb burst into life, illuminating the space, and Adelia wrinkled her nose at the smell of burning dust, so pungent she had no choice but to sneeze. Dan turned to her with a startled look, as though he had forgotten her presence.

"Bless you," he said in a near whisper.

She nodded her thanks, then examined her new surroundings. In the decades since her passing, Rose's art studio had never been touched. Supplies and brushes still lined the shelves, now cloaked in years of dust. Five or six tall easels, each carrying a covered canvas, filled the limited floor space. It was like walking into an abandoned mansion that had waited for the day someone would rediscover its long-lost beauty.

"I used to come out here quite a lot," Dan said, his shoulders slumped. "I felt closer to her here. I guess... I guess you just come to a point where even time fades that feeling away." He ran a forefinger down the side of the nearest canvas. "One day, she wasn't here anymore. I could no longer feel her presence. I haven't opened that door since."

"That must have made things even harder on you," Adelia said, her heart going out to her father-in-law. "It probably felt like losing her all over again."

He grimaced. "I shouldn't have said it like that. That's not what you need to hear right now, with Daniel's loss being so fresh."

"You didn't say anything that I don't already know, Dan."

"Maybe not, but you know what was between Rose and I. Things for you and Daniel were different. It won't be the same."

"I know time will fade my husband's memory." She looked around. "No, there's not much either of us can do about time."

When he placed his hand on her shoulder, his slight tremble passed through her. "You take as much time as you like out here. Daniel used to visit when he was younger, but not for long. I'll leave you to it. Move things around, if you like. It's just an old shed now. No longer a time capsule."

She understood all too well why he didn't want to stay. Too many memories. Still, it must have taken a great deal of courage to let her invade this sacred space. She moved over to the first easel and pulled up a corner of the cover, easing it back from the painted canvas it protected, doing her best not to disturb the layer of dust any more than necessary. One by one, she pulled the covers away from the treasure's underneath, until all paintings were revealed. She stepped back and surveyed them. Although she never had any skill as an artist, she recognized Rose's real talent.

From where she stood, the smell of oil paint from the closest canvas was strong, as if it had only been applied. This hideaway was the one place Rose felt a true sense of release from her world, and each of her creations contained deep emotions. Adelia closed her eyes and breathed in the fresh scent of flowers in spring air. There Rose stood, clad in some of Dan's old clothes, with bright-colored smears swiped across the front of her shirt, as though it doubled as a work rag. Her long golden locks were pinned back into a messy ponytail, with paint speckling a few loose strands that hung around her face.

She dabbed her brush into the dot of bright liquid on her old wooden palette, a gift from one of her favorite aunts before she'd left Robin Hood's Bay for good. Adelia had not seen the pallet at first glance, but was sure if she looked for it, she would find it here among the other relics.

When she opened her eyes to stare at the canvas before her, she was struck by the vibrancy of the colors Rose had chosen. It was a field of poppies, each of the hundreds of flowers crafted with great care. She almost felt the breeze pushing against the fragile stems in the infinite sea of red blooms. This was one of Rose's first paintings, back when love was fresh in her heart, her world rich in color. For a moment, she let herself be engulfed in the depth of that new love.

It filled her with a lighthearted heady sensation, a feeling she had experienced before, its intoxicating splendor unmistakable. She smiled as she remembered those early days with Daniel, when logic and sensibility took a backseat. It felt so long ago now and, somehow, she had forgotten elements of it along the way. Staring headlong into the painting, everything rushed back, bringing with it a sudden connection to Rose. All those whimsical hopes and dreams were much like her own.

She pried herself away from the euphoria of the poppy field, and made her way over to the next canvas. Soft shades of pale purple filled the better part of the painting, with row upon row of lavender plants stretched to the horizon, meeting with the light blue of the sky. A tiny stone house was set just off in the distance. The image radiated calm and security, much like established love gives. Once again, she was filled with the emotion Rose had poured into her work. By now, she'd been married to Dan for a few years, and the burning passion had cooled a few degrees as they settled into a somewhat routine existence together. This was the point in their relationship where trust became the foundation for all other things, and when deeper love began to emerge, leaving each with the knowledge that no matter what life threw their way, they never had to go it alone. For Adelia, this had been the best stage of her relationship with Daniel. A time when doubt and insecurity subsided, and she had felt safe.

Things were not so straightforward for Rose. Her gypsy spirit always fretted about safety. While safety should have left her feeling secure, it had a way of binding her too. Something in her wanted to stay suspended in the euphoria of new love, and that aspect refused to see it as an illogical desire. Had Dan ever really been in tune with his new wife's personality, he may have recognized the red flags then and there, but such was not the case. As he settled into their life of predictability with ease, Rose did the opposite.

As Adelia moved from painting to painting, the once-vibrant hues faded. At first, they weakened to muted pastels, until the colors diminished into the solemn grayness of a somber morning on the Yorkshire Moors. She felt the hollow lurch of loneliness creeping into Rose as surely as she could see it in her artwork. A deep desperation existed in the woman, and even with the birth of her only child, it never seemed to go away completely.

At first, she marveled at her son, believing he was by far her greatest creation. Yet it wasn't long before she felt as though she wasn't good enough to be called *Mother*, like being an imposter in her own skin. She knew Daniel should bring her infinite joy, and when being a mother didn't, it made her despair grow even greater. As a mother, she only wanted good for her son but, deep inside, she never felt worthy of his love. She could never love him as well as he deserved, and the idea that he would be better off without her became ever-present in her mind.

Looking through the window to Rose's most private thoughts was like watching the slow decay of an old house perched high on a cliff. It had been decades since Rose walked these floors, yet her thoughts and feelings were as raw as ever. Closing her eyes, Adelia allowed herself to sink into the spiral of delicate emotions. It was a lonely place, filled with fears and dreams that had never been spoken, but played on like a melancholy tune, each forlorn note scattering in the wind like a heart's desperate desire.

Falling out of love can be a slow and excruciating process. There is no one defining moment when it ends, but the realization comes as a sudden shock. Adelia never knew such sadness, yet here she felt every sharp edge.

It was on reaching the final painting that she sensed the shift in Rose's weary heart. Pale hues of the old familiar colors had returned in this work, filling it with renewed hope—a feeling Rose was convinced would never reemerge in her life. Adelia nodded to herself. Without a doubt, this was the moment Rose had met her secret suitor.

The sun was bright that day, with not a rain cloud in the sky. Her bike tires clanked along the road as she made her way into town that afternoon. As was her usual routine on Saturdays, she stopped by a few shops, tucking her purchases into the brown wicker basket on the handlebars. It was there, along the busy sidewalk, that she first met him. His face was hazy in Adelia's vision, but there was no mistaking the quickening of Rose's pulse. Something in this stranger evoked the same physical response she had felt on first meeting Dan. Adelia clung to it for a moment, remembering how it had been with Daniel once upon a time, and wishing she could drench herself in the euphoria of it all just once more.

Rose had craved this feeling for so long, and was powerless to resist. Soon, she was creating every possible excuse to make these excursions into town, and their secret meetings continued. Just as love had brought her here to Oxford, love would steal her away again.

The swirling conflict within Rose was tangible, coupled by the renewed feeling of some long-lost fire. It didn't matter what Dan did—he could never turn things around. She had switched off her emotions like a light, and love between them would never again return. Now, she was bound to a new fate, and the potential risks in her choice offered little hindrance.

Looking down at her blossoming abdomen, Adelia struggled to understand just where Rose's mind was at that time. For herself, it was unfathomable that she could have done such a thing to Daniel. Being unfaithful to a man who loved her so dearly was unthinkable. Though she had dug deep into Rose's thoughts, her reasons still troubled her. All the things Rose rebuked, were what so many other women dreamed of having. While she could appreciate Rose's need for freedom, there existed a selfish nature in her that could not be denied. To be fair, Daniel's mother had lived in a time when there was little in the way of help for someone in her position. A bout of melancholy could be branded as insanity in those days. She would have been prescribed a strong dose of Lord knows what, only to live out her existence in a blur of nothingness. It was doubtful she had anyone to turn to when it came to sharing her problems. Perhaps her parents would not have been sympathetic to her plight. Living way out here in the isolated countryside, and not being able to drive, would have made it difficult to visit friends. Even if she had tried to seek help in the parish church, she likely would have left feeling worse, for in those days a mother was expected to put her own needs aside for the good of the family.

All these things filled Adelia with a great amount of sympathy for the mother-in-law she never knew. Yet her own loyalty for Daniel was strong as ever. Rose's choices had put many people through years of pain, and that fact could not be denied. In the end, suffering was unavoidable, for one person or another.

Chapter Nineteen

C assandra had just sat at the table for her morning tea when someone knocked at her door. The sound jolted her and she spilled a few drops of the brew onto her pajama top.

"Shit!" She grabbed a napkin and dabbed at herself.

The knock came again, louder than before. She jumped to her feet and trekked down the hall, stealing a glance in the mirror by the door. Not good. She pushed back a few wild strands of her hair, grumbling to herself about not having time to even put on an ounce of makeup. When she peered through the peephole, she saw a young scrawny-looking lad in a delivery uniform. Not anticipating any package, she cracked the door open, the chain stretching out part way.

"Lady Cassandra?" the boy asked in a high-pitched voice.

"Yes..." she answered, almost laughing at his formality, which made her feel so old.

She released the chain and opened the door wider. The boy seemed paralyzed with nervousness. However, in the span of a few seconds, he washed over with a lovesick toothy grin—a reaction she was used to, and one she usually ignored.

He blinked several times in quick succession as he stared at her, as though his rush of thought had caused him to forget the reason he was standing at her door.

"Yes...?" she repeated, the word carried on a hint of a growl.

"Oh..." He snapped out of it and reached into the messenger bag slung across his shoulder. After a few seconds of rummaging, he pulled out a small square package that had been neatly wrapped in plain brown paper.

As he handed it to her, he regained his toothy smile, and she thought he might end up drooling if she didn't take control. In no mood for niceties, she nodded her thanks and closed the door in his face.

She continued grumbling to herself as she walked over to her pale-yellow loveseat by the window. Sunlight streaked across her as she turned the package over, searching for some indication of the sender. The only writing was her own name and address.

Curious, she pulled at the wrapping, tossing the paper onto the floor. She hesitated on seeing the small blue-velvet box, then traced the tiny bronze-colored clasp with her fingertips, aware of a strange energy pulsating through them. In that moment, she couldn't decide if it was real, or a manifestation of her anticipation.

Not willing to waste another second guessing, she flipped up the clasp and opened the lid. It snapped back, startling her so much she nearly dropped the box. It contained a small black pouch, also made of velvet, and she rolled her eyes at the inconvenience of yet another layer to this mystery.

She lifted the pouch out and ran her fingertips along its drawstring. The item's weight surprised her. She hesitated again, at a loss as to what she was about to find, but still anxious to know. Whatever it might be, it was firm to the touch. She loosened the strings and poured its contents into the palm of her hand.

There, by all accounts, was one of the largest sapphires she had laid eyes upon. The deepest blue she had ever seen. She turned it over, regarding the precision of its cut, unable to hold back a full smile, and needing no note to know the sender's identity. Her thoughts spun, like a child on a carousel, dizzy with the thought of him.

"Wait. How did he know where I live?" The realization that he should not have known her address hit her like a speeding truck. Everything about the gesture of the sapphire was amazing, and oh so sweet, but the fact that she had failed in keeping her personal space guarded was more than a little unnerving. She wanted to be angry at him for his deliberate intrusion into her world, but something held her back.

As she turned the magnificent stone over in her hand, the same tingle of energy resurfaced. She was a woman who relied on her intuition. It was instinctive, and had worked well for her over the years—a good reason to always be resistant to the second sight her family dubbed "the whispers." With her intuition being so strong, it was rare that she needed to call upon her abilities to see deeper or further. With Fulcanelli, though, she'd found herself more willing to be vulnerable, not so inclined to deny her ability but rather curious to see how far it could go.

She had a deep abiding sense that though he was infuriating and perplexing in his enigmatic behavior, he meant her no harm. His intentions were not clear yet, apart from his intense interest in Melusine, but she didn't doubt he needed her for something, romantic or otherwise. And now, more than ever, she was compelled to find out why.

Chapter Twenty

It was a weeknight, and by all accounts she had a long day looming ahead tomorrow, but Cassandra had always found that sleep wasn't nearly as important as an evening out on the town. One of the independent art galleries was hosting an opening for a local artist, and she had accepted the invitation to attend. Of course, she wanted to support local up-and-coming talent, but her attendance wasn't entirely altruistic. In her line of work, she was quick to understand that being seen was of paramount importance. Being a face people recognized, especially in important places, had helped to propel her career. Moving in what were often trendy circles, she'd built her list of connections and landed countless opportunities. And with her book just released, this was one more chance to solidify her name as an author. As always, such endeavors were strategic, and she would endure long-winded chats with complete strangers in the hope they produced something of value.

She chose a bright-pink dress for the evening, to ensure her presence in the room didn't go unnoticed. The subtle slit up the side stretched from the hemline to mid-thigh. It was a classy, tailored fit, with a touch of daring. Necessity required that she used her assets to her advantage now and again, and such was the case tonight. She was determined to make a name for herself in the fashion industry, too, and while she wanted it to be on her merit, she had to attract a bit of attention first. Attention led to conversation, and that was the only way to draw someone in long enough to convince them that she was not the flake they'd perceived at first glance. It was a sad reality.

After accepting a flute of champagne, she helped herself to a few things off the hors d'oeuvre table. The gallery had already attracted a steady crowd, so she stopped to make polite conversation as she moved through the throng. Like herself, many of tonight's guests were more interested in socializing than staring at a selection of canvases splashed with a few specks of paint. She didn't consider herself a connoisseur of art, at least not this contemporary stuff, much preferring Winterhalter's portraits of Queen Victoria or Empress Sissi. It was easy to lose herself in the fabric of those exquisite gowns or those neatly placed hair adornments. When it came to art, she had an old soul, with a true appreciation for fine craftsmanship. And when it came to fashion, she had an eye for good quality.

She had no idea where her career would take her, and saw nothing wrong with having so many aspirations. However, the fact that there were twenty-four hours in a day and only seven days in a week was a real hindrance, her dreams being far too many for one lifespan. Even so, from a young age, she'd resolved to do more things in this short existence than was humanly possible.

After circling the gallery a few times, doing her bit of networking, she planted herself in front of one of the uninspiring canvases, finger raised to lip, as though contemplating the artist's meaning. In truth, she wondered how long she should wait before revisiting the hors d'oeuvre table. She would lay off the champagne, though, already enjoying her third glass. Another five minutes or so should do it. Best to keep it classy.

As she pondered the canvas, a prickling heat moved up from the small of her back to the base of her neck, causing goosebumps to erupt across her shoulders. It was a feeling she didn't experience often, and never ignored. She gave her neck a light squeeze, having no need to turn as she sensed his tall form casting her in his cool shadow. An unmistakable scent came to her, so masculine and sensual the deepest breath couldn't pull it in enough.

"This is absolute merde, you know."

She remained still as the heat of his breath caressed her ear.

With her head tilted, she regarded the painting, then raised the glass to her lips and emptied it, the liquid losing its chill in the fire burning through her.

"Really? Those two splatters of yellow and that stringy line of blue remind me of a Caravaggio I once saw in Rome."

He gave out a muffled laugh, stepping forward to stand at her side.

She assessed him without turning. As expected, he was clad all in black, in a well-tailored suit, though with a far more modern look than the past few times they had crossed paths. She bucked against the urge to face him. If she were honest, something about those inkwell eyes and the crisp lines of his face weakened her knees. She knew better than to give him that satisfaction, for, try as she might to conceal it, her struggle would be useless. Fulcanelli would pick up on her every thought, relishing that he had chipped away at her resolve in any miniscule way.

"What are you doing here?" she asked, keeping her voice low. "You turning up everywhere I go is a touch concerning."

"I will let you know that I was invited." His tone carried a hint of defensiveness. "But to be fair, if I had known you were coming, I probably would have shown up earlier."

"Well, I hope you at least took the time to circle the room before coming over here to bother me."

"You are far too optimistic," he replied. "I found it impossible to wait. That's like telling a child on Christmas Eve to get a good night's sleep when there's a pile of prettily wrapped packages under the tree."

"I take it patience isn't one of your stronger qualities."

"I have far more patience than you can imagine, but I admit I am falling short today, in particular. I have had about as much of this place as I can take for the night. How about you?"

A glance over her shoulder told her the hors d'oeuvre's table was swarming with people, hovering there to avoid feigning interest in these dreadful paintings. She released a reluctant sigh. No chance of snagging a few morsels for the road.

"I should be heading home soon," she said, turning back to the painting, if one could call it so. "I have a long day tomorrow."

"Oh?"

"Yes, I have some finishing touches on an article I've been neglecting for too long." She toyed with one of her earrings, holding back another sigh at the prospect of ending the evening so early, for the sake of being a responsible adult.

"Will you allow me the privilege of walking you home?" He raised his forefinger, the corner of his mouth lifting in a half smile. "Or rather, close to home."

That renewed her suspicions about how he'd acquired her address. Hmm, perhaps I should thank him for the gift instead.

"Speaking of my house, the most remarkable thing happened the other day." Forgetting herself, she turned to face him, and realized her mistake too late. The gallery lights cast him in a luminosity that was beyond favorable, and she snapped her mouth shut on becoming aware that it hung open, in something that could only be construed as pure awe.

The man was sure of himself, as well he should be, but she wasn't convinced that extended to his physical looks. Fulcanelli was an accomplished gent—well-traveled—and for as much as she knew of him, quite intelligent. Even if he hadn't been breathtakingly handsome, and that was undeniable, his list of talents spoke for themselves, propelling him into an almost fictional realm of perfection.

He wrinkled his brow and pursed his lips as he regarded her straightforward glare.

"Please do share."

"A package arrived at my door. A most peculiar one at that. It was a little box with a velvet bag, and in that bag was a rather large sapphire. You will recall that those are my favorite." She paused just long enough to catch the corners of his mouth quirk. "I couldn't be sure of the sender—it was unmarked. I do wonder, though, how someone could have gotten my address."

"Maybe they just had the messenger look you up in the directory. I can't imagine there are too many people in this town who share the same name as you."

Her jaw slackened. No sooner had she opened her mouth to speak, she was forced to snap it shut, his answer being inconveniently logical.

"Hmm..." was all she could muster.

"Anonymous sender aside, did you find the gem to your liking?"

Something in his eyes, maybe hope, softened her to her core.

She shrugged one shoulder. "I can't imagine anyone would be displeased with such a gift. The cut was exquisite."

His smile made any attempt at words irrelevant. Despite his dark hair, eyes, and attire, he had a brilliant light about him. At that moment, she was sure she had never met any man who held her attention quite this fiercely. That scared her a touch more than she cared to acknowledge, and she was desperate for something, anything, that would divert her attention.

"I think I will just call a cab," she said, pointing to her high heels. He didn't know any better, but it was the lousiest excuse she had ever made. She'd worn high heels every day for years, and could bake a ham, run a marathon, and rescue a puppy from a burning building in them.

"It is such a pretty night." He made a half-turn to look out the front window. "What do you say, shall we walk for a bit? When you get tired, I will hail a cab and you can be on your way."

Her impetuous heart screamed *"Yes!"* but she was in no hurry to wave the white flag of submission. Never would she say it aloud but she had a soft spot for slow-burning tension. It sent a rush of something through her that she wanted to draw out and savor.

"Wow, a night stroll with you, or the cushy softness of my bed. Hmm, tough choice, but I think I might pick the latter."

His brow rose, and the energy swirling around them made her think mentioning her bed might have been something of a misstep. She couldn't read him nearly as well as she could others, but she had no doubt that something somewhat debaucherous was running through his mind at this moment.

"I won't keep you out late. You have my word. I was a perfect gentleman the other night."

"Maybe I regret it—the other night. Perhaps I am not keen on a night stroll with a perfect stranger."

He arched one eyebrow. "Well, I don't regret being with you. Not for a second. But I will—"

"That's because few people do," she interrupted, striding toward the door.

"Do what?" In seconds he had caught up, moving to push open the door, and holding it as she stepped out onto the sidewalk.

"Regret being with me," she said, giving him the hint of a smile. She believed herself to be as good at this game as he was, and tonight she would prove it.

"I have no doubt at all." He chuckled, running a hand through his dark locks. He glanced down the street. "Let me call you a cab."

"You know, on second thought, I think I have a block or two in me. I will let you trail along for a while."

They walked down the street at a slow rhythmic pace. The evening breeze was just right, and something about the pink and purple hues of the faded sky left her in no hurry to arrive at any destination. She couldn't be more content than if she were curled up on a rainy Sunday afternoon with a tantalizing book, though nothing in any bestselling novel could compare to her present company. He had all the mystery and intrigue she craved, but the ending was still unpredictable.

The low hum of a violin wavered in the air, and she looked up to see a street performer, perched on a stool just ahead. They stopped to listen as the musician doled out a tune or two. Fulcanelli's eyes were fixed on the young man's every move, as though silently assessing his skill. After dropping a few pounds into the open case on the ground, they continued on their way.

"He was good," Cassandra said, breaking the silence.

"He will get better with the proper amount of practice." Fulcanelli nodded once. "Like anything, it takes great concentration and dedication to be good. Nothing worth doing comes with ease.

None of us would stand out from the crowd if that were so." He looked at her for a moment. "I'm curious. What is it that you want to do with this life? What aspirations do you have for the future, Lady Cassandra?"

"Firstly, I do wish you would stop calling me that," she replied, a crisp cut to her voice. "I am not of the peerage. I have no lord to reign over me."

"My apologies." He bowed his head. "I doubt there is a lord worthy of your hand. All the ones I know are prattish pricks. Advantageous marriages are a thing of the past. You will do well to make your mark on your own, and it appears that you are well on your way. You have little need to align yourself with anyone who doesn't see your true value."

She swallowed hard to push down the lump in her throat. For as long as she could remember, she had been in a never-ending battle to prove herself. She was like a knight wielding a sword against the bloodthirsty dragon that represented first impressions. It was one of the reasons she had been so adamant to block out her use of the whispers. She hated knowing what people thought of her, and despised the way everyone assumed she was some mindless tart. Sensing that energy did nothing to bolster her self-confidence.

"Thank you," she mustered through a shaky breath. She focused on the sidewalk as they continued on, fixing on their shifting shadows. Invisible fingers strummed at her heartstrings as she watched those two forms move in tandem, teetered on something kind of perfect.

"I would not say what I do not believe."

His voice was far too full of conviction for her to mistake it for a sly attempt at flattery.

"I think," she said, her voice stronger, "what I want most of all is to find something that brings value to other people's sense of wellbeing. That's why I have always loved fashion. It's never been about the way someone looks, but how they feel. When I look in the mirror and see a polished reflection staring back at me, I feel polished. Perception becomes reality, though I can't say it works in everyone's favor all of the time. Take for example that woman walking over there." She nodded across the street to a woman clad in white.

"The nurse?"

"Precisely. One look at that uniform, and most of us could assume that she is a nurse. Automatically, you assume she is someone who is caring and understanding—one who has a passion for helping those in need. We make assumptions about her training and knowledge, and I am sure she is inundated with health questions from everyone she knows. Deep down, she might be lacking in any one of those areas, but her outward appearance makes you think otherwise. I think the same thing when I see a portrait of Marie Antoinette. She left Austria, bound for the French court, to a husband who was, by all accounts, uninterested. That could not have been a place that was warm and welcoming to such a young girl. Certainly, her extravagance in jewels and clothes was all a ploy to shield that inner turmoil from the world of prying eyes. She dressed the part, so she felt the part of that momentous role she was expected to play."

"Sounds like your Queen Elizabeth I. I never met her, but I heard she had a closet to be envied."

Cassandra rolled her eyes, giving him a reproachful grin. "I never met her either. Very inconvenient for her to die a few hundred years before I was born. Just the same, she was known to have a wardrobe of well over a thousand dresses. She had entire buildings just filled with them. Oh, what I wouldn't give to have a day in that closet." She smiled as she shook her head. "Save for her sister's short and turbulent reign, she was the first woman to be queen in her own right in England. If an extensive wardrobe helped her shore up the confidence she needed to lead this country, then, by all means, she had good reason to buy every bolt of fabric in the land."

"I think you have a great eye for the beautiful, but it is your understanding of human nature that will take you where you want to go. Don't ever underestimate just how powerful that talent is as you climb."

"Funny, we barely know each other, and yet, I feel like you might be the most supportive person in my inner circle."

"I see you," he said, his tone once again flat. "I see all the talents you haven't yet discovered for yourself."

Her legs trembled against the onslaught of emotion his comment evoked. It was as if he understood this ongoing war she had waging in herself, and knew the right words to bring it to a long-awaited peaceful conclusion.

"Might we...?" She motioned to a nearby bench. Feigning fatigue, she sat on the cool metal, slipping her feet from her heels and resting them on the sidewalk. She could almost hear her mother, appalled at such a tacky move. Thankfully, she was nestled back in the family's posh London townhouse.

He sat beside her, and her nose twitched with disappointment as she ran her tongue along the inside of her top lip. She wasn't sure what prompted such a reaction, but surmised it was the respectable distance he kept between them. In truth, she longed to be close enough to catch another faint drift of his heavenly cologne. She despised this addle-brained girl she had become. In the past two weeks, she had plunged herself shoulder-deep in history books, and became infatuated with a total stranger. She hardly recognized herself anymore.

She brushed down her dress over her lap. "It feels good to be getting out more, these days. I have isolated myself so much over the last few months."

"I can hardly believe that of you." He relaxed against the back of the bench, resting one arm on its frame.

"It was a rather lonely winter, in all honesty. I basically locked myself away in my flat, putting the final touches to my novel. I had such a tight timeline with the publishing company, and, of course, I still had my day job. Just when I finally started to get a handle on everything, my cousin lost her husband, quite unexpectedly."

"That's unfortunate to hear." He wiped a loose strand of hair from his eyes with his free hand.

"I went up to see her for a few days afterwards. Seeing her go through so much pain, I felt guilty coming back here and resuming life as usual. This probably sounds macabre, but it is so hard to wrap my head around death. It's like one minute your candle is burning bright and the next it is just snubbed out, as though we are nothing. It boggles my mind how that single moment, the instant we die, leaves years of sadness in its wake. The whole thing has made me really reflect on my own mortality."

"Death is not a singular event, Cassandra, it is a lifelong journey. For most of us, death is just an ending composed of every single minute spent getting there."

"For most of us? I think it is safe to say all of us." She cut her chuckle at the sight of his stony expression.

"Oh, but that is where you would be wrong. Not everyone lives just one life."

"Em, no. We are born, live our lives, however long we are blessed to be on this earth, and then we die. The end. Forgive me for failing to understand how that could be more than one life for anyone. Unless, of course, you are referring to the afterlife. Then that would be an entirely different conversation."

"Do you believe in the afterlife?"

"Yes. Well...in a way. It's hard to explain."

"If you believe in an afterlife, how is it so difficult to fathom that some of us live very long lives? Ones that do not end."

She shifted to turn to him. "Don't get me wrong. I am very open minded when it comes to a great number of things, but that goes entirely against nature."

"What if I told you that nature is simply a phenomenon that can be manipulated? That there are those who have discovered the secret to unlocking its code, in such a way that time can be extended."

"The alchemists, you mean? Those who use the great work for something far more intimate than the creation of precious metals and stones? I know about this. At the height of self-realization, they can enter a realm where it's possible to alter their own physical being—extend time, maybe even indefinitely."

His left brow furrowed. "How do you know this?"

"I have been cooped up in a library for days. As a distraction, I may have read a few chapters in a book on alchemy.

"So, do you believe it is possible?"

"On its face? No. But I have some experience wading through the realm of what most people wouldn't believe. If I look at it from that angle, then I suppose anything is possible."

"Experience?"

She swallowed, angry at herself for such a momentous slip. "It's nothing really." She shook her head, giving herself a moment to consider her situation. Having already said too much, with the conversation taking such an odd turn, she wasn't sure how to proceed.

He turned to face her, the fabric of his trousers grazing her bare knee, sending a delightful shiver along her thigh.

"We are sitting here having a discussion about immortality. Humor me."

With reluctance, she met his gaze, his intense focus locking her into the deep folds of a place she was hesitant to go. Thread by thread, she was untangling the mystery of Fulcanelli, and while still guarded, he was allowing her some liberties. Even though she barely cared to acknowledge the whispers, she had never been one to discuss her abilities outside of a few trusted acquaintances. As unthinkable as the prospect of blabbing her secret to Fulcanelli was, this situation felt rather different, to say the least. She sensed that his secret was every bit as explosive as her own. Its exact nature was gray and shaded, and far too elusive for her to get a solid read. They were both mysterious people—both existing in a way that unseated the normal balance of nature. The perplexity of how two people so equally matched in this way could have found each other in such a huge world, was no mere coincidence. For her, coincidence was a human notion, nonexistent in the elemental. Destiny had no room for chance.

"What if I told you that there are people who look out at this landscape and see something entirely different?" She opened her hand and made a wide sweep in front of her, pausing at a passing car, people on the sidewalk, a stray alley cat crouched against a building.

"They see beyond the here and now—back to a time that may be long ago. To them, time is something that ripples through the air like sound waves. It's both the old and the new all at once." She met his gaze again. "That is how I see the world."

"You see things from long ago?" He smiled, looking satisfied with her revelation, as if he had known it all along.

"I see things from the here and now as well. Sometimes, I can sense what someone is feeling, so intensely, it's like I can hear what they are thinking."

"What am I thinking?"

His question caught her off guard. He raised a finger to the underside of her chin, lifting it slightly. With his intense eye contact, her temperature spiked to something she was sure bordered on unhealthy. Trying to keep some shred of self-control, she gave him a tight-lipped grin, struggling against the full-on toothy smile striving to invade the stage.

"Right now,"—her voice came low and silky— "you are wondering about my lips. You like their shade, and you wonder if they are every bit as soft as you imagine."

"Wrong." Something about his low husky tone sent a surge of energy straight to her toes. "I was thinking about that more than a minute ago. I have since moved to your skin. I'm counting the freckles on your decolletage as we speak."

"I hate those freckles," she said, dropping her gaze like a shy schoolgirl.

"You shouldn't. They are lovely."

She looked at him again, peering through her mascaraed lashes for security. For a fraction of a second, or thirty, she thought he might move in to kiss her, and she inched closer in anticipation. Her heart was wrenching for release, and his lips on hers was the only answer. But then the energy around them shifted, and it was clear that, as much as he wanted to, he couldn't. She couldn't name what brought on his reluctance—maybe those three glasses of champagne had skewed her senses—but all she knew was that Fulcanelli, her dark handsome villain, was not going to put her out of this misery, and she felt like a capital idiot.

As she closed her eyes, allowing herself a moment of silent re-
buke, she caught the sound of him rising to his feet. Releasing a
sigh of defeat, she opened her eyes to see him standing out on the
curb hailing her a cab. It was just as well. She needed to go home
and swaddle herself in her bed, her head buried in her pillow, or
stare up at the ceiling for ages—anything to erase her humiliation
for being such a fool.

She was grateful that a cab pulled up in seconds. Fulcanelli
opened her door, then stepped back to let her slip into the backseat.

Without a word, he pulled out some type of card from his jacket
pocket, and placed it into her hands, its touch gentle.

"Saturday," he said, more as confirmation than a question.

She stared at him for a long moment.

"Saturday," she repeated as the door closed.

The cab moved off and she looked at the card, its black background and gold scrollwork the same as the one he gave her in the
library a few days ago. She ran a fingertip along the fine French
script of his name embossed on the front. When she flipped it over,
she gripped her bottom lip between her teeth, surprised at what
met her:

York Minster

Saturday, 6:15 p.m.

She read it over. He wants to see me again. The prospect filled
her with unparalleled excitement. Saturday was only a few days off,
but now it felt like a lifetime away.

Chapter Twenty-One

I t was late in the morning when Adelia dropped her bag by the door in the foyer of her father-in-law's house. Though her time here had been fruitful, she craved the comforts of her own home. Her bed most of all.

Dan had left earlier, apologizing for not being able to see her off due to his teaching a class at the college. She'd smiled, assuring him that it was no bother. Truth be told, she was glad to have more time to herself in the old house, having no idea how long it would be before she came back. She savored these last moments in a space that held onto Rose's spirit so strongly. This woman, who had so impacted her life these past years, even if she hadn't known at the time.

She let the warm rays of the sun tickle her face. Eyes closed, she released every thought, clearing room for the one voice she wanted to hear, besides Daniel's. At first there was nothing more than the frail buzz of white noise. She stood motionless, absorbing both the light and the energy of this place, breathing it in like the scent of lilacs in the air. It wasn't long before the pale hum of silence strengthened, and with each breath, as the noise became louder, the atmosphere grew thick and heavy. It sounded like a series of electrical sparks, some at random and others in perfect rhythm. The oxygen in the air seemed to fill with an electromagnetic charge, so prevalent that the molecules illuminated with each powerful surge.

As her body temperature changed, flickering from cold to hot in coursing waves, a figure came into view. At first it was a mass of pastel and iridescent light, hazy on the edges yet distinct. With each second, its shape took on a greater clarity, though it was the long golden tendrils of flowing hair that stood out. She smiled to herself as Rose's image materialized. Her flattering yellow dress had thin stems of emerald ivy adorning the bottom of the skirt. The yellow accentuated her deep-blue eyes, complementing the blanket of pale freckles on her nose and cheeks, and reminding Adelia of the shed. Rose tucked a loose strand of hair behind her ear with long delicate fingers. Everything about her was graceful.

What struck Adelia most was the woman's natural beauty. She didn't need a stitch of makeup to accentuate a thing. Just like Cassandra, nature had blessed her with the kind of beauty that must have stopped men in their tracks. Physical looks aside, there was something so exuberant about both women's spirits—ingrained and untamed. These qualities catapulted their outward appearance to another level, so high the average woman could only dream of attaining. This was the secret of their unwitting charm—their blessing and their curse alike.

Rose moved about in a rush, as though searching for something. Though she knew she could not be seen, Adelia still stepped back against the wall to give her space, not wanting to risk interfering with this coveted vision. Some sort of indecision was evident in the soft lines of Rose's face. Whatever was weighing on her mind had turned her tender features grave.

She picked up a thin silk scarf from the small table by the door, then sighed as she caught sight of the set of car keys. At last, she'd located what she had been so desperate to find. She grabbed them, then moved past Adelia, returning to the foot of the stairs where she lifted two small suitcases, one in each hand. Adelia blinked, realizing that this had to be the day Rose met her end on that lonely country road just a few miles out of town. She couldn't but feel somber knowing what she was about to witness. In a short time, she had come to understand so much about this woman, and even if they were different people, she still felt a deep connection.

Part of her wanted to stop Rose from leaving, to save her from this tragic end awaiting her, but it was impossible, and she knew that better than anyone. Even so, that knowledge filled her with such a deep sadness. Rose was eternally stuck in the fabric of time. Like an actor in an endless play, she was doomed to repeat her role over and over. Adelia could only watch this play out through time's thin veil.

It was her deep connection to Rose's story that brought a tidal wave of emotion to the surface. She felt every heavy-hearted thought, and wanted to close the window to the vision, but she couldn't bring herself to do something so rash. Having devoted so much time to deciphering every nuance of Rose's story, she was in way too far to turn away now. Despite her reluctance, she pushed through, opening herself to feel every ragged edge of Rose's experience.

This was the woman's last chance at freedom, but the cost was tremendous. She would be branded a fool—a harlot—and an unworthy mother. Her solitary days of torment and anguish would never be recognized by the gossipers, who would not understand what her life was like locked away in herself. They could only judge her for what she was about to do.

Adelia felt the tremble in Rose's hand as she clutched the keys. So much of her wanted to set them back on the table, because walking out that door, bags in hand, meant the end of everything. There could be no turning back now. The calling was too strong and time was running short. Just a few miles away waited the man who set her soul ablaze with a simple touch, the one who reignited something in her that had cooled years before. If she waited too long, he would be gone. In that moment, she understood that here a lifetime of unhappiness awaited, and just up the road lay the life she had dreamed of for so long.

She no longer hesitated as she opened the door and stepped out onto the driveway. The decision had been made in her heart. Adelia watched as she placed the suitcases in the trunk before sliding into the driver's seat, with every detail so vibrant. She sat for a moment, trying to adjust to the foreign feeling of being behind the wheel, with panic gripping her on seeing all the knobs and levers. Pulling in her breath, she slid the key into the ignition and turned it, flinching as the engine gave a low roar. She had watched her husband do this a thousand times, yet never once found the courage to try driving herself. By nature, she was a free-spirited soul, always seeking out the adventures that eluded her. Yet, deep inside, she was filled with cowardice. Trying something new had always been a deterrent to the life she wanted to live, proving that she was a dreamer through and through, not a doer.

After a jumpy start, she pulled out onto the road and took that fateful left turn, with little time for exhilaration. She was far too scared to even relish the moment.

She pressed on the accelerator with uneasy pressure, roughly shifting gear as the engine wound up. One minute she was creeping along at a snail's pace, the next she was jamming on the brakes to slow down. Here in the isolation of the country, she was free to make mistakes, with no one around to witness her perilous inexperience. Dread crept into her stomach at the realization that it would not be long before she reached the edge of the next town. The place where he would be waiting to take her away.

Her throat felt dry at the notion that soon she would be surrounded by other cars along the narrow streets. There would be traffic signals and signs, with people all about. She needed to find a place to park too. Her raving thoughts blinded her to the sharp curve that snaked along a high rise ahead, overlooking the serene fields below.

Panic gripped her as the car careened around the bend, and she realized she had misjudged her speed, her knuckles white as she clenched the wheel in an effort to regain control.

Adelia knew what was coming—the moment that would forever change the life of, not only Rose but all who loved her. She would never make it to the next town, or feel the warm caress of the man she was leaving her family to be with. Nor would she be able to explain herself to the husband and son she'd left behind. Two men and a boy would be left with no answers.

Someday, that boy would grow up to be a man, and go on to achieve a great many successes in his professional life. He would become a well-respected scholar, a published author, and a man of great prestige among his peers. In addition, he would marry, and carry on his legacy through a child he would not live long enough to know. Despite all Daniel achieved, he still spent his life pondering the unanswered questions about his mother. His love and devotion would never cease, and Adelia was thankful he never knew that she abandoned him and his father.

When she opened her eyes, she realized she was still standing in the foyer. The familiar pull of energy drew her outside, and she walked to her car, tossed her bags into the trunk, and seated herself behind the wheel. She didn't know the exact location where Rose had died, but it didn't really matter—the whispers would guide her there. As she drove along the quiet country lane, she recognized some landmarks from her vision. Not much had changed, even after all the time that had passed. As she neared a curve in the road, the steering wheel turned, veering the car toward a grassy berm. Knowing not to fight the energies, she pulled to the side as directed.

A low stone wall bordered the bend, though a large section of it was missing, leaving a clear view of the steep hill below. Its tattered remains spoke of great tragedy. Apart from Rose's unfortunate fate, Adelia didn't feel the smoldering anguish of loss here the way she might on an old battlefield. Rose's accident felt singular. As macabre as that may sound, she was somewhat pleased, because there was no one else's calamity to muddy her view. It allowed her an unblemished view of the poor woman's final moments.

She got out and leaned against the hood, staring down at the valley. When she closed her eyes, she felt the countless hours Daniel had spent at this spot. He came here often as a boy, slipping away on his bicycle, sometimes on a muggy summer afternoon. The steep slope of the hill had him drenched from sweat, but he would still push on. Against the low hum of insects, she heard the click of his bike's medal kickstand after he parked on the grassy verge. His youth permeated her bones, bringing her back to her teenage years. Over and over, he would come to this spot to gaze out at the rich green fields bathed in golden sun. Besides the old photo of his mother that remained, this was all he had. He felt close to her here, the site bringing him both sadness and peace in equal measure.

In his mind, he'd painted many different scenarios why his mother drove out this way, none of which came near the truth. For him, she was eternally angelic, and he couldn't remember one quality about her that wasn't perfect. She was faultless in every sense. Even as time wore on, and he no longer recalled the sound of her voice, he somehow always remembered its tenderness. As each year passed, the only thing that remained of her were faded images tucked away in the back of his mind, and that one photo in his father's album. To rectify that, he would draw her, scraping together every detail from his memory until she came back to life on the page.

Adelia thought of the sketchbook that lay on the backseat of her car. How carelessly she had dragged it around as she journeyed, dismayed for a time even at its existence, when it had been a priceless treasure to Daniel. The thought pinched at her heart.

As though she were arguing with someone other than herself, she became defensive. At the time, she assumed the images were of some secret love interest of her husband. Shame weighed on her now over her treatment of something Daniel held so dear to his heart. For a moment, she sensed a far deeper connection to Rose than she had before. Love was nothing without loss, just as loss was nothing without love.

Chapter Twenty-Two

Having remained too long at the curve, Adelia knew she would arrive home to Middleham far later than anticipated. Not that it mattered, with no one waiting for her return. The big house she once loved at the end of the long lane didn't hold the same appeal now. She looked around one last time, sad in a way that her quest was over. It had given her something to occupy her mind—an escape from her constant sorrow. She'd come here for answers, and the whispers helped her find a certain closure.

She got into the car, smiling as she thought of the night in the apothecary shop. Meredith assured her that healing would come in time, and work would be its vessel. She searched her heart, seeking out those feelings that had been so crippling. The pain at losing Daniel was still there, but not as it had been before. Now, it felt muted, dulled around the edges—manageable. Just as the beautiful Yorkshire Rose had broken so many hearts, she had helped put one back together too.

Ready to go, she reached out to adjust the side mirror, and flinched on seeing the image reflecting back at her. Not her own, but of a man, faded and blurry, all for his sorrowful eyes. They weren't Daniel's—she would have known that shade of blue anywhere. She blinked, glanced behind, then looked back to the mirror. The man was gone. She had no idea what she'd just seen, or if it had any meaning at all. The whispers were always unpredictable. This was an old road, traveled by many people over time. It may just have been a weary traveler who passed this way long ago.

She had traveled down the road no more than a mile or so when a pulling sensation gripped her hands. Maybe it was nothing. As she approached an intersection, she looked up at the signage, ready to continue the long drive to Middleham. About to make the left turn, a gentle pressure pulled the wheel to the right. She groaned, not happy with already being delayed, and not in the mood to exhaust herself with more visions. But she knew from experience that the whispers always came to her for a reason, so she gave in and followed the pull, turning right and driving away from her initial destination.

In about five minutes, she came to the edge of a village surrounded by a patchwork of fields and small family farms. It wasn't much to speak of, its main street consisting of little more than a block or two of old shopfronts and a tiny square. She drove on, being led to an open parking spot in front of a hardware store. When she stepped out onto the sidewalk, she looked around, waiting for the whispers' next clue. A slight push on her back nudged her forward, and she found herself standing at a red-painted bench

outside the hardware store's front window. Taking the whispers'
lead, she sat on the bench, took a deep breath, and soaked in the
quietude of the street. Only a few people were about—a world
away from her life in Oxford.

She shuddered when a tingle frittered across her skin, and closed
her eyes as it spread through her. The store window materialized,
though its modern signage melted away, the façade revealing a café
in place of a hardware store. Unlike all the places she'd visited
during this quest, this was the one that changed, as if in real time. It
reminded her that nothing in life remains untouched. The exterior
was rough and weathered, in need of a good coat of paint, and the
window was glazed over with a light film of dust.

He sat at a table inside. A gray haze shrouded his face but his
figure was clear, showing him to be a lean man, dressed in a neatly
pressed military uniform. His demeanor told her that he was not
at leisure to stay long, no doubt expected to return to his post
soon, wherever that may have been. His hands wrenched together,
as though he might tear them to shreds with his obvious anguish.
She sensed a depth to his thoughts, and an unmistakable pit in his
stomach. The man was racked with indecision. He was waiting for
Rose, yet he wondered what he was doing here. His heart had led
him to a place his head didn't want to be.

This man was not prone to going through life without a solid
plan, unlike Rose. Nor was he the type who allowed emotion to
get in the way of better judgment. Yet, this once he had, and now
his heart and mind fought each other in a battle fiercer than any he
had seen as a soldier.

The room felt like it was spinning, so hard his stomach began to churn. Over and over, he told himself that everything was wrong. Things he once thought so perfect were now showing their ugly flaws, and the darkness of it all swept through him like a flash flood.

Then the haze that blurred his features subsided, and Adelia gasped, recognizing him, like she would a dear friend. It was none other than Paul, though he was far younger than the man she had befriended back when she rented a room at Middleham Manor. The Paul she knew, retired from his life as a military pilot, worked part time in his brother's antique store. He had been a treasured friend and confidant, a father figure of sorts when she was so far away from her own. Paul had known Daniel too.

Shook by disbelief, she studied the youthful curves of his face. He had always been a peculiar sort. Carefree one moment, aloof and down the next. She remembered how he'd once spoken of a love lost to him years before. His words struck a chord with her then, especially as she and Daniel had hit a bit of a rocky patch at the time. She sensed that Paul, though guarded in his words, had suffered a great loss, one he never fully recovered from.

Indeed, he had lost something of great value to his heart. Rose. Dan's Yorkshire Rose, and Daniel's beloved mother. Love can be a cruel mistress, never content in leaving just one heart in pieces. In more than one way, Rose became another of its casualties. How was it that she could be loved by so many people, yet still never know love for herself, or at least the lasting kind? Maybe there was too much discontent in her to ever be satisfied for any length of time. Perhaps it was her fault, perhaps it wasn't. Was there something in her that kept her from ever fully connecting to any one person or place? Maybe her natural wiring prevented her from being at peace.

There comes a point in life when a person is no longer bound to their past, and happiness becomes a choice. Rose could never seem to grasp that Camelot wasn't real. Maybe she was always searching for some idyllic love that could never exist. That endless quest to procure some phantom existence would, in the end, prove her personal undoing. She could never find this holy grail, and thus would never be satisfied. Adelia supposed there were a great many people like Rose—never satisfied with their lot.

While she could comprehend Rose's angst at the direction of her life, her failure to take accountability was glaring. Adelia had spent the better part of her career studying the lives of notable women, from the days of the crusades to present day, including women of noble birth and those of humble origins. Despite her given subject, the one common thread for all of these women had been strife. No human being has ever been exempted from life's sharper edges. Society had long prescribed rigid expectations for women and, more often than not, those edicts limited their options in life. Even if Rose had lived in a time of stricter social standards than today, she ultimately failed to use what freedoms were available to her.

Perhaps seeking guidance outside her marriage was not an option, but she still could have sought it with the person who might have done the most. Dan. She never spoke to her husband about her unhappiness. Instead, she avoided the subject altogether, putting on a fake smile and giving the illusion that all was well.

If there was a breakdown between the two, she made no effort to repair anything. While her husband was aloof, he might have made an effort to change if he saw there was a real need. Dan Brown was not a man content with mediocrity, least of all in himself, and if Rose had attempted to share her feelings, he might have endeavored to make things right.

The question had to be asked: Did Rose want things to change with her husband? She was far more willing to place herself in the arms of another man than to make her own marriage work.

That brought on another question: Are we wrong to give up on dreams? Was there shame in trading our heart's desire for a comfortable existence?

In the end, whether it had been Adelia or Daniel who discovered the truth about Rose, they each would have come to the same conclusion: Rose was nothing more than a human being, comprising layer upon layer of complexity—a product of our decisions, our triumphs, and our failures.

Chapter Twenty-Three

The towering York Minster hovered above the rooftops as Cassandra walked toward it. It possessed a mystical quality. When she first came to the city, the building served as her navigational beacon, giving her a much-needed sense of direction as she found her way around. The original church was built in about 627 A.D., with the current Minster constructed between 1220 and 1472. Its austere presence stood as a gallery of wonders, displaying the mastery of centuries of skilled craftsmanship. The unparalleled beauty of the gothic façade was a constant reminder of the days when the church was the beating heart of the community. A time when chivalry, honor, and faith were the center point of life from the humblest peasant to the highest of nobility. Faith had always been the thread that held humanity together, only to tear it apart in the same breath. Every square inch of the Minster told a story, from its towering vaulted ceilings to the large expanse of stained glass, with each detail serving as a beacon of the glory of heaven and the threat of the perils of hell. It was a place of life, death, and rebirth—a constant reminder that while there was the promise of the next kingdom, the time spent in this one mattered most of all.

It was impossible to enter the building without being filled with awe. In reality, it was more than just a religious establishment. The Minster was a refuge for souls. For more than 1300 years, it had heard the plight of all who walked its floors: the cries of the wronged, and the sins of the wrongdoers. Just to stand in its shadow was to feel the energy of the lives it had touched. Even if Cassandra hadn't been to church in ages, she still appreciated this edifice's long history, and could love the sacred old building as much as any York native. It was a crowning jewel meant to be shared with the world.

The usual crowds had dwindled, leaving the grounds sparse with visitors. She walked around, taking in the calm beauty of the evening. As she tired, she found an empty bench that faced the main entrance. It was her first chance to really examine the striking beauty of the arched windows. There was nothing to not appreciate about the old building, its painstaking construction something to revere.

Her quiet appreciation was interrupted by the sound of footsteps approaching, though she didn't tear her gaze away from the majesty in front of her. Even as he sat beside her, she continued her appraisal for a wordless moment longer. When she turned to face him, he was also taking in the building's magnificence.

"I never tire of this place," she said. "It fills my head with a thousand questions that can never be answered."

"Cathedrals and minsters are like storybooks. They hold more answers than you can fathom if you look close enough." He nodded once and sighed.

Cassandra motioned up to the massive structure. "It would take a hundred years to examine every detail, and another hundred to decipher the meaning of it all."

"Not everyone has that kind of time."

She laughed. "I, for one, do not have that kind of time. Still, it would be nice if I did. I think I would stay right here in this spot for all my days."

"No, you wouldn't," he said. "You should make the most of your days. You should travel the world and see all the other things this tiny planet has to offer."

"I think you're right." She wagged her forefinger once at him. "I have never been one to stay in the same place too long." It was more of a figurative statement; she had only ever lived in London before coming to York.

He looked straight ahead. "That, we have in common."

That topic concluded; Cassandra wrestled with what to say next. Fulcanelli did not appear to be in a hurry to explain why he wanted to meet her here. Her curiosity was killing her, but she didn't press him for an answer. The evening was calm and peaceful, and he would get to it in time. No need to rush a moment so perfect. The past few days had been such a blur, with every waking minute dominated by another thing to do. Between work and the research, she had been doing for Basil Duncan, she was struggling to make time for herself. For now, she was content thinking of nothing and doing even less.

"I trust that your week has gone well, since we last spoke," Fulcanelli said, not nearly as willing, it seemed, to sit too long in the beautiful silence, maybe because he thought it awkward.

It was a boring pleasantry, devoid of any hint of the utter fool she had been the other night. Nonetheless, she appreciated his attempt to sooth her wounded pride.

She had spent the past few days deep in her studies, succeeding in matching the heraldic badge to the respective familial line. For her, it was a momentous milestone, and she was elated at her accomplishment. She still hadn't been able to get hold of Adelia, and was bursting at the seams with the desire to share it with someone. Fulcanelli just happened to be near, and as he possessed some modicum of knowledge about the project, he was probably as good as anyone to share in her excitement.

As she turned to face him, she was hit with the realization that she'd never so much as bothered to learn his first name. It was true that they didn't know each other long, but it still struck her as odd that she'd never thought to ask, or he'd never offered it.

"I'm sorry, I don't know that I ever caught your first name." Once the words were out, she winced at how rude the comment sounded.

"It's just Fulcanelli." He continued staring forward.

"It's just Fulcanelli?" she repeated, raising her brow. The evasiveness of his answer thrust her back to the first few times she had met him, before she decided that he might be tolerable after all.

"I don't think I ever caught your surname, Lady Cassandra."

She glared at him, having no doubt he had taken it upon himself to discover her full name. How else did he manage to ensure the package was delivered to her address, or ensure the doormen at the Treasurer's House knew who she was? She imagined he took great pains to find out far more about her than he would ever confess or she might care to know.

"It is just Cassandra," she quipped. "You see, I was branded an idiot at birth, so my parents thought it would be simpler if they just gave me one name. Easier to spell."

He huffed, folding his arms. "You are difficult."

"I have been told that before," she replied, unphased by his agitation.

"Good. It brings me peace to know that people haven't lied to you."

She shot him another glare, only to be met by his sly smile. He had a way of making her think he knew something she didn't, which made her feel inferior. Just the same, it was obvious that he needed her for something, which led her to believe she had the upper hand. Since the day she had met him, it was as if she were suspended in some perpetual state of confusion. She was always hanging off the cliff, waiting for some dramatic revelation that would set the earth back upon its axis.

For her, Fulcanelli crossed over into both of her established categories. He was undeniably attractive, which she liked, yet there was something of an eerily elusive quality about him, which she was convinced she could come to detest. Even if, of late, she'd developed a fondness for him, he still had a way of keeping her at arm's length. Was this intentional, or some subconscious protective measure that activated whenever someone came too close to breaching his guard?

His cool demeanor reset the stage, moving them back to the days when they were virtual strangers. Perhaps she cared about the sudden shift because she'd spent the past few days with a head full of fanciful dreams. Leaving that euphoric high only to crash back to earth was deflating. Then again, maybe she didn't care so much after all. She was no stranger to a guarded heart. She'd never let anyone command her thoughts as much as Fulcanelli over the last while. A dose of reality like this reminded her of the dangers of losing sight of herself. The whimsy-filled girl she had turned into was far from the sophisticated worldly woman she wanted to be. To date, she'd never had to beg for a man's affection, and she was sure she never would. Or was she? If she had misread something between them, she could accept that momentary lapse of judgment, placing the blame squarely on that third glass of champagne the other night.

"Well...are you ready for the good news?" she said, looking at him as though her inner thoughts had not been setting her mind aflame.

"Knock me off my feet," he replied, giving her a devilish smile.

She shook off the unwanted distraction of just how nice his smile was. "The necklace was designed for John, Duke of Bedford. I traced the heraldic badge back through the archives and found it to be a perfect match. Now, if I can just find some evidence of it being in his household inventory, I think I can give Basil Duncan the information he needs to establish its official provenance."

"This is remarkable news indeed," he said, his eyes twinkling with satisfaction.

From the beginning, it was clear that he had some unshakable faith in her ability to find these answers. It was both flattering and perplexing. Finding the origins of the necklace was a big accomplishment for her, and a real boost. No matter how hard she strove to project an aura of confidence, she always fell short of believing in herself. To be surrounded by people like Fulcanelli and Adelia, such cultured and educated people, could be intimidating, and their presence often left her feeling like a work in progress. Her habit of sizing herself up, irrespective of what she managed to achieve, left her believing it wasn't enough.

"Given its pristine condition, I believe it has been in the care of someone who fully appreciated its importance. Once I can connect it to Bedford, I plan on tracing its journey from there."

"I think it is fair to say there was a great deal of effort made to keep it safe," Fulcanelli said.

"It's more than five hundred years old, yet still looks as though it was made yesterday. The craftsmanship is truly remarkable."

"I know. I made it." His statement was as matter-of-fact as one could make.

She leaned back, her neck going cold as she stared at him. "You made a necklace for John, Duke of Bedford...who died in the fourteen hundreds?"

"Fourteen thirty-five," he said. "It wasn't for him, but a wedding gift for his wife."

"Which one? He had two." Shook and confused by his declaration, she was nevertheless chuffed at knowing that detail. Her countless hours in the library had paid off.

"Jacquetta of Luxembourg."

"Right. So, you made a necklace for a wedding that took place in the fourteen hundreds?" The challenge in her voice was clear. Just what was he trying to pull with such an outlandish declaration?

"Fourteen thirty-three," he clarified again.

She groaned inside. "That's quite annoying, you know."

"That I made the necklace?"

"Actually, I was referring to spouting out those dates like a text-book, but the fact you expect me to believe any of this is annoying too. Just how old are you, Mister Fulcanelli?"

"I am very old, Cassandra," he replied, with not a hint of jest.

She tilted her head to the side as she took him in. "You look remarkably good for a man who is centuries old." She had heard a good many egotistical exaggerations in her time, but immortality took the cake.

"I adhere to a strict diet and stay quite fit," he said, with clear pride.

In response, she just nodded, tempted to ask him what his skin care regime consisted of, but decided against what might be construed as a facetious response.

She shifted, uneasy at the realization that the man she so foolishly became smitten with was just another fabricated version of himself. That was fitting, really. The one time she fell for someone wholeheartedly, he turned out to be a fraud. Whatever honesty she had sensed in Fulcanelli was little more than a carefully crafted sham. Damn it all to hell.

"Look, I am all for a good story, but what kind of fool do you think I am, sir? You waltz into my life, all dark and mysterious, then have the audacity to feed me some rubbish story that you are hundreds of years old. Just what do you want from me?"

He blinked twice, as if considering his next move. Then, without warning, his gaze locked on hers, and it was as if everything around them fell away. Cassandra shivered, with every hair standing on end.

"You and I are different from everyone else, Cassandra. The world moves around us, unaware of the enormity of the secrets we keep locked away. To let them know would be fruitless. The scientists would prod us, and the skeptics would crucify us with relentless ferocity. We can do nothing for them, but we can help each other. Just this once, we should let our guard down."

She scrutinized him. All at once, it was as if a gust of wind swept through her and a flash of light blurred out the intensity of his stare. A flurry of visions, too numerous to count, rushed at her, coming too fast to process. The whispers had broken through his wall. She struggled to steady herself against the miasma of light, each eruption fading into a scene that took her to a different time and place. The window to his life had opened, revealing all she deemed fiction to be true. She reached out and gripped the metal arm of the bench, using its coolness to pull herself back to the present. After what felt like an age, her vision cleared and, once again, she found herself staring up into his black eyes.

"Okay," she choked out, striving to control her breathing. "Let's be honest with each other."

"What we see as the natural world, is only the surface. Science, as you know it, comes nowhere near the reality. Innumerable things are possible when you understand the inner workings of nature—hidden secrets that are just waiting to be decoded by the right person. I was an apprentice once, to a man of great knowledge."

"Did he uncover the secrets, this great man?"

"He did far more than that, and then he passed this knowledge onto me. When I say I am very old, Cassandra, I mean I am far older than you can imagine."

"So, what happened to your tutor?" she asked, needing to press him further. "Have you outlived him?"

"It is possible. I do not know for sure. Flamel was said to have died in fourteen eighteen, but I have never believed it was so."

She shook her head, not sure she could withstand all that was coming at her. "You were an apprentice to Nicolas Flamel?"

"One and the same." His eye contact remained firm. "A great amount of suspicion started to come upon him, and his sudden wealth led to much speculation. He had discovered the elixir of life long before he shared it with me. One day, he sent me on a journey, and while I was gone, I received news of his death. I never believed it for a moment. I knew him too well. It is far more likely that he faked his death, slipping off into obscurity. Like myself, he has probably reinvented himself time and again to evade anyone knowing the truth."

Cassandra shifted on the bench—just an inch or two, but enough to give herself time to refocus. "So what does any of this have to do with me?"

"It was foretold to me that the gem would lead me to a woman of great power and wisdom. When I met you that day in the shop, I knew you were the one."

"I'm a fashion writer," she said, her voice flat. "I think your soothsayer may have been a little off in their prediction."

"Melusine speaks to you, Cassandra." He leaned closer. "You have heard her cry before. That day in the jewelry shop was not the first time. You are the one."

She sat still, dumbfounded. He wasn't wrong—she had heard that cry before. She took a breath and looked into his coal-black eyes. The absolute insanity of the conversation aside, she sensed the truth in him again. This wasn't some shabby pick-up attempt. The man was far too serious to employ such a lowly tactic.

"Just what makes you think I am *the one*?"

"Your eyes. They betray your every thought. You couldn't lie if you wanted to, though I scarcely think you do. Melusine speaks through her descendants. They have the great ability not just to see the past, but to foretell the future. You are a scribe. With practice, you will find that your ability is greater than you know."

"I can see the past, but not the future," she said, needing to set him straight. "My abilities have never let me see beyond the here and now."

"Think hard, Cassandra. Think back to her voice. You have heard it before."

She looked at the Minster, letting the gravity of everything he'd just said sink in, and allowing herself a much-needed breath or two. Part of her wanted to deny it all. But what was the use? She was sitting here talking with a man who was, by all accounts, immortal. What did she have to lose?

"I have heard that mournful sound twice before," she admitted. A shiver gripped her spine as she recalled the bitter melody. "I was a child the first time. Barely out of my toddler years. We had a townhouse in London, just off the banks of the Thames. I woke up to the painful sound of a woman's sobbing. More of a howl, really. I can remember crawling out of my bed, and looking out the window to the river below. I searched the night for the sad woman but all I could see was the shimmer of moonlight on the black water. The next day was The Blitz."

"And the next time?" he pressed, leaning toward her, as though he couldn't wait another second for her to speak.

"Just a few months ago. I was walking home from a party, not too far from here, near the River Ouse. It had been so long since I first heard it as a child, I didn't remember the sound. I looked around, trying to find her, thinking she must be a woman in distress. I was so concerned, I found the nearest phone booth and called the authorities. Then I ran the rest of the way home. Two days later, I got word that my cousin's husband had been killed in an accident."

"She warns you of things to come," he said, his words soothing and warm, quelling the chill prickling her skin.

"But none of this makes sense. Again, I have never had any visions of the future." She grimaced at a throbbing in her temples. "Maybe those were just accidents."

"Scribing has been a gift passed down through generations of her line. It is an ability that takes practice to be intentional."

"Just like the whispers."

"The whispers? That's what you call the visions?" He leaned even closer. "What does it show you?"

His presence was overpowering, and she had to ease herself away, if only by an inch or so. "I...was always an imaginative child—always daydreaming and telling stories. The visions started when I was young, as far back as I can remember. I was probably in early grade school when I finally had the courage to confide in my aunt. I had been frightened of something—it was so long ago I can barely remember what it was now. My aunt told me not to be afraid, as it was a special gift shared by the women in our family."

He nodded twice, his eagerness for her to continue clear.

"For most people, the concept of time is a linear notion, like an object always moving straight ahead. It's not that way for those of us who hear the whispers. Time is like strips of fabric, laid on top of each other. Sometimes, I find that those layers somehow slip out of sync. That's when the whispers are strongest. I can feel the images with such intensity, they materialize before my eyes."

"Do you understand what all this means, Cassandra?" His voice was filled with such intensity, she could barely muster the courage to formulate her response.

"Not...exactly."

"You, my lady, are the one. You are descended from the line of Melusine. Only those who are of her blood can hear her cry. Everyone else is deaf to her voice. It has long been said that her descendants have the gift of a second sight, the power to see all the things that were and all that is yet to come. Your gift has been passed down through your family line, but I believe it stretches further back than you realize."

"That is impossible. It's just an old myth from the days of the Plantagenets. Some ancient legend to brand them the devil's brood."

"The very fact that I am sitting here could be deemed impossible," he said, raising his brow in challenge. "I know a great many things. I have been to places that today's scholars can't even prove are real. I am but one man, and yet, have had a thousand names. I assure you, Cassandra, nothing is impossible."

She shook her head, then looked toward the west, with its hints of a sunset to come. Fulcanelli was right, most people would say her gift was impossible. Most people would scoff at such a notion, and yet she had lived with it, albeit begrudgingly, her entire life. Her abilities were real. What he was suggesting could be possible.

Nervous, she glanced around to make sure no one was close enough to hear.

"What is it that you want from me, Fulcanelli?" she demanded, impatient to know.

"I want you to wait for me."

She straightened in her seat. "Wait for you?"

He brushed an invisible fleck from his knee, then turned to her. "You much remember everything I'm going to tell you."

As she stared at him, it was as if the space between them disappeared. With his guarded wall down, she sensed more honesty in his eyes than with anyone before. There was nothing to hide between them anymore. Destiny had brought them together for a reason, and Fulcanelli was about to reveal its plan.

Chapter Twenty-Four

Adelia watched from the front window as the small blue car made its way up the long gravel approach to the house. Two months had passed since discovering the truth about Rose, and this was the final step to putting it all to rest. One she had been avoiding. She pulled in a breath, trying to muster all the courage she'd still not convinced herself she possessed. Though willful at times, confrontation had never been her strong suit. However, her incessant need for answers always put her in the position where facing this weakness became inevitable.

The car came to a halt and the motor stopped. She smoothed back her dark waves as she walked toward the front door to greet her awaited visitor. With trepidation, she tugged on the heavy wooden door, pulling it back in time to see him closing the driver's door.

They smiled at each other, but the moment she laid eyes on him, she couldn't help but see the young soldier in the café. His once short-cropped hair had for some time been replaced by long frazzled strands of steely gray, and the smooth outline of his jaw was now creased with the fine lines of age. Despite the changes a couple decades had brought to his looks, there was no mistaking that these men were one and the same.

As he pulled her into a friendly embrace, her thoughts could not be quelled. The whispers taught her early on that there was no such thing as coincidence, with every minute detail of fate being by design. Nothing could convince her otherwise.

It was fate that had veered her fortunes to the doorstep of Middleham Manor all those years ago. How else could one explain this man's appearance in her life? Even at a time when her life seemed unreasonably unfair, she understood that it was always meant to be this way. No act of her own could have changed anything that led her to this day. Nothing she could do would change tomorrow. Her mind echoed the prophetic words of Shakespeare:

"All the world's a stage, and all the men and women merely players."

No words could be truer at this point.

"Welcome back to Middleham, Paul." Her words came wrapped in the warmth of a longtime friend.

"What a grand place it has always been," he said, his smile nostalgic as he took in the stone façade. "I quite like my flat in the city these days, but this old place holds many fond memories. Such great conversations we used to have here. I suppose I miss that most of all."

They hadn't seen each other in such a long time. After Daniel's passing, Paul had reached out with his condolences but this was the first time they'd seen each other face to face. Knowing Paul as she did, these simple pleasantries were his way of easing his way around the obvious, focusing on the old days while offering her the chance not to have to acknowledge all that was missing here now. She was grateful for that gesture. It made him an even truer friend.

"I miss our evening chats in the library. There was something about the sound of a jazz record on the player and your cigar smoke in the air that always had a way of putting my restless mind at ease. Those were good days."

He took another turn in the driveway to soak up the old familiarity of the house before following her inside. She led him into the library, which he might think was for old time's sake. Not so—she had good reason to choose this room.

She turned to see that he had moved over to the overstuffed oak bookshelves.

"When Ross and Laura sold you this place, I never thought you would be able to fill all of these again. Looks like you proved me wrong."

"Between Daniel and I, we found we were in possession of a great many books." She laughed. "I'm not going to lie, I have probably bought just as many titles since we moved in. My collection is not nearly as old and rare as what Ross owned, but I stumble upon new treasures almost every day. In fact, my latest acquisition is a book written by none other than my cousin Cassandra."

"You are kidding me?" he said in surprise. "That's remarkable."

"She has done quite well for herself these past few years. I really am very proud of her."

"As you should be, and I'm happy to hear of her success." He eased an old tome back into its place, then turned to her. "Tell me, Adelia, how are you doing...?" His voice trailed off, conveying his hesitancy in approaching the inevitable.

They had remained friends long after Ross and Laura sold the property. Paul moved to the city to be closer to his brother's shop, and she and Daniel took over Middleham Manor as its new owners. They managed to stay in touch, sending the occasional card or letter, but over time their contact diminished. Word of Daniel's passing had not reached him until after the funeral, and she still regretted her failure to phone him. She did, however, appreciate it when he phoned her to convey his condolences. Throughout their friendship, she always held a high regard for his council and the sensible way he looked at things.

Now, she recognized confusion in his eyes, no doubt wondering about her urgency in wanting him to visit. He carried the look of a concerned father.

"I am well, Paul. It has taken some time but I am where I need to be now. The baby will be here in a matter of weeks, and things will change quite dramatically."

"I should say they will." His laugh was deep. "As an antiques' dealer, I must insist you start putting up some of these things sooner rather than later." He picked up a heavy gold-plated inkwell from one of the side tables.

"Oh... I-I suppose you have a point. See, there are so many things I haven't even begun to think of yet. Not to worry, my mother is coming for the birth of the baby. She will be here for a few weeks, and I have no doubt she will let me know everything that is to be done."

"That is the gift of mothers," he said, sitting into one of the plush chairs in the center of the room. She sat opposite him, and a momentary silence filled the space between them as they looked off in different directions. Just like the day with Cassandra, she struggled to find the right way to approach the subject.

"I was overjoyed by your invitation, Adelia." His impatience had no doubt got the better of him, saving them both. "It is just as nice to see the old manor house as it is to see you. I must be honest, though, I can't seem to shake the feeling that something might be wrong."

She allowed a half smile. "These past few months, I have been on a journey of sorts—"

"I can only imagine the passing of Daniel has been most hard on you." He leaned forward.

"Not an emotional journey. Well, yes, of course, but that's not what I am talking about—"

"Oh...I'm sorry for the interruption."

She smiled back. "It took me a few weeks at first but I finally built up enough courage to go through Daniel's things. That's when I found something." She got up, walked over to the desk, and retrieved the sketchbook. It wasn't that she found it difficult to be in Daniel's study, the library just felt like the right place to keep it, for now. She handed it to him. At first, he just gazed down at the cover, reading the words to himself aloud. His brows were wrinkled in confusion as he looked back up at her. She nodded for him to open the cover. He did, and as he stared down at the images, his demeanor changed, with a wash of sadness enveloping him. He didn't look back to her, his focus glued to the golden-haired beauty on the page.

"You never told me you knew Daniel's mother."

He blinked several times, his mouth hanging open just enough to see his bottom teeth. The page crinkled as he ran his thumb across it.

"I never put two and two together until the day I...attended your wedding," he said, his voice cracking. "When I recognized Daniel's father, it all came together."

Paul had always been a man steady with his emotions—at times difficult to read—but now, as he stared at Rose's picture, a brokenness in him was clear to see. She recounted the rest of the story, sharing as much as she dared, avoiding all mention of the role the whispers had played. Despite their years of friendship, she had never shared her secret with him. She pondered why he didn't ask how she knew.

"Why didn't you say something?" She failed to curb the demand in her voice.

He puffed a breath out and shrugged. "What was I supposed to say? To the best of my knowledge, Daniel's father didn't know who I was, or at least he gave no indication that he did. Did you want me to spoil your wedding by revealing some long-held family secret?"

"I suppose not," she replied. "I guess I am just trying to process all of this right now."

"Would you really have wanted Daniel to know that I am the reason his mother died?"

"N-no," she stuttered. "It's best that he didn't know the truth in the end. He must have taken her loss so much harder than he ever let on. It haunted him to the very end, I guess. It really is better that he didn't know. You're not the reason Rose died, anyway, Paul."

He sat up. "I am the reason she died, just as good as if I killed her myself. She would never have been out on that road had it not been for me."

She almost grimaced at the pain in his voice—in his eyes. While she understood how easy it was for him to blame himself, he had no need to shoulder the entire blame.

"She loved you, Paul. She was going to meet you at the café. She knew you would be waiting, and she made the choice. It was hers alone to make."

"I w-wasn't at the café for long, though," he sputtered, his face reddening, his eyes misty. "I went and I waited, but I didn't stay. I knew Rose would be giving up her entire life to be with me. She had a husband and a son. I couldn't ask her to make that sacrifice in the end, so I didn't stay. I honestly thought she would see that I wasn't there and return home where she rightfully belonged. I hoped she would see what a big mistake it would have been, and ended up hating me for almost taking her away from everything."

Adelia stared back in shock at the broken man before her. Rose had indeed made her choice, but little did she know it would have been the wrong one either way. Had she made it to the café, she would have discovered the truth. Paul loved her enough to want to protect her life. He did the most honorable thing he knew to do: break her heart. Fate had other plans for Rose and Paul, and neither would escape unscathed from their secret.

"I can understand your feelings. I truly can. But you are not to blame for what happened to Rose that day. She has haunted you long enough. It's time for you to let her go. You have to forgive yourself."

"Have you forgiven yourself, for Daniel?" His accusing tone struck deep.

His immediate reaction told her he regretted his words, but it was too late, her eyes welling with hot tears. She had struck a nerve with Paul—digging into some long-plaguing memory he wanted to keep locked away. Though she could not blame him for his harshness, it hurt her all the more that he'd used her feelings against her.

When Paul phoned her after Daniel passed, they'd had a long conversation, and she had confided in him, telling him about her guilt. Had she not been so tired that night, she would have just cooked dinner at home. After a long week, with her newly dis-covered pregnancy leaving her drained, laziness got the better of her and she'd agreed to Daniel's suggestion that he drive to the pub to grab something for dinner. If only she had insisted they slap together a couple of sandwiches, her husband would be alive today. There was no hiding the fact that she shouldered deep guilt for what happened to him. Paul was one of the few people she felt comfortable enough to confide in after his death. Now, hearing those words used against her, like a sharp-edged knife, was almost more than she could bear.

"Fair enough," she said, rising to her feet and avoiding the urge to look into his shame-ridden eyes. "We both are destined to be haunted by our mistakes. 'Tis but another thing you and I have in common."

"I did not mean that," he said, lowering his gaze to the floor. "I am an utter fool for ever saying such a thing to you, after all that you have been through. Forgive me, Adelia, please. I can't bear another heavy weight on my conscience."

That nudged at her shell. "Paul, we have both been through a great deal of pain in our lives. There is little reason we should add to it by being cross with each other. When I set out to learn more about Daniel's mother, all I wanted was to find some closure. And it helped that it occupied my mind long enough to get through my grief."

"I don't want us to hurt each other," he said. "We have been friends much too long. I am sorry for my insensitive words, and I am sorry for not telling you about Rose."

"I didn't bring you here to be critical of something that happened so long ago. To be honest, I have been torn on whether to even bring it up." She chuckled. "I have never been very good at letting things go, you know."

"No, my dear, you have not. I suppose a burning question such as this has lingered on your mind."

"Yes, it has, actually." She raised both hands to her temples. "I guess this was the last piece of the puzzle. I am relieved to say that I feel as though I can put the whole thing to rest now."

From her experience, there was a dishonesty about grief—a certain veil upon the truth. One's memories become selective, and there is a subconscious ability to block out all the things that were imperfect. It is as if there is far too much guilt in daring to allow flaws to enter your mind.

From the outset, she and Daniel had shared some storybook love, the kind any outsider might view with envy. Yet theirs was a love not unlike any other, full of trials that could strengthen or break it down if they hadn't been careful. They could have become like Rose and Dan; in some ways, they were already heading in that direction. The ravages of time may have thrust their relationship into decay, if they'd lost sight of what was important. They both had the propensity to be self-absorbed—consumed by their own ambitions. Had things not ended as they did, they may have found themselves growing apart.

Like a love story ripped out of a Shakespearian play, a twist of fate changed the scene, and their future was scattered on the wind. Maybe this was the best ending destiny could offer them. What lay down the road may have been a far more heartbreaking outcome.

All she could do was trust that what she had been given was the better plan. Paul, in his own time, would have to do the same.

After another hour or so, he said his goodbyes. She felt a true sense of lightness in her heart, possessing all the closure she required. Though she was tired, she wasn't quite ready to go to bed yet. She propped her feet up on the ottoman in the front parlor, letting the day's activities come to a quiet end. As she pulled a lap blanket from the back of the sofa to cover her legs, she caught sight of something out of the corner of her eye, and a warm glow swept through her.

There, just outside the door frame, stood Daniel. He unbuttoned his overcoat, then hung it on the hall tree, as he had done nearly every day he'd lived in the house. His image was in full color, as real as if he were standing there in the flesh. A moment later, he passed by the doorway, bound for some other area of the house, probably to make tea for her in the kitchen. At last, the whispers had brought him home.

Chapter Twenty-Five

Adelia pulled her wool coat tighter as she walked along the desolate road, shuddering on arriving at the spot where Daniel had spent his last moments. It took a long time to amass the courage to come here, but tonight her resilience was strong.

The narrow shoulder was uneven and somewhat overgrown, and did not look to have been traveled by foot much in recent times. Loose stones snapped beneath her feet like the cracking of thin ice. As the clouds slid along above her, a ray of fading sunlight cast itself across the rocky fields, and she stopped, her breath catching at the radiant vision of blankets of purple heather covering the jagged landscape. This place, that had veiled her life in such darkness, now felt full of light. She could sense him—as if he was there, pushing away the stray strands of her hair dancing in the cold breeze. As she moved further along the broken trail, his presence became stronger, and with the last threads of daylight slipping away beneath the heavy bank of gray clouds, she knew he was there to protect her—wary of her falling prey to his own fate.

A car approached from behind, and she stepped further away from the road. Its wheels crunched the gravel as it came to a stop. She pulled her blowing hair back behind her ear, and squinted against the glare of the headlights.

"What the hell are you doing out here?" Cassandra demanded. "I swear to God, you need a babysitter."

Adelia laughed, surprised and delighted that her cousin had shown up like this. She walked toward the car.

Cassandra stood there, hands in her own hair, making as though she intended to pull it out from frustration. With Adelia returning to work in the fall, and Cassandra entrenched in her own endeavors, it had been a while since they'd last spoken. Their phone calls and letters back and forth since her visit to York had been rare and brief. They were both busy women, making their way on their own. Yet, the fact they had lost touch made her feel guilty. She had plenty of time for her cousin—she just hadn't made it a priority with all she had going on.

"What the hell are you doing here in Middleham?" she asked, somewhat baffled at her appearance. "I had no idea you were coming this way."

"Just as well," Cassandra snapped. "I should have known I would need to scold you for something when I arrived. You shouldn't be gallivanting around on this road. Have you forgotten you are pregnant?"

Adelia groaned, motioning to her round belly. "None of my clothes fit anymore. I can't even button this coat. And all I want to eat are rashers and sausages all day. I assure you, I haven't forgotten that I am pregnant."

"Hop in the car," her cousin ordered, her tone similar to that of an infuriated mother. "Let's get you back home."

Both women gave each other a well-deserved roll of the eyes as they got into the car. Adelia studied her young relative's face while she chatted about some road work that had delayed her arrival. She looked great, as always, but something about her eyes was different. Her mindless chatter was little more than a distraction from the real reason for her visit.

It didn't matter what the woman needed, her company was a delightful reprieve from the deafening silence of the old manor house. Adelia had always been a person content on doing things alone. Whether it was an afternoon shopping, or an evening curled up with a good book, solitude was something she embraced. However, that was back in the days when those quiet moments were few and far between—back when to be alone with her thoughts was a rarity and didn't feel like her every waking minute. No longer prepared to allow her grief to swallow her whole, she found herself wanting to be around people more and more. Though now heavily pregnant, being back on the university campus, surrounded by students, helped lift her mood. She always downplayed human interaction as something she could take or leave, but being alone over the last while taught her that she needed people far more than she realized. Soon, her mother would arrive, ending these days of domestic solitude, and she would take her maternity leave from work.

Once they pulled up in front of the Manor, Cassandra cut the engine, and Adelia barely had a chance to reach for the door handle when her cousin ran around to her side, swung it open, and helped her from the car.

"Seriously, Cassandra," she growled, shaking her arm loose from her cousin's gentle grip.

Cassandra stepped back, thrusting her hands in the air as though admitting defeat. "I just want to help."

"I appreciate it, I really do, but I am absolutely fine. Come see me in a few more weeks and we may be talking about a different story."

"Fair enough," Cassandra said with a spirited giggle. "You win, you stubborn mule. Walk yourself up to that door while I grab my bags."

She retrieved her bags from the back of the car, slinging one over each arm before following Adelia into the house. It was uncharacteristic of her to pack so light for the trip. Even though she was only expected to stay a night or two, her two bags were still more than the average person would have brought, but quite minimal for Cassandra. It was a break from the norm, which had Adelia wondering what was up with her.

"You go prop your feet up," Cassandra ordered, pointed off into the direction of the library, "while I throw a kettle on the stove for us. That will give me time to get changed."

Adelia knew there was no point arguing so she sat in the library and waited for her cousin to get settled in. The girl knew her way around the house better than anyone, having stayed for an entire summer the year before they'd bought the place, so she hadn't bothered to show her up to her room. Whenever her college breaks allowed, she made an effort to visit. Their relationship had grown over the years and, by now, they acted like sisters, with the expected occasional squabbling mixed in.

Cassandra breezed into the room, refreshed from her travels and donning more comfortable attire. After handing Adelia a steaming cup of tea, she perched herself beside her on the couch, her own cup in hand. She fiddled with the handle, her focus locked on something in the distance. As she sipped her tea, Adelia eyed her cousin's uneasy demeanor over the rim of the cup.

"What ails you? Something's up. I can see it in your eyes." There was little reason for Cassandra to try to hide her thoughts, as Adelia could puzzle them out without effort.

"I have met a man. Not just any man, though." Her initial excitement disappeared as her shoulders slumped.

"I see. That is a predicament, to be sure." She tried to hold back a grin. Cassandra's face held both anguish and excitement—all the trademarks of blossoming love.

"He is almost too complex for an explanation," she said, waving off the subject as if she wasn't sure what else to say. "Tell me, Adelia, have you ever heard a woman's cry in the middle of the night? Like a howling moan that floats on the wind?"

"A howling woman? Like a banshee?"

"Similar, I suppose." Cassandra's voice quivered.

"No. Thankfully, I have never seen a banshee, kelpie, or a changeling. My gift only allows me to see the dead. Well...they were very much alive when I saw them, but they are...dead."

"Yes, I know, I have that same gift, too, remember?"

"Yes, I guess you do." She laughed. "What can I say, I am a teacher by trade. I always feel the need to explain things a little too much. How did you meet this man?"

"It all started with the necklace. You see, the day I went to see it, I had a strange sort of vision." She went on to explain all about Melusine and her encounter with Fulcanelli, recounting the details of each of their meetings and how much time she had spent tracing the heraldry of John, Duke of Bedford.

"Cassandra, this is an adventure straight out of a book." Adelia placed her cup on a side table. "I am sorry that I wasn't around to help you, but I honestly have to admit that I am impressed with your diligence. I know tracing it back so far took a great amount of work on your part."

"I didn't exactly do it alone," Cassandra confessed. "Fulcanelli provided me with a great deal of information. You see, once I established that it had belonged to the Duke of Bedford, it was Fulcanelli who shared that it had actually been a gift for Jacquetta, the duke's second wife."

"That necklace belonged to Jacquetta of Luxembourg? *The* Jacquetta of Luxembourg? How on earth did you prove that?" She couldn't hide her delight.

Cassandra sat straighter, and it was clear that she was chuffed.

"Well...the duke commissioned Fulcanelli to make it for her." She sat back, looking down at her cup.

"Wait... What? Fulcanelli was a jeweler in the fourteen hundreds?"

"No." She grimaced, as if fully understanding how ludicrous she sounded. "Fulcanelli was an alchemist in the fourteen hundreds. The duke had a great interest in alchemy at that time, and wanted to learn the art of turning base metals into gold. Fulcanelli proved it could be done, creating the gold necklace and the ruby pendant."

Adelia shifted, leaning against the armrest to face her cousin. "I have heard tales of the duke's interest in alchemy. There are some who say he had quite an impressive library of books on the topic. Yet, you see how I am having trouble getting behind the notion that the mysterious man you met in York, this Fulcanelli, was alive at the time and knew John, Duke of Bedford."

"Believe me," Cassandra said, "I thought the very same thing. He gave me these..." She pulled out an envelope. "These are the documents that support the purchase of the necklace. There is an inventory list that shows the necklace was among the jewelry owned by the Duchess of Bedford at the time of her husband's death. From there, I had to follow its trail. For a time, it was surrendered to the crown, but I was able to trace the line all the way up until Fulcanelli came into possession of it, not long ago, and brought it to Basil Duncan's shop."

"Why did he want it back?" Adelia still wasn't buying the story, but she pressed on anyway.

"He said the necklace was the key to connecting the descendants of Melusine."

"Melusine, the water goddess?" Adelia asked, fragments of the myth coming to her.

"Yes. Fulcanelli said it had been foretold, however long ago, that these descendants—women—possessed the ability of Melusine to foretell things that were to come."

"Hold on, I've read about this. The old legends say that Jacquetta was said to have been descended from the Lusignan family line, but in truth I never actually dug deep enough to check the validity." She raised her brow as she smiled. "The whole half-woman, half-serpent thing doesn't hold much weight in the academic world."

Cassandra's eyes lit up. "Actually, I have done the research. If one is to believe the story of Melusine, there is a direct link to Jacquetta through the Lusignan, Luxembourg, and Plantagenet families. Descending from all three lines, she no doubt had a connection to Melusine."

"The devil's brood," Adelia said. "That's what they always called the Plantagenets. There have been several interpretations as to how they inherited such a moniker, but the connection to Melusine was certainly one of them."

She sat back, considering what she'd heard so far. "It's a lot to take in, but as far-fetched as it sounds, the fact is our ability to hear the whispers is no less incomprehensible, at least to most."

"I agree, but there is so much more to this story."

"So, if Fulcanelli did know the duke, and they were alchemists together, what happened?"

"They never finished their work together. You see, the duke wanted to create the gold to help fund a war. Fulcanelli believes in using his knowledge to better the world, not to destroy. As a result, he ceased working with the duke. But Bedford knew of Jacquetta's connection to Melusine. It's probable he thought she could help him as he continued on his own. Perhaps she had the sight herself, and was able to help propel his work forward, but when the duke died shortly after, everything came to a halt."

Adelia thought back to all the rumors that swirled around Jacquetta in her lifetime. She had been accused of witchcraft at one point and imprisoned. Though historians claimed those accusations to be false and politically motivated by the Duke of Warwick, these new revelations lent some truth to it all. Thankfully, Jacquetta escaped unscathed, but her reputation as a witch remained long after.

Cassandra recounted her vision of Melusine and the other times she'd heard her cries. Adelia appreciated her sharing what happened before Daniel's death, knowing it pained her, but they were details she couldn't leave out.

"The story of Melusine has been around for more than a thousand years or more," Adelia explained. "I can't deny that I have always chalked it up to being little more than a fable. Yet, you have encountered her at least three times in your life. I know you far too well to think this is all in your imagination."

"There is absolutely no doubt in my mind that she is real. I know it sounds crazy, but what I have experienced is not a trick of the mind."

Her earnest response left Adelia with no doubt either.

"Help me connect the dots here," she said. "If Fulcanelli, the alchemist, created the necklace for the Duke of Bedford, and the duke was married to Jacquetta, and knew of her gift as a descendant of Melusine, where exactly do you and the present day Fulcanelli come into play?

"You see, Fulcanelli knew something about Jacquetta's gift. He has spent a great many years searching for someone with the same ability. That is another story. Anyway, as time passed, he came to the conclusion that his mission cannot be completed without this sight. He can see a great many things, but not everything. He needs someone who possesses the ability to see beyond what he can. Someone like Jacquetta."

"And this someone is...you?"

She shrugged one shoulder. "That's what he said."

"So, you will work with him?"

"I can't," she said, her expression turning somber. "He's gone."

"He's gone? What does that mean?" The story was taking so many twists and turns, she could barely keep pace.

"He wanted to find me, but now isn't the time for this work to continue. He said he will return again to me, someday."

"Someday? How far away will that be? I suppose time doesn't matter to him, but it certainly does to you." She realized she was incensed that her cousin had been abandoned.

"I have absolutely no idea. All I know is, he assured me that Melusine will continue to work through me, even more so now if I accept her presence."

"So, he just disappeared," Adelia said, working through the details. "This reminds me of a story I heard long ago. The Count of Saint Germaine, some mysterious aristocrat in eighteenth-century France. In fact, I believe Daniel had a book about him, which in itself is surprising. He was never the type to believe fanciful stories like this. Let me see if I can find it." She struggled up and walked over to a shelf, scanning a line of books before locating the right one.

"The who?" Cassandra asked.

"The Count of Saint Germaine." She cracked open the cover and returned to her seat by Cassandra. "This story is one of the most intriguing ones I have ever heard, if I say so myself."

Cassandra's brows furrowed. "Story?"

Adelia flicked through the book, stopping at several pages before she found the one she wanted, showing a copy of the count's engraved portrait. She handed it to Cassandra, who studied it in silence for a long moment.

"His face is unmistakable. Those eyes. Those incredible eyes." She chuckled to herself as she traced her fingertips across his hair. "His black locks weren't covered by this ridiculous powdered wig of an eighteenth-century man, but the resemblance is uncanny." She looked at Adelia, who glanced at the etching but remained silent.

"Then again, don't we all look a little like someone else? Perhaps the man I know is a descendant."

Adelia tapped the page. "The count went by many names, they say. He traveled the world, always reinventing himself. The time and place of his birth are quite murky, but many said he hailed from some line of royalty."

"He was a prince then?" Cassandra asked, still staring at the etching.

"That has never been confirmed, but given his unparalleled education and infinite financial resources, it's safe to say he came from royal stock. He was well adapted to courtly life, wherever he turned up." She flipped back a few pages, scanned the text, then tapped the page. "It was thought that he may have been the son of Prince Rackozy of Transylvania. Apparently, he stated this himself. One of the three sons who escaped imprisonment. The only thing that was documented about his youth is that he was raised under the protection of the last Duc of Medici in Italy."

"If he was indeed the son of a prince, why did he not claim his birthright as he grew older?"

"Why should he? He lived a life of absolute luxury. He was renowned the world over for his skills as a musician, scholar, and alchemist. His financial resources were unending, and when he tired of a place, he simply moved on to another. He lived a life of pure freedom, far from the constraints of any responsibility."

"I guess that does sound appealing," Cassandra said, releasing a long sigh. "I kind of like that lifestyle myself."

Adelia smothered the urge to roll her eyes. "While the timeline of his life has been debated, there are a great many documented encounters with him. These include a wealth of letters and stories of his exploits, given by prominent figures of the day. If you cast all of the speculation aside, it's safe to say this was a real man who did exist. This engraving is proof in itself. They say he could play the violin like a virtuoso. He was fluent in many languages and had extensive knowledge of every country's history. What he is most known for, though, was his practice of alchemy. It is said he could turn several small jewels into perfected larger ones. His clothing was littered with gems, and he often gave them as gifts. His wealth was so great, it far exceeded many of the powerful figures in which he paid court to."

"An alchemist," Cassandra said. "The count was an alchemist. Was there anything he couldn't do?"

"Age, apparently." She took the book and flicked forward, then back a few pages to a panel of small sketches that looked to be of the same man but in different manners of dress. "Here, of all those who knew him, over and over it's said that he never aged a day. He remained perpetually youthful. Even those who knew him more than fifty years said he never looked a day over forty."

"Forty," Cassandra repeated. "If I had to guess, Fulcanelli was near that age. So, when did this mysterious man die?"

"Well, that is even more peculiar. It is said that he died in seventeen-eighty, though no known grave exists. Furthermore, it seems that a man like him appeared in a variety of countries years after his supposed death. He was appointed as grand master of the masonic order in seventeen eighty-five, and spotted at the execution of Marie Antoinette eight years later. All of these alleged happenings have led to the widely held belief that in his work as an alchemist, he somehow managed to discover the elixir of life, rendering him immortal. If one is to believe the well-preserved evidence, then you must admit it is something worth pondering. It is a great story to be sure, fictional or not."

"It's him," Cassandra said, no doubt in her voice. "It's Fulcanelli. Obviously, he isn't sporting the powdered wig these days, but this is definitely the man I know as Fulcanelli."

"So, your Fulcanelli was the Count of Saint Germaine?" Adelia leaned against the armrest, glad to take the pressure off her back. It felt like all of the legends she had known as a child had just been proven as truths.

"I know it sounds crazy, but I would know him anywhere. I mean, again...that hideous powdered wig aside, he looks exactly the same. It is him."

She held her hand to her chest. "My goodness, my heart is racing. I feel such a strong connection to this man. It's as if... It's as if he's calling to me, like the whispers but more. Deeper."

"Are you okay, Cassandra." Adelia touched her cousin's arm, leaning forward to make direct eye contact.

"Yes, yes, I am. This is quite overwhelming, to be honest."

"You said there's more to this story...?"

"There is, but I'm not quite ready to go into it. I'm just grateful that you don't consider me a complete idiot."

"Don't be silly. Of course not. I'm just glad that you are okay."

Cassandra wiped the corner of her eye. "I think I might have fallen in love with him." She said this as though she were admitting some great sin.

"Oh, I see. That does complicate things a bit."

"How is it possible that I could have done that so easily?"

Adelia pointed to herself. "I can honestly say, from experience, it's not so hard to do. Now, the problem is we both are in love with someone who is gone from our lives."

"It is the worst feeling in the whole world, isn't it?"

Cassandra's eyes held such sadness, her own heart was pained. She understood that feeling far more than anyone else could at that moment.

"Yes, Cassandra, it is, but it does get easier in time." She rubbed her enormous bump. "You see, they both made us a promise that they would never be gone for good, and drawing from my own experience, I can say with certainty they will keep their word."

****

There was so much more Cassandra wanted to say, but now just didn't feel like the right time. Her cousin had faced so much in these past months, and there were even bigger things that lay ahead. For all his searching, Fulcanelli had never expected to stumble across her that day in Basil Duncan's shop. More than anything, he wanted to know what had become of his old mentor. It was reasonable to assume that if Flamel had passed such an intricate secret on to his apprentice, he would have secured his own life's longevity for himself. The fact that Flamel simply disappeared, without any warning, was something Fulcanelli had never been able to fully accept, though he understood it later, having done the same himself many times. There were still pieces of the puzzle he wanted to uncover, for never had he believed that Flamel was dead. These things that needed to be resolved before Cassandra could be brought into the fold. Deep down, she knew he didn't think her entirely ready for what lay ahead. Had she not felt the same, she might have resisted his departure with more fervor. She had spent so long rejecting her gift, she was now, quite frankly, out of practice. If she was to help him find answers, she had a tremendous amount of fine tuning to do to make up for all that time. As it stood, her feelings for him to the side, she knew in her heart that now just wasn't the right time for either of them.

Chapter Twenty-Six

Avilynn Rose Brown arrived in the early hours of the day. Nothing about her was imperfect to the doting mother who held her to her chest. She had the brilliant blue eyes of her father, and tiny strands of dark chestnut hair, like her mother. Adelia could already see the deep fiery soul of the newest member of the Babbington line. This precious jewel would be the next keeper of the long-held family secret. The whispers would carry on through Avilynn, just as they had for generations before with her ancestors, revealing the stories of people long forgotten in time.

For all the strife this ability gave Adelia through the years, she had finally learned to look upon it as a genuine gift. In time, she would teach her daughter to do the same. Through the whispers, Avilynn would come to understand the many layers of herself.

Learning about Dan and Rose's marriage taught Adelia a great many things about her own. It brought to light not only her own failures, but also the things that deserved to be cherished. Things hadn't always been perfect, but they were never broken either. Daniel had been such a rock of security, and at times she took it for granted. Even if they didn't share every single inner thought with each other, their life together was filled with an honest love. They were strong people, both as individuals and as husband and wife.

She no longer wanted to cry when she thought of him, her tears replaced by the immense pride she felt to have been married to such a remarkable man. Daniel had done what many people struggle to do their whole lives: taking the pain of the past and channeling it into something beautiful. He paid attention to the little things, understanding that when those around him thrived, he did too. Without doubt, he cared for others' well-being, but still knew how to care for himself. These were qualities that made him the man he was, and ones that made her love him all the more.

Dan had conditioned Rose to be alone, but in weakness, and she never found comfort in her own strength. Daniel conditioned his wife to be without him, too, but in a different way. He taught her to trust in herself, and to always persevere. Though her time with him had been all too short, he gave her something that would last a lifetime—Avilynn—this tiny baby now wrapped in her arms, and the strength to raise her, just as if he were still there. Avilynn Rose Brown would always know where that strength came from.

About the Author

As a child, Tasha Sheipline wanted to be a ballerina, marry a doctor, and have a pony. Since none of these dreams came to fruition, she became a teacher instead. Teaching others has proved an empowering endeavor.

An avid reader, Tasha has a long held belief that you can never have too many books. Her favorite authors include Alison Weir, William Shakespeare, Edgar Allan Poe and Jane Austin. She is certainly not opposed to sprinkling in a good Tessa Dare romance novel when time allows.

She began writing as a creative outlet, and it soon blossomed into a real passion. A lover of history, Tasha has a specific fondness for the medieval through early modern eras. She loves to infuse characters and events from these areas into her writing.

Her favorite pastimes include traveling, watching historical documentaries, and adding to her growing collection of antique books. Tasha lives in a small town in Ohio with her husband, children, and three corgi's.

The Whisper Series